Cairo

Victoria Pitts-Caine

Published by Prism Book Group
ISBN: 978-1-940099-06-4 First Edition, 2013
Published in the United States of America
Contact info: contact@prismbookgroup.com
http://www.prismbookgroup.com

FOREWARD

In many ancient cultures, man created stories to explain his beginnings and even his everyday surroundings. Stories were handed down from generation to generation, ranging from petroglyph figures in the caves of the Native American Indians to intricate hand-painted scenes on the walls of the Egyptian pyramids. The architectural masterpieces of temples and shrines honored beings both of the earth and the underworld. Kings who rose to high supremacy were buried there, waiting to enter the afterlife of their grandfathers.

The sarcophagi have long since been emptied and the wealth of the tombs taken, but three of those monuments stand against the bright blue Egyptian sky at the edge of the great city of Cairo.

On April 01, 2009, Addison and Gary Wright traveled to Cairo to celebrate the second anniversary of their marriage. Gary's one desire was to fulfill Addie's dream of visiting Egypt...but without explanation, the anniversary couple disappeared.

GLOSSARY

Galabayas: Long flowing robe.

Hennak: There.

Kaif halik: How are you?

Klaft: A kerchief, usually striped horizontally, which wrapped around the front of the head and fastened at the back of the neck. Later it was cut away so that it fit over the shoulders and was decorated heavily with beads.

Marhaba: Hello.

Moya: Water.

Naja haje: Egyptian Cobra.

Ney: It is an end-blown flute with seven finger holes: six in the front and one in the back. The Ney is made of a nine-segment section of reed.

Oud: It is a pear-shaped, stringed instrument, similar to a modern western lute and distinguished primarily by being without frets, commonly used in Middle Eastern music and East African music.

Taieb: Okay.

CHAPTER ONE

Six Days Later, San Francisco, California

A SUDDEN BREATH of early spring filtered through an open window and scattered the papers on her desk, but before she could stifle the breeze, the telephone rang. "Liz McCran, San Francisco Museum," echoed across the empty room. The garbled message of the international connection caused her to wrestle with each word. She understood the caller's name as Rayhan. His deep, masculine voice intrigued her, but his message did not, and as the conversation ended, a cold chill settled over her. His name meant *favored by God*, but had God chosen this man named Rayhan to deliver such unsettling information? His voice lingered in her ears.

She fought for control before she made the dreaded calls to repeat what she'd been told, knowing she'd burden the hearts of others. The window stood open. The cool current whisking over her skin delivered a small measure of stability to her now spinning brain. Her chest constricted with an emotional crush as her trembling fingers drummed the desk. Liz reached for her upright file and pulled a bright purple folder from the stack marked *itinerary and important numbers*. Her gaze moved to the bookshelf as she opened the file and her eyes rested on her best friend's wedding photo. How could Gary and Addie Wright have disappeared on a well-planned vacation to Cairo?

The authorities had waited two days for them to return from a trip to the Great Pyramids at Giza. Liz envisioned the open desert to the back of the necropolis. Addie's brilliant research skills and awareness of her surroundings left her far too smart to venture out on her own. Liz feared something terrible had happened. She sighed. Now she had to call Addie's relatives, perhaps starting a chain of events which couldn't be stopped.

Addie's immediate family lived scattered between the east and west coasts, and she had appointed Liz as her contact. On the "in case of emergency" line on the card the travel agency provided, she had carefully printed: Liz McCran. Relationship: friend.

Friend encompassed far too much. Their kinship ran deeper, sisters maybe, but more, something hard to explain. Addie and Liz grew close when Addie's work as a document restorer crossed paths with Liz's job at the San Francisco Museum. Even after Addie and Gary had settled into married life, the two women remained fast friends.

Cairo, Egypt

RAYHAN SHENOUDA DREW his hand through his hair and leaned against the side of a white-washed building as he waited at the edge of the marketplace for his young cousin, Jahi. At six years old, the boy announced he could retrieve his mother's shopping list by himself and told Rayhan he only allowed him to walk the distance to the market for company. Jahi had left his prize possession with his cousin, a football. One Rayhan had bought him for Christmas. Rayhan fingered the white stitches on the leather and glanced at the gold ring on his finger. It had belonged to his father. His parents had exchanged rings in a betrothal ceremony prior to their wedding. Both his mother and father had honored and touched the ring, all Rayhan had of their existence.

Marriage, he thought as he let his mind aimlessly stroll back to a breakfast conversation with his uncle less than two hours ago. He heard his uncle's words. "Don't you think it is time you found a nice young woman, Rayhan? You're thirty-three, and all the pretty ones will be gone. They don't want an old man." Al Abdul smiled and laughed at his own joke, but Rayhan knew truth lie there, too. Egyptians believed in family and marriage, but he hadn't found what he knew his heart wanted. His views of women were swayed by his first few dates with American girls before he returned to Cairo. They were free, opinionated, and excited about their futures, something he didn't experience at home.

Many Egyptian women expressed their forward thinking, but the ones he knew were steeped in their practices. They hung back in the shadows, wearing their traditional black dress, quiet and unobtrusive. A few of them, without caution, hoped they would be chosen by his Uncle Al Abdul as Rayhan's betrothed. He had learned this bit of gossip from Jahi, who often sat perched in the kitchen during family gatherings, listening to hushed whispers. Rayhan, grounded in his upbringing and culture, the very thing he loved and cherished, found it difficult to liberate himself from tradition. He wanted something more, something close to forbidden.

His desire compelled him to make a different choice, someone like the American woman his employer, Mr. Aston, had asked Rayhan to call. Her kindness, even though he delivered bad news, left him surprised. He tried to envision her somewhere in San Francisco, half a world away. A familiar longing pulled at his chest, and his thoughts drifted.

San Francisco, California

LIZ CALLED ADDIE's brother, Eric, but he had flown to France on business earlier in the week. Her sparse conversation with his wife, Sarah, ended as Liz told her not to worry. Hanging up the receiver, Liz doubted she had sounded convincing. She had done nothing but worry herself. She grew more uncomfortable, weighing her thoughts on the next call to Addie's two male cousins in Arizona. Addie's four cousins were her closest relatives next to Eric. Donnie had proven himself Addie's favorite. Liz stared out the window at the Bay Bridge, exhaled a pent-up breath, and dialed their number.

The ringing ceased and, breathless, Clay answered the phone, "Hello."

"It's Addie's friend, Liz." She paused, not sure Clay remembered her. "We met at her wedding."

"Yes. Is something wrong?"

"Addie and Gary are missing."

"No. Wait—let me wake Donnie," echoed in Liz's ear as Clay's footsteps pounded the staircase.

Donnie took the phone after a muffled exchange. "What's going on? I thought Addie and Gary were in Egypt. What happened?"

"They are, and nowhere to be found. One thing that concerns me, and I doubt if they mentioned this to anyone, but their pastor asked them to carry some papers to Egypt for the church."

"What papers?" Donnie grumbled.

"Information about a building project."

"Did you call the Embassy?"

"They called me. I only received the information myself twenty minutes ago."

"Why didn't anyone call me?"

"I am, now." The few times she had met him, Donnie rubbed her the wrong way. He had a chip on his shoulder and seemed to be asking for someone to knock it off.

"I'm going to catch the next flight over there."

"Do you think I should call the police?"

Donnie's voice rose. "No. Did they take their cell phones?"

"Yes. Addie called me once after they arrived."

"I hope they don't use them. They can be traced."

"Traced? Do you really suspect something might have happened to them, other than—" Liz measured her thoughts. Addie and Gary weren't just lost. Disappeared or missing meant something quite different. Donnie's concern escalated the fear which coursed through her veins. "I'd planned to go myself."

"What? No," he objected.

Liz drew in a sharp breath. She didn't care to ask him along, but she could put herself at risk by being a woman alone in Egypt. "Come to San Francisco and fly out of here."

"It could get rough if we have to find them ourselves. I don't play by the rules."

"Playing by the rules is out of the question now. I'm doing this for Addie, and I know what I'm up against. I've been there, you haven't, and I'm fluent in Arabic."

"You may be, and I don't care how many times you've been there. I'm running this show. We need to move before the trail disappears." Donnie stopped and the line grew silent. Liz wondered if they'd lost the connection.

"Donnie?" *Did Mr. Arrogant just hang up on me?*

"Sorry. Just thinking about what I need. Call me back." He hesitated. "At noon. We both should know something by then."

Liz cradled the phone. She regretted the conversation, but she did need his help. Her mind raced at a frightening clip as she flipped through her address book. She searched for the number of the church in Fremont that Addie and Gary attended. Liz had time to make one more phone call before she made her own preparations to leave the country. She had met the pastor a couple of times when she'd visited, and if Michael Waterford gave Addie and Gary the papers, perhaps he knew more.

Liz dialed the number and a pleasant female voice answered, "Fremont Community Church, may I help you?"

"This is Liz McCran, Addie Wright's friend. Could I speak with the pastor?"

"He's in a meeting right now."

Her heart raced and, not wanting to say the words. "It's urgent. I've received information which makes me believe Addie and Gary are in trouble."

"Michael Waterford." The strong voice of the pastor resonated in her ear.

"Pastor Waterford, it's Liz McCran. I'm not certain if you know who I am."

"Yes. How can I help you? Addie's in some sort of a fix?"

Liz knew no other way to break the news than to state the facts, keeping it simple, her emotions in check. "They're missing. I understand they had some papers to deliver?"

"For the building of a church south of Cairo. They were supposed to locate a Mr. Moustafa. I'm sorry I don't know more.

Mr. Hamaka, the builder in San Francisco, wanted the contract taken to the church there."

"Then it wasn't between the two churches for the work you're doing?"

"No. We're just volunteering. Nothing contracted. I offered to do it as a favor."

Her heart sank. Gary and Addie, and perhaps even Mr. Moustafa, had been unknowing pawns in someone else's game. "Pastor Waterford, did you think anything could have been wrong with the situation?"

"Not at the time. The company wanted a head start on shipping some crates over there. They needed some paperwork signed."

"Crates? Crates of what?" An uneasy worry gnawed at the back of her consciousness. The situation had just taken an ugly turn.

"Some tools, maybe. I don't know. Oh yes, I remember, there was a large wooden box of Bibles, too."

"People are arrested over there for less." Liz bit her lip. Unwarranted incidents often spiraled out of control in foreign countries. "There weren't any guns?"

"Guns! What do you mean?" The pastor took a deep, audible breath before he spoke again. "I don't think so, but there could have been anything in those boxes. What are you going to do?"

"I'm leaving for Egypt with Addie's cousin, Donnie. We need to find them before they wind up in some kind of international mess. Do you know the contents of the envelope?"

"I didn't even ask. I just assumed…" Pastor Waterford exhaled with a discernable groan. "I'm sorry if I implicated the two of them. I had no idea."

"It's not your fault. Did they question you about the envelope?"

"No. I thought it was nothing more than an innocent request on Mr. Hamaka's part."

"I'm sure if Gary and Addie are being held by someone, it won't take them long to realize they don't know about any shipments."

"Their circumstances are worse than I thought. Please be careful." The pastor hesitated. "The God of Peace be with the two of you."

She appreciated his concern. "And with you."

LIZ MADE THE necessary phone call to the American Embassy in Cairo. She questioned a sudden twinge of disappointment which flickered through her thoughts when Rayhan didn't answer. He had been compassionate and caring. She found herself eager to talk to him again, but instead she spoke with the American Ambassador himself. She checked on an overseas flight after a brief exchange alerting him of their plans.

Liz considered her risks, ran a hand through her hair, and with a quick glance in the mirror, stood from her desk. She pulled as much height into her five-foot-two frame as possible, smoothed her skirt and walked across the hallway to the director's office.

A chair scraped after her light rap on the wooden casing. "Come in." When she opened the door, the director quickened his stride to meet her. "Liz. Is something wrong? What's happened?"

"You know Addie Wright who restores our documents?" Liz asked, but didn't wait for an answer. "She and her husband are missing in Cairo."

"When did you find out?"

"An hour ago." She paused, drew in a deep breath, and continued. "I'm going with her cousin to find her."

The director rubbed his chin and studied her with soulful eyes. "Liz, you work on a grant, which is coming up for renewal in two weeks. I can't hold your job if you aren't here to do it. Times are hard. There are plenty of people seeking employment."

"I know, but Addie is like a sister." Liz gave him a weak smile as she fought back tears. "I need to find her." Liz turned and left the room, not stopping to catch the director's expression.

The wall clock reached twelve as she picked up the receiver and called Donnie. He answered on the first ring. "Will your flight arrive by six this evening?"

"Yeah, sure. It's just a hop."

"Then book a flight on Lufthansa 9530. We're leaving for Frankfurt at nine tonight."

"What's your seat number? Should I try to sit near you?"

How could I possibly sit next to him that long? "It doesn't matter. We just need to be on the same plane."

"When will we get there?"

"The flight is eighteen hours. Cairo is ten hours ahead of California, so we'll arrive in two days."

"Did you call the Embassy?"

"Yes. I spoke with a Mr. Aston. He's sending his Egyptian assistant to meet us. His name is Mr. Shenouda. In fact, he called me this morning."

Two days later, Cairo, Egypt

"RAYHAN. YALLA. YALLA," tumbled from Jahi's lips and jarred Rayhan from his thoughts. The boy stood at the other end of the street where the market ended, holding up the bags. He bent down, set his groceries on the ground, and motioned for Rayhan to throw the ball. "Yalla!"

These trips to the market with Jahi were becoming a daily habit, as fetching his mother's groceries made the boy feel grown up. Rayhan enjoyed the time with his cousin.

He brought his hand up to shade his eyes. He wanted to throw the ball at just the right angle for Jahi, not too hard, but with enough force to land in the boy's arms. Rayhan smiled and wrapped his large hand around the oval-shaped object, bringing the stitches in line with his palm. "Ready?"

"Yalla!" the boy said, growing impatient.

Rayhan's cheeks crinkled around his eyes as he smiled, drew back his arm, and threw the football. He followed the arc as it soared and descended into Jahi's outstretched fingers. He made a perfect catch as Rayhan walked toward him. Rayhan decided on the way home the time had come for another English lesson. "When are you going to speak English? Don't you remember what I've taught you?"

Jahi shrugged and ran in front of Rayhan. The boy's sandaled feet slapped at the well-trodden dirt road. Rayhan shook his head. He found it hard not to love the mischievous carbon copy of his Uncle Al Abdul. As Jahi's white tunic disappeared around the corner, Rayhan glanced at his watch. He had enough time to change from his own traditional clothing and meet the two Americans at the airport.

Rayhan often picked up dignitaries for the Embassy and could maneuver through the airport parking lot with ease. He pulled the black sedan into a stall and checked the time. The Lufthansa flight 9530, if on schedule, would land in thirty minutes. He walked into the cavernous glass and metal building, past the long, narrow windows parallel to the runway, followed the row of live palm trees to a lighted, wooden felucca, and then to the area designated for those awaiting incoming passengers.

He checked the flight monitor and noted the plane would land a few minutes behind schedule. Mr. Aston hadn't told him much about the two people he had been instructed to pick up. He knew they came to search for a missing American couple. Rayhan had heard nothing on the news or read anything in the papers. It must be a minor incident. The cousin and family friend were distraught, the missing couple would be found, and all of them would head back to the States by the end of the week.

An overhead speaker announced the flight had landed and Rayhan moved into position near the arrival gate. Mr. Aston had told the Americans they could identify Rayhan by the official American Embassy sign he carried. The board, not much larger than a sheet of legal paper, rested in his hands. He stood with ardent awareness, a smile plastered on his face.

Passengers came down the ramp in a slow string of twenty or thirty from customs and into the lobby. An American couple walked through the door, ending the procession. The woman stood behind the gentleman and when she spotted Rayhan, she raised her hand, indicating they were who he waited for. The gentleman moved aside and Rayhan's eyes drank in her small, delicate features. She glanced in his direction and he startled himself when he gasped. He memorized every feature. She stood a hint over five feet, small-boned, but fit. Her short, dark hair suited her oval face, and her porcelain skin appeared almost translucent in contrast. He forced his eyes away from her when the gentleman spoke.

"I'm Donnie Barnes, and this is Liz McCran," Donnie said, gesturing to Liz.

"I am Mr. Shenouda." He shifted the sign under his arm and offered to take the carry-on from Liz's hand.

"Thank you." She smiled. "I hope you haven't waited long."

My entire life ran through Rayhan's head, but he mumbled, "No. Not long at all."

CHAPTER TWO

L IZ, D ONNIE, AND R AYHAN walked to the parking lot. He opened the rear door and she slid into the passenger seat behind the driver's side, tilted her head, and smiled. Donnie waited for Rayhan to release the trunk lock, loaded their luggage, then sat in the front across from Rayhan.

"How much do you know about your friends' disappearance?" Rayhan asked as he eased the car onto the busy highway.

Liz caught his eye in the rearview mirror. "Not much, Mr. Shenouda. They'd been missing for two days when you called me." Her heart pounded against her ribcage and she fought to breathe. "I had been instructed to call her family if anything happened, and when I called Donnie, he and I agreed to come here."

"This is all you know?" Rayhan murmured. *"Fil-mišmiš!"*

Liz sat on the edge of her seat and bent forward as she gave Rayhan a gentle, but firm message. "It did happen. Don't be so skeptical, Mr. Shenouda. Just to let you know, I understand every word you say. We can speak either Arabic or English."

"I'm sorry, Miss McCran. It is just odd they disappeared with no other information." Rayhan fixed his eyes on Donnie, who shrugged his shoulders.

"They were here on vacation. I don't know any more." Liz sat back in her seat and speculated how she could spend the next few days with not one, but two, headstrong men.

She fell into silent thought as she remembered the weeks right before their vacation, and Addie's excitement about her first trip to Egypt. Her husband, Gary, as a hobby compared early Christian writings and Egyptian mythology. Liz wondered if this had gotten them into trouble. Had they asked the wrong questions of someone? Addie and Gary were good, decent people. They wouldn't have knowingly stepped into a smuggling situation. Or could it be an issue of Christianity? They would have been arrested, not missing. Unless…Liz shuddered. She glanced out the tinted window of the sleek, black vehicle and recognized the streets approaching the Embassy. She found an inner strength and forced down the panic rising in her throat.

Donnie and Rayhan discussed something trivial about the weather and she joined their exchange. "Spring in Egypt is a beautiful time, isn't it, Mr. Shenouda?" Forgiving him for his earlier assumption, she continued. "We shouldn't have a problem, unless there is a spring sandstorm."

"It's a bit early for the Kashmin," Rayhan offered. "It will not be a problem in the city."

"No. However, we may not stay in Cairo." Donnie shifted in his seat to include Liz in the conversation as he continued speaking to Rayhan. "We need to find a gentleman named Mr. Moustafa."

"It is a very common name," Rayhan said. "Do you know anything else about him?"

Liz rummaged through a stack of papers she'd brought and hesitated. *Should I tell Rayhan about the letter?* "His first name is Abubakar."

"I know of a man with the same name. He lives very close to my Uncle Al Abdul."

"Can you arrange a meeting with him, Mr. Shenouda?"

"Yes, after we've met with Mr. Aston." Again, Rayhan locked eyes with Liz in the mirror. "Miss McCran, Mr. Barnes, if Abubakar Moustafa is who you are looking for, I believe you are going to be here a while. I think we need to at least be on a first name basis. I request you call me by my given name, Rayhan. May I have permission to use your first names?"

Liz nodded and acknowledged his request. She understood the formality of the tradition. "Who is he and why would he extend our stay?"

"Do you know anything about the Christians here, Liz?" Rayhan glanced at her.

"Some. I've worked mainly with the ancient Egyptian culture, but have also studied the beliefs and customs. I probably don't know as much as I should."

"And you, Mr. Barnes?" Rayhan questioned.

"I know absolutely nothing. I'm still working on my own Christianity. Go on, though. I find this all very fascinating. Do you think there's some religious connection to their disappearance?"

"I am a Christian, as is Mr. Moustafa, and we have learned to live secretively. With a population of over eighty million, there are roughly eight to twelve million Christians. We are, and have been, persecuted by our fellow Egyptians and the government." Rayhan paused as he approached the gate of the Embassy parking lot. He showed the guard his identification, and the entry gate swung open.

"At any rate," Rayhan said after he'd drove away from the gate, "we are generally careful, fearing danger for not only ourselves, but our community. Mr. Moustafa gambles with his own existence. He is being followed closely. There could be a problem if he is involved in this, even accidentally."

Liz moved back in her seat as Rayhan approached the parking stall marked: Ambassador Aston. "They were doing a favor for their pastor by delivering an envelope from a builder. Their church planned to volunteer during the construction. Why would something so simple have caused them to vanish?"

Rayhan grew silent. He parked the car and quickened his pace to the rear door to offer Liz his hand. "The involvement of Abubakar Moustafa makes me uneasy. He isn't careful."

Rayhan took Liz's hand and pulled her to stand beside him. They hesitated for a moment, facing each other, inches apart, until Liz moved away. She had been drawn to him from the beginning, mysteriously intrigued by his smooth, dark skin, brown eyes, and black hair, which glistened in the sunlight. The stylish cut of his suit accentuated his muscular build. He stood a good foot taller than she, and Liz slanted her head to explore his face. *Another time*, she thought, *different circumstances, but not now.*

"Donnie, Liz, come this way." Rayhan indicated to the large back door just beyond a small courtyard. "We'll use the employee entrance."

The sizable concrete building, the color of sand, loomed before them. Liz had been there many times, but it always struck her as odd. A pillar to Americanism in a country so different from her own, yet she'd been drawn to Egypt by those differences and now, to find her friend.

Liz and Donnie followed Rayhan. On previous trips, she frequented the Embassy to deal with visas or passports for the crew she'd brought from the museum, but never to meet the ambassador. On occasion, there'd been a problem with their rights to enter a dig and the Embassy would become involved in any relations with the Egyptian government. The museum staff ranked among a handful of outsiders allowed onto the archaeological sites of the various ruins.

The U.S. Embassy stood across the Nile, tucked into an area close to its shores. Mr. Aston's large, mahogany desk sat in front of an oversized window which offered a commanding view of the blue-green water of the river. He rose from his chair and extended his hand to Donnie.

Mr. Aston smiled. She appraised him with one quick glance and observed his full head of gray hair. She put his age about sixty. He'd spent too much time behind his desk the last few years and not out playing golf, his sport, as hinted to by the trophies displayed on a matching bookcase to his left. He exuded a warm and pleasant persona, but Liz caught a lack of conviction in his voice as he turned and shook her hand. She wondered if he hid his true feelings under his professionalism. Did he think they came here on a whim? Would he help them?

"Miss McCran, Mr. Barnes, it's good to meet you." He gestured to twin brown leather chairs with brass buttons down the front of the arms, ending at the wooden legs. He put a hand on his jacket, and in one swift motion unbuttoned it and smoothed his tie down, while he returned to his seat. "I have done some investigation this morning, and no group has come forward claiming they are holding your friends or wanting any demands. I'm not exactly sure how we can be of help to you, other than the normal routine. We will check where Mr. and Mrs. Wright have been and where they were supposed to be. Unless we hear word from some militant faction, it's about all the Embassy can do."

Liz turned to see where Rayhan had gone, but he had disappeared when they entered the ambassador's office. "I'm concerned about them, as is her cousin, or we wouldn't have come all this way because they changed their vacation itinerary. I've been in touch with the travel agency. I filled out papers for them to contact me in case of emergency. They obviously thought there was one."

"We might bring in the Legats," Mr. Aston offered.

"The who?" Donnie, raising his eyebrows, stared at him.

"The Legal Attaché for this country. Legats are assigned to the forty-five countries we work with by the Federal Bureau of Investigation."

The thought of the FBI connected with Addie and Gary's disappearance made Liz concerned the ordeal might be more serious than she'd thought. "You must not think it's necessary, or you would have already notified them."

"Not just yet, but ..." He hesitated as he groped for words. "Let us say, we may." He placed his hand on his jawline, touching his perfectly trimmed white beard. "I'm really sorry I can't help you more. There are many things which come into play when two countries are involved."

"You mean you're done?" Donnie blurted out. "We're on our own?"

"Please, Mr. Barnes, you must understand. There's a lot at stake," Mr. Aston answered in a calm, polished manner, which revealed the character trait Liz questioned. "I'm sure you two read the newspapers. The government here is shaky at best. I cannot draw the Embassy into this on supposition and no concrete evidence that your friends haven't gone off on some lark. I need evidence, not hearsay."

Donnie shifted forward. "How much do you know? Do you know about the letter, the shipment of crates here from the States, or this elusive Mr. Moustafa?"

"What crates?" Mr. Aston's voice escalated, which caused Liz to think he had come close to losing his tranquil façade. "There is a letter and a contact in Egypt? How were your cousin and her husband involved in this?"

"We don't know. It appeared to be an innocent request." Donnie rose from the brown, leather chair. "Addie told Liz they were delivering a letter from a Mr. Hamaka. The Wright's pastor gave it to them, and he wasn't sure, either. He perceived it as a favor, but he mentioned a building project and the crates"—Donnie paused—"I don't want to go to the police, the Egyptian government, or whoever else is tangled up in this. I just want to find my cousin and take her and her husband home." He reached across the desk to shake Mr. Aston's hand. "Are we finished here?"

Mr. Aston stood and shook Donnie's hand. "I'm sorry. This is a very difficult situation. I have nothing to go on. If I get a ransom note, anything for me to conclude they're in some kind of danger, I can proceed in an official capacity." Mr. Aston exhaled, his face sober. "It may be possible Rayhan can offer you some assistance. Please use him as much as you need. I will help where I can."

Liz caught a glimpse of a gold-framed picture as she extended her hand and glanced at the two blonde cherubs sitting on a young man's lap. "Your grandchildren?"

"Yes," Mr. Aston smiled. "Their mother, my daughter, was a Legat." Liz noticed a softened sadness around his eyes. "You remind me a lot of her. She, too, disappeared right after young Julia was born."

"I'm so sorry. Here?"

19

"No. At home. There are evil people everywhere." He took Liz's hand with such an unusual measure of warmth, her caution dissolved. She'd found an ally, even though she knew Donnie would not agree.

Mr. Aston walked from behind the desk and stood next to Liz. "I regret I can't help you more." He pressed his business card into her hand. "You might find this useful. Where are you staying, in case I need to find you?"

"The Mena House where Addie and Gary were registered." Liz slid the card into the pocket of her short-sleeved, linen jacket. She'd been in the same clothes for almost two days, and exhaustion crept into her bones as she grasped the enormity of their plight.

"Let me call Rayhan's office. He can drive you to your hotel." Mr. Aston clicked the intercom and asked his secretary to have Rayhan join them.

Liz's thoughts traveled to the handsome man sitting somewhere in an office nearby. She had pictured him as Mr. Aston's assistant and wondered what he really did at the Embassy. *What brought on this sudden interest?*

Rayhan appeared in the doorway. He had removed his suit jacket and his white shirt made a striking contrast to his dark skin. He flashed a smile at Liz.

"I would like you to take Miss McCran and Mr. Barnes to the Mena House," Mr. Aston directed Rayhan. "Also, are you available to help them? Your project on antiquities trafficking could be delegated to someone else, but what about your studies?"

"The current trafficking project is almost wrapped up, and I can work around my classes."

"Very good then." Mr. Aston paused and turned to Liz and Donnie. "He's at your disposal."

The trio left the ambassador's office after another round of handshakes and goodbyes. Rayhan took the lead and walked a few feet in front of Liz and Donnie. Her heels clicked on the highly polished tile floor and echoed through the empty hallway. Apprehension overtook her with Mr. Aston's hesitation. He could do no more considering the situation, but his reluctance caused her to think he might be more worried than any one of them cared to admit.

Rayhan walked to the parking lot exit and nodded as he stepped aside for Donnie. When Liz approached Rayhan, he reached out and touched her arm. The comfort of his warm skin on her forearm startled her. She waited, standing in the doorway, close enough to smell his aftershave. She brought her eyes to meet his.

"Don't be disappointed with Mr. Aston. His hands are tied," Rayhan said. He bent close to her. "I will help you." She felt his warm breath on her cheek and brought her fingers to touch her face. He gestured to the car where Donnie waited. "We must go."

Rayhan unlocked the car and Donnie took the back seat. "Let Liz ride up front. I need to think," he said.

"I know you're mad, and I appreciate you holding your tongue, but Mr. Aston probably couldn't help us any more than he has," Liz offered.

"Liz is right. There is only so much he can do. I can be of assistance."

"Doing what? Running errands?" Donnie fumed.

Liz scowled. "Donnie!" She couldn't believe his disrespect when Rayhan only offered his support. "It isn't going to help find Addie and Gary if we're all fighting." She let out a heavy sigh. "Rayhan knows Mr. Moustafa. We'll start there. We can arrange a meeting after we're settled."

"I'm just annoyed the Embassy can't help us." Donnie cleared his throat. "You're right. Sorry, Rayhan."

"Mr. Aston is a good man. Give him a chance. He might be doing more than he's telling you," Rayhan offered.

"He gave me his card." Liz pulled it from her jacket. She turned it over and noticed he had written on the back. *Call me at home: 02-8871645.* She slipped the card into her pocket and said nothing to the others.

Rayhan maneuvered the car into the circular drive at the Mena House. The verdant foliage at the front entrance gave an appealing oasis feel to the resort-type hotel surrounded by forty acres of lush gardens in the shadow of the Giza Pyramids.

Donnie and Liz checked in at the front desk with a young, Egyptian woman. Liz wanted to ask about Addie and Gary's room, and wondered whether or not she could convince the hotel staff she needed to get in, but decided to wait. Rayhan carried her bags, while Donnie walked ahead of them to the elevator. She noticed he hadn't said much since they left the Embassy and tried to anticipate if he brooded over the conversation with Mr. Aston, or if Donnie had actually decided on a plan. They walked across the large, marble-infused lobby and Liz pressed the button for the fifth floor. "Are you still mad?" she asked.

"No. I understand. I have a lot to think about. We need to figure out if Addie and Gary are here in the city or if they're somewhere near the church the pastor mentioned. I want to call Waterford and find out exactly where it is located, and if he found out anything else." The elevator opened and Donnie squinted at his room key then glanced up at the sign on the wall. "Well, it appears I'm down this way. Where are you, Liz?"

She turned the key over in her hand. "I'm in the opposite direction, but not far. Addie and Gary's room is 520. We'll need to convince someone to let us in there."

"I know the night clerk. His name is Ini-Herit. He can help us and let us know if anything might have happened while your friends were here." Rayhan glanced at his watch. "You two must be tired. Why don't I come back later this evening and we can talk with Ini?"

Donnie, who had moved down the hall away from them, hesitated as he said over his shoulder, "Call my room thirty minutes before you're coming over, or ring Liz and she can locate me." Donnie stopped, left his bags, and walked back toward Liz and Rayhan. "Could I have Pastor Waterford's number?"

Liz fished in her purse, jotted down the number, and handed it to Donnie. "Here. Have you met him?"

"Yeah, a couple of times when I visited Addie. I'm not sure he knows any more than he told you."

"Perhaps not, but maybe he remembered something else."

She and Rayhan continued down the hall. He extended his hand for her key when they reached the room, opened the door, and carried in her bags. The display of chivalry, something rarely seen in her male friends in the States, impressed her, and she enjoyed it more than she wanted to admit. He raised his hand, indicating for her to remain in the hall. After he checked the adjoining rooms, he motioned for Liz to enter.

"Why the room search?" she asked.

"Liz, there's something not right about this situation with your friends. I'm uncomfortable with it. At first, I thought they had just wandered off and they'd show up, now I'm not sure. Mr. Aston was hesitant, and rightfully so, but Mr. Moustafa's connection with this

23

has me worried." Rayhan moved closer. "I'm very troubled for you."

"I appreciate your concern. I'm worried, too. I don't even know Moustafa, but I do know Gary and Addie, and they wouldn't have willingly vanished into thin air."

"I should go. Do you want me to have the front desk call when I'm back?"

Liz thought for a moment. She trusted Rayhan, and his genuine concern for her friends touched her. There had been something else there, too, an electric spark which caused a ripple deep inside of her, but she could not yet acknowledge it. Ignoring Donnie's warning, she said, "Let me give you my cell."

They exchanged numbers and he walked to the door. "Is Mr. Barnes your…" Rayhan stopped and regarded Liz.

"My what?" Liz glanced at him, not understanding. A warm rush flushed her cheeks. "Oh, no. We're not anything. I met him at Addie's wedding and a couple of times at her home in San Jose. I hadn't talked to him at any length until yesterday."

"I see." Rayhan smiled. "I'll come back in a few hours. Rest well."

Liz pushed the door closed and wondered why Rayhan had asked his last question. The very last person on earth she wanted to belong to was Donnie Barnes. She realized people in other countries perceived Americans differently. Now Rayhan, he could be her type. Handsome, intelligent and eager to help. Protective, too, as proven when he had expressed his anxiety for her wellbeing. Maybe she could find a moment to speak with him somewhere in the turmoil. Perhaps after Addie and Gary were found.

The smell of jasmine wafted through the open window as the sheer gauzy curtains billowed into white floating clouds. The aromatic scent of flowers and fresh air stirred her thoughts. *Was he just interested in who Donnie and I are and our relationship to each other...or is he interested in me in a more personal way?*

She walked to the bed and sat on the edge of the moss-green spread. The numerous multicolored fabric pillows cascaded from their precarious positions near the headboard and one landed next to her. She picked it up and drew it closer, pulling a small amount of comfort into her arms. Liz surveyed the grand and impressive décor of the suite furnished with just the right mixture of old Egyptian and contemporary design. Warm earth tones filled the room and several large, native plants graced the entryway.

She found a sense of calm and lay back against the pillows. She remembered Donnie saying he had to think. So did she. Thoughts of how they'd accomplish their task swirled in her brain. She would just close her eyes for a moment and rest before this evening. Her arm tingled from Rayhan's soft touch. His musky aftershave and the closeness they shared in the doorway at the Embassy played over again as she drifted off. She needed to focus on finding Addie and Gary, but the mysterious Egyptian man who had vowed to help her filled her thoughts.

THREE HOURS LATER, she awoke with a start when her ringtone echoed from across the room. Shaking off sleep, she struggled to adjust to her surroundings. The song had played almost all the way through when she stumbled to the dresser and answered, "Hello?"

"Liz?" Rayhan's deep voice mixed with the melody lingered in her ears. "Did I wake you?"

"It's okay. Jet lag. Are you here?"

"Yes. I'm in the lobby. My friend is on duty."

"Give me a few minutes and I'll be down." Liz stretched and yawned. Her mind moved faster than the rest of her. She didn't want to waste the opportunity to check out Addie and Gary's room. "I'll call Donnie. One of us will be right there." Liz snapped her cell shut and went to the hotel phone to call Donnie's room.

She almost hung up when he answered. "Yeah?"

"It's Liz. Rayhan's in the lobby. Can you go down and meet him while I take a quick shower?"

"I guess. I was in the middle of a nap." Donnie hesitated and Liz wondered if he'd refuse to meet with Rayhan, then Donnie said, "Okay. Sure I'll go."

"I'll be there in just a bit. We may be able to search Addie's room. The night clerk is a friend of Rayhan's. We might find a clue as to where they are."

Donnie exhaled heavily on the other end of the line. "I called Pastor Waterford and he told me the church is south of Cairo. The more I talked with him, the more I doubted they went there." He grew silent for a moment and then continued, "Liz, the pastor didn't have any further ideas about the content of the sealed envelope. He did a little research on the contractor, Mr. Hamaka. He has ties in Egypt, and he may have been using Addie and Gary to deliver a message Hamaka knew he couldn't do it by phone or email, but at this point it is all supposition."

"We'll find something." Liz forced herself to believe her own words. "Go down and meet with Rayhan. I'll be right there."

She hung up the phone and rummaged through her suitcase until she found her favorite light blue dress and matching sandals. After a quick shower, she pushed her damp hair into a quick style, dressed and headed for the lobby.

The elevator, filled with occupants from higher floors, stopped on the next level, and when a group of people nudged their way to the exit, she followed them. Impatient, she used the spiral staircase she'd seen earlier to reach the lobby. She stood on the top step and spotted Donnie and Rayhan speaking to the desk clerk, an Egyptian man about Rayhan's age. She moved down the staircase just as Rayhan turned and caught her eye. Liz hesitated in her descent, both amazed and unsettled by the way he held her in his gaze.

Rayhan broke away from the conversation, crossed the lobby, and waited at the bottom of the stairs. He extended his hand to Liz. "You're quite a vision this evening." He took her hand and placed it into the crook of his arm. "I want you to meet Ini."

Liz did not want to appear rude, but the bold move to take her hand, again, came as a surprise. Her mind raced to what she knew of his beliefs. He possessed some traits of westernization, but with all of her conscious energy going into finding her friends, Rayhan's actions confused her.

He gestured to the man behind the desk. "This is Ini."

"Hello. I think I may be here a while. You may call me Liz."

"Oh. No. Not allowed." He smiled, which caused his eyes to twinkle.

"May I call you…" Glancing at his name tag, she strained to pronounce it correctly. "Ini-Herit?" She examined his smooth, round face.

He laughed. "You may call me Ini."

"What does it mean?"

"He who brings back the distant one."

Liz glanced at him, puzzled. "I haven't heard the name before."

"My parents are very traditional, and when I was born, my older brother traveled many kilometers to return home, therefore the name."

"Oh. I see." Liz caught Donnie's eye. "Would it be possible for us to see Mr. and Mrs. Wright's room? Did Rayhan tell you Donnie is family? I don't think we'd be breaking any rules." *Probably just bending them*, she thought.

"I have given the key to Mr. Barnes. Under the circumstances, I understand. Just be quick." Ini glanced behind him. "I really don't have permission."

"Thank you. We won't be long."

Ini reached underneath the mirror finish, black counter and produced a box wrapped in brown paper and tied with ordinary string. "Here, Miss McCran, this came yesterday for your friends."

Liz tore at the edges of the small box as they talked. She removed the lid which revealed a beautiful golden pendant—an ankh.

Ini eyed the symbol and cleared his throat. "The Egyptian symbol for life, unless…" His voice trailed off.

"Unless, what?"

"It is also a Crux Ansata, an eyed cross." His solemn eyes burnt into her. Just above a whisper, he said, "The symbol of the early Egyptian Christians."

"Who sent this?" Rayhan asked. "Do you know where it came from?"

Ini turned to Liz. "A small boy brought it. I thought, perhaps, Mr. and Mrs. Wright had it sent here from the market square. It is a common thing for the tourists to do. They will purchase something and pay a child a small token to deliver it to their hotel." Ini paused. "You may not want to let people see it, Miss McCran. Tell anyone who asks that you don't know what it means."

"I've studied Egypt for years. I do know what it means. It's a symbol of life and fertility, and one of the most popular hieroglyphics."

"Yes," Ini said as he placed his outstretched hand, palm up on the counter. Without hesitation, he moved his white shirt back away from his wrist, revealing the tattoo of a cross. Their eyes met as he smoothed the sleeve of his jacket.

Liz thanked him, her voice kept to a whisper. She hurried to replace the lid on the box and motioned for Donnie and Rayhan to follow her to the elevator. *What does the ankh mean? Should I be bold enough to wear it? Does it suggest someone wants to lead us to Addie and Gary? What else had Ini been trying to tell me when he showed me his tattoo?* Liz had too many questions and nowhere near enough answers.

THE ELEVATOR REACHED the fifth floor and Liz stepped out. She didn't delay as she made her way to room 520, Rayhan and Donnie on her heels. She took the key from Donnie and slid it in the lock. Rayhan moved next to her and put his hand over hers. "Let me. It may not be safe."

Lost in his eyes for a moment, she removed her fingers from the knob. The door creaked open into a darkened room. Rayhan reached in to click on the light and Liz gasped. "The room's destroyed." The threesome surveyed the upheaval—drawers turned upside down, cushions removed from the furniture, and Addie and Gary's suitcases overturned.

"My guess is someone didn't find what they wanted." Donnie stepped past the doorway and stooped to pick up the handle on a suitcase. "This is Addie's. Her jewelry is hanging from this inside pocket. This wasn't a robbery. Someone is after the letter."

"Do you think they were taken from here?" Rayhan asked.

"No, beyond this mess there's no sign of a scuffle, and no one reported any noise or unusual behavior to the desk clerk. I've already asked Ini if he knew of anything unusual."

Liz turned to Rayhan. "Now what should we do?"

"Check papers in the trash. See if anything's written on the notepad on the table. We need to find out where they went," Rayhan instructed.

"After we're done here, I'll pay Ini for housekeeping to straighten up. I don't think anything is missing, and I don't want the authorities to know about this." Donnie hesitated and stiffened. "The police here are known world-wide for their corruption. This break-in should go unmentioned."

Rayhan nodded. "If they weren't here, then someone had to gain access to their room. It may have been an employee," Rayhan said from the table where he'd upended a trash can.

"I don't know who we're dealing with. These rooms are easy enough to get in. They aren't electronic, just old-fashioned keys. I've jimmied a few locks, believe me." Donnie smiled ruefully. "Find anything?"

"Nothing. Mostly candy wrappers and a newspaper from four days ago."

"Why would their room not have been cleaned by housekeeping for four days?" Liz questioned.

"Whoever managed to break in here probably told the hotel not to clean so no one would be looking for them." Donnie shuffled through a stack of magazines and travel books on the coffee table. "Why did the tour agency call you, Liz? When did they suspect something?"

Liz searched the drawers of a small desk. "Addie and Gary missed a couple of the planned tours and no one could find them. The agency called a couple of hours after Rayhan."

Donnie frowned, eyeing Rayhan. "Do you know who called the Embassy?"

"I believe it was the contact from here, Exotic Tours."

Donnie nodded his head. "The time difference may explain why Liz wasn't notified by the travel agency first."

Liz rubbed her neck in an effort to ease away the stress-rooted tightness. She walked to the phone and picked up a blank notepad. "I think I've found some phone numbers," she said, spotting a slight indentation on the paper.

Donnie took the tablet and a nearby pencil. He sat at the table where Rayhan had dumped the trash can and rubbed the pencil lead back and forth until the information appeared: El Dar Restaurant on Sakkar Road and the phone number 02-2889007.

Donnie slid the pad to Rayhan. "Where is this place?"

"It is a popular restaurant, perhaps where they were to meet Mr. Moustafa."

"Can you take us?"

"Yes." Rayhan glanced at his watch. "It is some distance, and it is too late now, but we can go there in the morning. We must be careful." Rayhan shifted his attention from Donnie to Liz. "Very careful."

"I guess tomorrow is soon enough." Donnie folded the paper and gave it to Liz. "I don't think we're going to find much else here. We might as well go."

"Wait." Liz stopped them before they reached the door. "I want to ask Rayhan some questions." She removed the ankh from the box. "What does this really mean, and why did Ini show me the tattoo on his wrist?"

"Where your friends are concerned, I'm not sure what the ankh means, other than the obvious. It is a symbol of the early church as well as my people. You could be questioned if you display it in any fashion. Ini is afraid it might tie you to us." Rayhan paused and moved to the door. "We should go."

"What about the tattoo?" Donnie questioned.

"It is Ini's way to let Liz know he is a friend. He's willing to help. I have one as well." Rayhan moved his shirt sleeve away from his wrist to show them the sign of the cross above the palm of his hand. "We are different from a large majority of the population here, tolerated by some and persecuted by others."

The threesome walked into the hall and Rayhan locked the door. Liz turned to him when they reached the elevator. "How does all of this implicate Addie and Gary?"

"The church comes into play if Moustafa is their contact. Don't misunderstand. Abubakar Moustafa is a decent sort. He just takes risks and he may have done so by his participation in this envelope exchange and didn't know what he'd gotten himself into."

"Then why did he do it, and how does it concern your people?" Donnie punched the elevator buttons and waited for an answer.

"He probably thought he could make as much as a thousand-pound note."

"Over one hundred and eighty dollars in U.S. currency?" Liz asked. "Why would it have been so much?"

"Depending on the contents of the envelope and Moustafa's involvement. Most likely he had only been a messenger."

Liz noticed Rayhan's careful avoidance of the last part of Donnie's question. Did Moustafa hold the key to Addie and Gary's whereabouts?

The elevator reached the first floor and they stood in an alcove near the staircase. Liz took in the glittering golden lobby, high columned pillars and welcoming velvet furniture. The marble floors sparkled in shades of black and rich brown. This would have been such an idyllic place for Addie and Gary's vacation. She wondered if they enjoyed their short stay before—

"Liz?" Rayhan jolted her from her thoughts. "I just asked you if you'd like some dinner. We might find a few places still open."

"You two go ahead." Donnie wandered toward the elevator. "I'm beat. I need a clear head and there's a lot to do tomorrow. The longer they're gone, the harder they're going to be to find."

"Liz?" Rayhan turned to her. "Would it be all right?"

She knew it wouldn't be all right, considering his background, unless he had an interest in her which extended to far more than finding her friends. Liz weighed her thoughts. He should not have touched her. She knew this much of his culture, but he had many western traits which also puzzled her.

He placed his hand on her elbow and moved her away from the elevator. "Well?"

Liz smiled. "Are you sure?"

"Very," he said in a breathy whisper.

His response stirred something in her. An awakening of feelings long since put aside. They strolled through the massive double doors of the hotel entrance and out onto the circular drive. A large veranda sat to the left. Rayhan drew her there and took her hand. "Wait here. I have a wonderful idea."

"What?"

"This is perfect. I'll be right back."

Liz walked into the dimly lit patio and seated herself in a wicker chair near a glass-topped table. She wondered what he had planned as Rayhan disappeared around the corner. Liz gazed into the still night and saw the outline of the pyramids. They stood against the darkened sky like stone guards, each one taller than the next, knowing the secrets of thousands of years. What had happened to her friends? What secrets did she need to unlock to find them?

Rayhan returned with three large, white paper bags. Liz smelt the wonderful aroma of grilled chicken. The intense bouquet tickled her nose. From another package he pulled warak enab and she marveled at the perfectly rolled grape leaves. The final bag produced a small container of baklava and two large Styrofoam cups of mint tea.

"Where did you go?" Liz asked, amazed.

"Just around the corner my friends have a small, walk-up restaurant. They were closed, but I convinced them to put this together for us."

"You're full of surprises." She had been on her own too long, dealt with men very much like Donnie, who were full of themselves and, to her, quite boring. "I like surprises."

Liz took a bite of chicken and indulged in the bouquet of the meat and garlic mixture cooked to perfection in olive oil and sprinkled lightly with oregano.

"I hope we're not interrupting your life. Mr. Aston said you were working on an antique trafficking project and going to school?"

"I'm taking postgraduate studies in Egyptology and ancient cultures. I should have my masters shortly. I would like to work on some of the digs."

"Really? I've been on several digs, mostly in the Valley of the Queens. I work at the museum now in procurement." Liz surveyed Rayhan's face as she spoke. She had found a common interest and the conversation flowed easily. "Trafficking, too? Isn't it dangerous?"

"Well, not the part I do. I verify suspicious objects taken from tourists. Mostly, nothing comes of it, but once in a while we do arrest someone trying to smuggle something out of the country. Mr. Aston becomes involved when they are Americans."

Liz felt her pulse quicken. She found Rayhan incredibly interesting. He most likely downplayed his job for her benefit. Trafficking could be extremely hazardous. He came off as gentle and kind. Humble, not proud, but he had strength, too, at least in his convictions, or she wouldn't be here, on a moonlit veranda with him.

"May I ask you a question?" she asked between mouthfuls.

Rayhan hesitated. "I am assuming you will anyway."

"Do you mind?" She glanced at him before she continued and he nodded in agreement. "I have studied Egypt for many years, and I've been here numerous times. I know some of your culture and you surprise me. You seem very westernized." A quick smile danced across his face, even though they were shadowed from the moonlight.

"I lived in the States from the time I was two until I was sixteen. My parents were killed and my Uncle Al Abdul brought me back to Cairo and raised me as his own. I have no brothers and sisters, but I have two cousins who are close to my age. Then there's Jahi. He's only six and the little brother I always wanted."

"I'm sorry. It must have been a frightening experience."

"It happened long ago. I have the best of both worlds. I love this country and my people, but I also lived part of my father's dream of going to America." Rayhan grew silent.

Liz pondered over her next question. She didn't want to upset him, but she also needed to satisfy her own curiosity. "May I ask you something very personal?"

"Only if I have the option not to answer your question," he teased.

"You're very much a gentleman, which I truly appreciate, but Rayhan, doesn't your culture only permit you to touch the woman you intend to marry?"

Rayhan didn't answer. He gazed out into the street, then back at the meal in front of him, then finally his eyes rested on her. His jaw tightened before he spoke. "The answer to your question is yes.

However, our culture isn't as strict with men as it is with women. Your father would be disappointed with me if you were Egyptian. I do exhibit a lot of my western upbringing. I'm sorry if I upset you."

"No. I'm just curious. I don't want to offend you either." Liz lowered her eyes, grateful he couldn't see her cheeks flush.

"I had barely turned sixteen when I came back, but I did date some. I liked American girls. They were free with their ideas and thoughts. It is different here. Many of the women my age are very traditional, in some cases, even betrothed."

"Is it what you want?"

"No. My Uncle Al Abdul brings up the subject often. I want to make my own choice. You are a very beautiful woman, Liz, asking me all these crazy questions." He laughed nervously. "I want to make my own decision and it will be because the woman I pick fits me as well as my culture and my life. I must obtain Uncle Al Abdul's approval if I move outside the cultural circle. I'll be separated from my family without consent and it is something I also need to consider before I make my choice."

"Has your uncle tried to arrange a marriage for you?"

"It has been mentioned. Women come around at parties, offer me a smile, and hope we'll become betrothed."

"Have there been many?"

"It isn't important. I'm well beyond the proper age, and my uncle reminds me often. The important part is the last woman who catches my eye, not those who preceded her."

Liz's mouth went dry. What was he telling her? "Then what part of your culture allowed you to touch me, your western, or your Egyptian?"

Rayhan stood. "You must be tired. Have Donnie bring you to the El Dar tomorrow at noon. I'll meet you there." He busied himself picking up the bags and clearing the table from their meal.

He walked her to the edge of the veranda just short of the entryway door.

She turned to face him. They stood inches apart. "You didn't answer me, Rayhan. Which part of you?"

He reached up and gently brushed his hand across her face, trailing a finger down her cheek, and rested it on her lips to silence her. "Both." He turned and walked into the night.

CHAPTER THREE

LIZ WOKE AS the first stream of morning light fell upon the terracotta-colored tile of her bedroom floor, glad to be free from her restless night of dreams and memories. Fresh fears revisited her, knowing they had less than a precious handful of clues to find her missing friends, and more than she cared to admit, the dinner with Rayhan had left her unsettled.

She glanced at the alarm clock. Seven. She had several hours before their meeting at the El Dar, and Ini would still be on duty. Could she find anything to explain what had happened in room 520 just a few days before? Someone had to see or know something. Who had broken into Addie and Gary's room and who had kept it from being cleaned?

Liz dressed in a royal-blue silk shell, light-blue cotton blazer, and matching slacks. Struggling into her sandals, she brushed her hair away from her face. A few quick strokes with a makeup brush, a touch of lip gloss, and she headed to the door, but remembered the ankh and returned to the dresser. Liz dropped it into her purse, and once in the lobby, found Ini at the front desk.

"Good morning, Miss McCran," Ini called. "Did you have a good night?"

"I'm afraid I didn't sleep well worrying about my friends." Liz let her thoughts travel briefly to Rayhan, but she could not concern herself with him now. "Do you know anything, Ini? Did someone see anyone around their room, and why did it go unnoticed by the maid service?"

"I did some checking last night as Mr. Barnes requested." Ini glanced behind him. Liz's eyes scanned the lobby for other prying eyes. "There is an entry in the computer. Mr. Wright called and requested they not be disturbed. No housekeeping or room service during the rest of their stay."

"Mr. Wright requested it? Isn't that a bit unusual?"

"Yes, but not unheard of."

"Are you sure Gary called?"

"I didn't take the call. It happened during the day shift four days ago. It is noted that the call came from room 520, and possibly whoever took it assumed it was Mr. Wright."

"Do you know the address to the University Library? There's some research I should do."

Ini tapped a few keys on the computer, and then turned to Liz. "The American University in Cairo, 113 Sharia Kasr El Aini. You'll need to ask the driver to take you to the side entrance." Ini glimpsed up from the keyboard, and then again over his shoulder. "There is a tour forming to go to the pyramids." He nodded toward one of the golden columns where a young woman stood, a small group of tourists gathering around her. "You might find out more by going with them."

Liz's eyes questioned him and didn't understand this sudden change in the conversation. Why did he want her to go visit the three towering pyramids which stood in plain view from the Mena House? "I've been there several times. Not today."

Ini leaned over the desk and whispered, "Moustafa will meet you at the necropolis."

Liz frowned. Common sense told her to go back and wake Donnie. He'd be angry, but her fearless determination won out. "When did he contact you?"

"Early this morning." Ini cleared his throat while his hand tugged against his collar. "I was just about to call you."

"How did he even know we were here?"

"News travels fast in our community." Ini gazed across the room to the group forming for the tour. "He's your connection. They're leaving. Go with them. You'll find him at the Tomb Robber's entrance of Khufu's Pyramid."

"Maybe I—"

"Hurry," Ini said as he thrust a ticket into her hand.

Liz stood, torn between staying where Addie and Gary might find her, meeting with Rayhan, and leaving with the tour group. She trusted Ini's instincts, and perhaps Moustafa had some answers. Liz rushed to join the group as she called over her shoulder, "Charge the tour to my room."

The young woman dressed in a casual pantsuit directed the group to a waiting bus at the front entrance to the Mena House. Liz, one of the last to board, peered around at the smiling faces of the other Americans and Europeans. Her heart sank, heavy with the growing awareness of her desperate mission. The short ride brought them to the edge of the plateau. The assemblage gathered at the Great Pyramid of Khufu.

"It is of interest to learn none of the Pyramids in Egypt were built alone, but always with many other tombs and buildings surrounding them." The tour director held up her slight, thin hand and spanned the surrounding area of monuments and burial grounds. Liz, half-listening, launched a quick search to locate the Tomb Robber's entrance.

"We will now enter the burial chamber of Khufu. The foyer to the Great Pyramid leads to a corridor. Please watch your step as the ramp slopes downward."

Liz waited in the morning shadows and stepped back as the others passed. The group filed into the main tomb as she reached into her pocket. She handed one of the young Egyptian boys, who were waving maps in her face, a small coin and unfolded the layout of the burial grounds.

Liz walked toward the western edge, studying the diagrams when her name floated over the dry, still air of the desert. Startled, she turned toward the sound. A gentleman in a white suit, stout and shorter than she, approached. He smiled broadly, but her eyes focused on his eyebrows. They reminded Liz of large, furry caterpillars.

"I'm Abubakar Moustafa," he said, and nervously grabbed her hand.

Liz fought the impulse to wrench herself free as he pulled her to a waiting car. The driver drove in the direction she had come on the tour bus, toward the palm trees of the Mena House in the distance. She wrestled to control her nervous, quaking hands, and pounding head. She sat perched on the edge of the rear seat, behind Moustafa. Placing her hand on the door handle, she considered whether or not she should jump.

The car slowed after a series of rapid turns and the driver deposited them on a quiet street lined in whitewashed buildings with blank, windowless exteriors. Men huddled in the solitary doors. Children sat at their feet, hungry mouths waiting to be fed. Liz and Moustafa exited the vehicle during a quick stop. The driver left them in a cloud of dust. A cough convulsed from her throat, and Mr. Moustafa put his finger to his lips.

He searched the road they'd just traveled and motioned for Liz to follow. She, too, glanced around before she ducked her head and entered the building. She wanted some sort of mental picture of this place, in case she had to find it again.

"Come, Miss McCran, we don't have much time." They entered a small set of rooms jammed together in a senseless fashion, which would grate an interior designer's last nerve. The dark interior offered a cool respite from the early morning heat. He directed her to sit on a contemporary couch surrounded by old, wooden, inlayed tables. "An attempt was made to kidnap your friends, but there has been an intervention."

Kidnapped? Intervention? The statements registered as cold fingers gripped her heart. Perspiration rose on her upper lip and she drew a shaking hand there to stifle an unwilling scream. Mr. Moustafa rose and returned with a cold, bottled soft drink. As she took it, the shape of the familiar bottle in her hand forced Liz to understand his small gesture. *Hope.* Moustafa had given her hope.

"Can we find them?" Liz asked, her voice shaky.

"There is a plan to rescue your friends and it has been arranged for them to be removed from Cairo by a small group of men who will take them to a church in the south."

"Are they still here?"

"I do not know when the action will take place. It may have already happened. I only know the plan." Mr. Moustafa placed his hand in front of her like a brown, callused stop sign. "You must stay out of this, Miss McCran."

"I've been to the Embassy. They already know the Wrights are missing," she protested.

"That may have been an unwise choice. Your country doesn't understand our people or our ways. Can you tell them their services aren't necessary?" He considered her pensively, pushing Liz for an answer.

She hesitated with her reply and feared she shouldn't implicate Rayhan. "I'm sorry. I cannot. I'm working with a man from the Embassy, Rayhan Shenouda. He contacted me concerning their disappearance."

A spark of recognition danced across Moustafa's eyes. "Ah… Al Abdul's nephew." Moustafa thrust a note into her hand. "You will need this if the men are able to move your friends. I will send you word if and when they are safe." Liz unfolded the paper when Moustafa shook his head. "It will mean nothing to you now, read it later."

"Is this your home?" she queried.

"Yes. Humble, but my own."

"How would I find it again? The streets and houses all seem to be the same."

Moustafa didn't answer. "I will call a car for you. You've been here much too long. I have no doubt we're being scrutinized. God be with you."

No more than five minutes later a yellow Honda screeched to a stop at his door. Moustafa instructed the driver, and once Liz had settled in and closed the door, the car rumbled down the dirt road. She opened the paper Moustafa had given her. He had been correct. It didn't mean anything to her.

All built in one straight line.
Cubic by cubic, time by time.

At the vanishing point you'll find a shelter built from stolen stone.
Ask the ancient dweller there.

He knows of many things, of God's whispered breath and angel's
wings.

AFTER THE HONDA deposited her at the Mena House and sped away, Liz rushed through the lobby to the elevator. She glanced toward the desk, but Ini had left. When she reached the fifth floor, she ran down the hall to Donnie's room and banged on the door.

"I'm coming," Donnie grumbled from behind the entrance, opening the door.

"It's Liz. Hurry."

"It's only ten o'clock. What's going on?" Donnie glanced at the bed where he spread the contents of the black, concealment pack he wore around his waist. He took the comforter and threw it over the contents.

"What are those things?" Liz questioned.

"Stuff I might need." He addressed her head-on. "Don't worry. Nothing illegal. In fact, some of it is quite ordinary."

Liz decided not to question him. "I've been out to the pyramids."

"You went sightseeing?"

"No. I went to meet Moustafa."

"You met him?" Donnie glared at her in disbelief. "When did that happen? Why didn't you call me?"

"The tour group was leaving and there wasn't time." Liz paused. "I tossed and turned all night and finally gave up on sleeping. I dressed and went down to the lobby to ask Ini for the address of the library at the University of Cairo. I thought I might find something about the ankh and what it has to do with the

Egyptian religions." Liz met Donnie's gaze. "The tour group was ready to leave. Ini told me to go with them."

"Moustafa contacted him?"

"Yes. I asked how Moustafa knew about us and Ini told me they had a tight underground network."

"Rayhan probably told him." Donnie walked over to the window and Liz followed. Below, they viewed the verdant grounds of the Mena House. The hotel guests had ventured out, breakfasting on the verandas or walking the compound.

"I don't like Rayhan. He doesn't seem like someone we should trust."

"You don't like anyone, and you can't find one thread of worthiness beyond your own." She turned to face him. "You don't like Rayhan, you're mad at Mr. Aston. Can you just stop?" She crossed the room.

"I can see I'm not winning any popularity contest with you either."

He has that straight. "I don't think Rayhan notified him. Moustafa acted surprised I knew Rayhan, but Moustafa knew Rayhan's family. He gave me this." Liz thrust the note into Donnie's hand. "It doesn't make sense, but he said it wouldn't, unless Addie and Gary are rescued."

"By whom? Us?" Donnie questioned.

Liz reclaimed her self-control and weighed her words. She did not want Donnie to coordinate a search party until all the pieces were in place. "There was an attempt to kidnap them and someone intervened. A group of men will, or have by now, taken them to a church south of here."

Donnie handed her the note. "Then we need a jeep, and I'll need to find supplies for a trip across the desert. We should leave immediately."

Liz fought to gain control over the anxiety rising in her throat. "I agree, but we don't even know where to go. We should solve this riddle and find out what the ankh means in all of this."

"Do you have to go to the library? What about the Internet?"

"It would work. I can access the San Francisco Museum database. The archive research papers will have the information." She hurried to the door. "I have to locate a computer, and we only have a couple of hours."

Donnie pointed to a small alcove with a chair and roll-topped desk. "There's one in the credenza. Don't you have one?"

"No, they were short on rooms. Yours is the business suite. I guess it came with a computer." Liz made her way to the desk and pulled out the chair. She sat down and brought up the Internet. "Where do you want to start?"

"You know more about Egypt than their religious perspective. I think you should focus your search there," Donnie said. He pulled a chair beside her and settled in.

"You're right. I should know what I need to solve the puzzle. I just have to analyze it." Liz logged into the museum's records and searched on the Christian religion in Egypt.

Donnie gave her a wry smile. "As we learn more about the church, maybe the riddle will solve itself."

"Perhaps."

"Here it is." She tapped the screen with her finger. "The ankh is the symbol for life, fertility, and the early Egyptian Christians."

"Yes." He gave her a thumbs up. "See, you know more than you think. You told Ini about it last night."

"I'm uncertain about the eyed cross, the Crux Ansata, as he calls it." Liz turned and focused on the screen and read aloud. "Christianity was brought to Egypt by Saint Mark and spread in the next half-century. However, now the Christians are very few." She stopped briefly as she scrolled down the screen. "There are approximately two million registered Christians, but many more do not acknowledge their faith to the government."

"I guess that's why Rayhan and Ini are careful about who sees the tattooed cross on their wrists. It is a symbol of their church and their unity to each other," Donnie said. He held out his hand and asked, "Let me see the ankh."

Donnie turned the pendant over in his hand. "This has so many meanings. It's doublespeak. I believe whoever sent this wanted you to see the Crux Ansata."

"What do you mean?"

"Okay. Tell me what you know about the ankh as an Egyptian symbol, then tell me what it means in Christianity."

"Maybe I should call Rayhan. He's taking courses at the university on this very subject. We'll see him in a little over an hour, but I would like to ask him some questions."

"The jury is still out on him. Just wait."

Your jury, not mine.

"In Egyptian history, it's a looped cross. It's the symbol of life and is supposed to give the wearer wealth, power, and intelligence. It was formed from the hieroglyphic RU. It appears as an O set on a cross. The RU loop represents the opening of a fish's mouth giving birth to water and the Nile," she repeated from a long ago Egyptology lecture one of her professors had given.

"Go on," Donnie coaxed.

"The fish is an early symbol of Christianity. The meaning of life is represented as eternal life, and of course, the cross for the crucifixion. Why do you think I should see it as the church symbol?" Donnie's analogies still hadn't convinced her.

A small, etched mark caught her attention as he turned the cross over in his hand. "There's a verse inscribed on the back, Isaiah 19:25. Are you familiar with it?"

"No. I'm not sure I am." Donnie shook his head.

"We need a Bible. There aren't any Gideons here," Liz said.

Donnie scraped the chair on the wooden floor as he moved from the desk. He made his way to the closet and unzipped his duffle bag, which sat on the suitcase stand, and came back with a black, leather Bible, his name inscribed in gold on the front. The sight of the book impressed Liz. It appeared expensive and well-worn. "What a beautiful Bible."

"Addie gave it to me," he said almost in a whisper.

Liz stopped a tear trickling down her cheek. Once Addie married, she had such a renewed faith, she made it her mission to bring her friends and family to Christ. Liz knew the exact inscription Addie had written in Donnie's Bible. The same line from a song had been written into hers: *The hour I first believed.* The difference between Liz and Donnie's Bibles would be the date when they took their step in faith.

Liz glanced at the glass partition and the dancing patterns the mid-morning orb made as it marched across the sky. She waited for Donnie to locate the passage. Her stomach reminded her it had been a long time since dinner with Rayhan the night before. She wondered what he might be doing now. *Could he be thinking about me, too?*

Donnie interrupted her thoughts. He picked up the ankh and turned it over. "This is quite interesting."

"What?"

"See the etching where you told me you saw the verse? There's a name there, too. Talmar. Does it mean anything to you?"

"I am supposed to find someone. It's in the riddle. Here." She handed the folded paper to him again. "Line four: find the ancient dweller. Maybe that's his name." Glancing at the Bible, she asked, "Did you find the verse?"

"Yes." Donnie read the passage out loud. "In that day there will be an altar to the Lord in the midst of the land of Egypt, and a pillar to the Lord at its border... Blessed is Egypt My People."

"There are several old, fifth century churches in Cairo. Maybe a priest could answer our questions."

"Any of them built of stolen stone?" he asked.

Liz pulled away from the desk and walked to the window. She unfolded the note from Moustafa and read the first line. "*Cubic by cubic.* Why cubic? The pyramids were built in cubits. Cubic means weight, place, space, three-dimensional. I've read that somewhere." Liz went to the desk where she'd deposited her purse, dug deep into the side pocket, and found a small book she'd brought to read on the plane. "The pyramids are the earliest structures of man. The base is larger than the top, which provides a sturdy structure which has lasted thousands of years. A three-dimensional triangle to survive the ages, constructed by the Egyptian, Incan, and Mayan cultures."

Donnie joined her and followed her gaze toward the three towering pyramids. "Volume, weight, place, space—that explains three-dimensional, doesn't it?"

"Oh," she said. "There, in front of us, the necropolis. It is an interesting effect. The pyramids are almost as one, an illusion. Khufu's alone was one of the Seven Wonders of the Ancient World, the only true survivor. It is six city blocks at the base, and the tallest manmade structure until the Eiffel Tower. Addie and Gary are out there somewhere, right under our noses."

"Then what does this mean?" Donnie said. He pointed to the second line. *"A shelter built of stolen stone."*

"Stone robbers took the outside blocks of the pyramids to build the city of Cairo. That's why it's whitewashed. Everything is made of limestone. There must be a building at the vanishing point." Her enthusiasm soared. Perhaps solving the puzzle wasn't going to be as hard as she'd thought.

Donnie glanced at her. "What's this vanishing point?"

"It's a theory which is embraced by some archaeologists and not by others." She turned from Donnie and viewed the graduating sizes of the triangular monuments. "The vanishing point of the Giza Pyramids is believed to be a geometric designation and where many think there are additional burial grounds or tombs of lesser members of the Pharaoh's families, or even important treasures."

"Where is it? Do you know?"

"It's beyond the smallest pyramid, where the curvature of the earth takes the line of site out of view." She motioned for Donnie to follow her to the table. Liz inked a quick sketch on hotel stationery. "Assuming all three tombs are in line, it should be about…" She drummed the spot on the paper map she'd just drawn. "There."

"It's away from the city and the normal tourist routes. Should we hire a guide?"

Rayhan's name came to mind. She had tried to dismiss him and their dinner the previous evening. What he had said about both his Egyptian and his American culture allowing him to touch her, the way he trailed his finger down her cheek and rested it softly on her lips... "Maybe Rayhan can take us."

"I guess, but I didn't want to involve outsiders," Donnie grumbled. "I told you I wanted to call the shots here."

Liz sprang up from her chair. "You're in uncharted territory. You may have lived on the streets and toughed your way through lots of situations, but you cannot do that here. I've tried to explain their way of life is different." Liz dug her clinched fingers into her palms. "There are places we can't go and things we won't be allowed to do." She turned to the window and the view of the pyramids.

"Okay." Donnie came to her side and drilled his eyes into her. "Maybe he can, but he doesn't strike me as the type to..." Donnie hesitated.

"To what?" She glared at him. "He isn't afraid to get involved, and he's offered, so let him."

"Isn't he just a clerk or something?"

"Do you know how dangerous his job is? Trafficking of antiquities is a serious offence."

"You certainly found out enough about him last night."

Her stomach knotted. Liz hated this constant battle raging between her and Donnie. He had to be right, the one to find the answers, the one to lead the way. She longed for Rayhan's gentle approach and would insist he be included. "I'm not going to argue this point any further. I think he'd be a valuable asset. I'll show him the note once we're at the El Dar."

"Fine," Donnie hissed. "What are we looking for?"

"According to the riddle we must find a shelter of some sort, a white building, and hopefully, someone who lives there—maybe this Talmar." Could it be so easy? She would just walk up to a total stranger in a foreign country, hoping he knew how her friends had disappeared, when she had trouble, at first, getting Mr. Aston interested in helping them.

She remembered Mr. Aston's business card and the phone number he'd jotted on the back. Liz had hesitated telling Donnie the day before, and the uncertainty kept her from mentioning it now. "Maybe we should call Mr. Aston again."

"He didn't want to help yesterday."

"Rayhan told me Mr. Aston may be doing more than we know. He has to be careful."

"I think we're wasting too much time solving riddles and doing nothing about locating Addie and Gary. Aren't you a bit chummy with this Rayhan character?"

Liz ignored his question. "We don't have enough information. Moustafa said they would be rescued and then moved. We don't even know where."

"You believe Moustafa?"

"I don't think we have much choice."

Liz glanced at her watch. She needed an out from arguing with Donnie. "We should go to the El Dar. We'll arrange to find the house at the vanishing point once we've met with Rayhan."

Donnie turned and walked to the bed and threw back the comforter. "I'll put this stuff together and meet you in the lobby. Have the front desk call a cab."

Liz moved to the door, and as she reached the entryway, she turned. "I'm sorry, Donnie. We don't need to argue. I want to find them as much as you do, but we have to follow a methodical plan."

"You're right. We don't have enough information, but every day, every minute matters. We'll go locate that mythical white house this afternoon, and maybe Rayhan knows where the church in the south might be. We'll be on the road no later than tomorrow."

She wondered how everything would come together in time, but nodded in agreement. "No later than tomorrow."

Liz took the stairs to the lobby. Her heart pounded, but the exertion didn't bring on her increasing nervousness. At the thought of Rayhan, an electric spark ran down her spine, leaving her surprised at her angst. She had tried all morning to push him from her mind, but she had to admit, the idea of seeing him again pleased her. Liz ignored Donnie's statement a few minutes ago. *Could he be jealous? Two men interested in me? Most of the time, I can't find a single one.* Her clear choice would be the dark, mysterious Rayhan. She continued to speculate. If she and Rayhan did fall in love, which one of them would be willing to give up their culture and country for the other?

She approached the desk clerk and asked for a cab. Liz went to the ladies' room to freshen her makeup while she waited for Donnie. She fluffed her hair and stole a glimpse of herself in the mirror and reapplied the blush and lipstick she'd pulled from her purse. *I could live here. I love this country. My family would visit. I'd visit them. Why am I even thinking these thoughts? He only touched me...but through to the very nucleus of my being.* However, she knew his actions were forbidden, unless he had sincere intentions. She studied her reflection. *If she could see into the future, would it be with Rayhan?*

Liz returned to the lobby just as the elevator opened. Donnie strode toward the door. "I've called a cab," she said from behind him. "It should be out front by now."

They found the taxi waiting in the circular drive and were whisked away to the El Dar. The eatery, located in a two-story brick building, sat wedged in among the businesses on Sakkara Road. The used brick facade and red tile roof made it stand out in the midst of the other, gleaming, white buildings. The restaurant spread over a full city block, and reminded Liz of a western frontier establishment, instead of one in downtown Cairo.

Liz and Donnie were greeted by a gentleman inside the cool, dark entrance. Dressed in a green, embroidered Egyptian vest, flowing, white kilted pantaloons, and a red fez, the man escorted them to a table. Mesmerizing music echoed through the room. Liz recognized the sound of the ancient flute, the ney, and the strings of an oud. The wistful melody, taped on a never ending loop, played over the restaurant's sound system.

"Someone else will join us," Liz instructed the host in Arabic. She and Donnie were seated in a small alcove near the entrance.

After a quick inspection of the room with its white walls and leaded glass windows, nothing seemed foreboding or dangerous, but her apprehension grew. Each of the door openings, exiting and entering the main dining room, were covered with colored, plastic beads. She kept her eyes on the entrance from the kitchen. *Did Addie and Gary leave through those doors?* She rose, scanned the restaurant, and without a word, walked past Donnie.

"Where are you going?" Donnie asked.

"Wait here for Rayhan. We know this was the last place Gary and Addie might have been. I want to check something out." She pushed back the beads and entered the preparation area. The aroma of spicy foods greeted her, but the kitchen appeared empty. The door to the alleyway stood open. Liz froze. Nothing out of the ordinary—a kitchen, a doorway, an alley—but Addie and Gary had been there. An alarming sense of awareness flooded over her. A sixth sense told her they had been abducted from this very spot. Tears welled in her eyes. She turned, startled by someone yelling in Arabic.

Liz raised both hands in front of her, palms out. "Sorry. I took a wrong turn," she mumbled. The menacing expression on the dark face in front of her jerked her thoughts back to the kitchen with its aromas and vegetable bins. With a large meat cleaver from the chopping block, the chef pointed her in the direction of the restaurant's main seating area. She shuddered, her unsteady fingers parting the swaying beads. Liz clung to the back of her seat and collapsed into it, hands clasped together to halt the tremor. She spotted Rayhan as he made his way to their table, Mr. Aston on his heels.

"Are you okay?" Rayhan asked. His face grew dark.

Her heart knocked against her ribcage. She closed her eyes and ran a quivering hand through her hair before she answered. "I wanted to see the last place Addie and Gary might have been. This is where they were to meet Mr. Moustafa, and where they may have disappeared. All this has left me shaken." A waiter appeared by the side of the table, his pen poised over a notepad to take their order. "Please decide for us, Rayhan. I think you'd be a better judge of what we should have." She gave him a weak smile and kept the encounter with the chef to herself.

Rayhan spoke to the server in Arabic while he jotted down the order for their meal. Another waiter arrived within minutes, carrying several small bowls of vegetables and fruits and strong, black Egyptian coffee. The final plates of mashed fava beans and pita bread were in place when Liz told Rayhan and Mr. Aston about her meeting with Moustafa and the riddle.

Mr. Aston didn't speak. He pushed his plate aside and brought his hands together to form a steeple with his index fingers. He brought the point to his cleft chin and spoke thoughtfully. "There isn't much I can do for you in my capacity at the Embassy, except tell you not to go looking for your friends, and to let us contact the police. You should not go out into the desert. Not as two American citizens. Understood?"

Hot tears she'd kept pent up for the past two days rolled down her cheeks as his betrayal shrouded her. He rose from the table, then glanced at Donnie, whose face had turned to stone.

"I should return to the office. Rayhan will go with you this afternoon and see whatever it is you think this riddle is about." Mr.

Aston offered his hand to Donnie, then he turned to Liz and said, "Do you still have my card?"

"Yes. I do," she answered him.

"Then I suggest you use it."

Donnie's eyes followed Mr. Aston through the entryway. "What was that supposed to mean?" Donnie asked.

"He gave me his home phone number."

Rayhan considered them across the table. "I told you he'd find a way."

"First, take us to this place mentioned in the riddle." Donnie gestured to Liz. "Show him the note."

Rayhan returned the paper to Liz after he read the riddle. "I believe I know where this is. Meet me at the edge of the marketplace in an hour." Rayhan brought his eyes to meet Liz. "You'll need to change. We'll be walking through the sand, and if the building is the one I know about, you'll need a scarf to cover your head."

"Where should we meet you?" Donnie asked.

"You'll find me two streets over from the Mena House. I will be waiting at the fruit vendor's stand." Rayhan stood and held Liz in his gaze for a moment, then turned and walked away.

"What's with him?" Donnie asked.

Liz silently acknowledged the ember ignited by Rayhan, struggling to hide a smile as it formed on her lips, as she said to Donnie, "I have no idea."

CHAPTER FOUR

DONNIE AND LIZ returned to the Mena House and agreed to meet in a half hour near the front entrance. Liz arrived first and paced back and forth across the lobby for an additional fifteen minutes before Donnie exited the elevator. "What took you so long? Men always complain about women being slow."

"Sorry." He held the door open. "I tried to make a couple of calls back to the States."

"Anything I should know?"

"Not yet. I could only leave messages with the time difference." He adjusted his Stetson and brushed his hands over his faded jeans. His cotton cowboy shirt, with pearl-snap buttons, made Liz think he appeared out of place. "Ready for a safari?" He pointed to her multi-pocketed shorts and light pink polo shirt.

"Whatever." Liz smiled as she glanced between his alligator skin Tony Lamas and her old, high-topped boots with pink socks jutting out from the top. "Each to his own."

The walk to the open market took less than ten minutes. Rayhan hadn't arrived and they waited at the vegetable and fruit vendor. The stand overflowed with bananas, peaches, melons, and grapes, all neatly arranged in colorful rows. Shaking her head at the offer to try the sweet delicacy at the end of a sharp knife in the entrepreneur's extended hand, Liz moved closer to Donnie. She reached into her bag for a scarf, swirling it around her head and neck to partially cover her face.

A young boy approached on a bicycle. He circled around Liz, his eyes never leaving her, but as he pedaled away, up the center of the marketplace, he stole a quick glance over his shoulder.

"Wait," Liz called. Nothing. "Saadni," she tried again in Arabic before his slender brown legs spirited him away.

His sandaled feet stopped and drew back on the pedals. The bike spun around, raising a cloud of dust and a quizzical spark crossed his face. He dropped the bike and walked toward her.

"Rayhan Shenouda?" she asked.

He pointed to the end of the street at the last house on the left. Liz smiled, but he didn't move. She reached into her pocket for a dollar and the ankh, which she'd place around her neck, slipped from beneath her shirt. The boy's eyes grew wide. *Is he aware of the Christian connection?* He took the dollar, grabbed his discarded bicycle, and disappeared down a narrow pathway between two buildings. Liz tucked the ankh away.

"Did the kid know where Rayhan lives?" Donnie asked as he munched on a banana.

"Yes. Down there somewhere." She nodded in the direction the boy had shown her. "Where is he? I thought he would be waiting for us."

No sooner had the words left her lips than Rayhan emerged at the end of the street, followed by an older man. His Uncle Al Abdul,

Liz assumed. They appeared to be in an argument. Rayhan walked toward Liz as his uncle stood near the doorway, unmoving.

Rayhan came to stand in front of her, eyes clouded, his lips in a tight, thin line. He brought his hand to his face, rubbing his jaw. "I'm sorry. I had to talk to my uncle about what I am doing."

"He doesn't seem too pleased," Donnie said.

"He isn't, but he will be." Rayhan drew his lips into a forced smile. "I just have to convince him otherwise. Donnie, would you mind if I took Liz back to the house for a moment?" Rayhan gestured in Donnie's direction. "Is there anything you need? The marketplace is the world's biggest supermarket."

"Now?" Donnie set his jaw as he stepped closer to Liz.

Her eyes shifted between the two men. She had no idea what Rayhan wanted, and Donnie was right—why now? Her gaze rested on Rayhan's imploring face and she crumpled. "We'll just be a minute."

"Okay. There are a few things I want. Could you two hurry?"

Rayhan nodded and indicated for Liz to follow. "My uncle and aunt want to meet you."

"I'd like to meet them, too, Rayhan, but we really don't have time." Liz, annoyed, wondered why he wanted to introduce her *now*. Rayhan knew the urgency of the trip to the vanishing point. She glanced up and saw Al Abdul, his feet squarely planted on the ground, his arms crossed over his chest. "Is this necessary right now?" she demanded.

"I'm afraid it is. I told him I was going to marry you."

"You what!" She stopped in the middle of the street and refused to move any further. "What were you thinking? I hardly know you," Liz sputtered.

Rayhan turned and his smoldering, deep brown eyes caused her to lose her resolve. She quivered as he reached for her, then he stopped. "It is our custom," he whispered. "You know I cannot court you unless I announce my intentions and you meet my family."

"Court me?"

"I want to explain how I feel, and I can't unless—"

"You've talked to me plenty already. Why do you need permission? You've even touched me." Liz glared at Rayhan. "We just met yesterday. I'm here to find my friends. This can't happen."

He moved so his uncle couldn't see him stroke the back of Liz's arm. "My Egyptian side is winning out, Liz. If there is any chance for us, I have to do this properly." He gazed into her eyes. "You don't have to meet my uncle if your heart does not speak to you. I will help you find your friends and you can go home."

She could not deny the distinct and unmistakable tug at her heart. Perhaps they'd planted the first seeds of love, but marriage? She knew his customs. To gain approval from his uncle, Rayhan had to announce their engagement. He could not touch her, let alone talk to her, other than about the business of finding Gary and Addie, until the betrothal had been announced. The normal custom would be followed by a short courtship and the marriage soon afterward. The betrothed, under most circumstances, would be a childhood friend or a distant relative, not someone he'd met the day before. *None of this fell into the normal category.*

Liz peered around Rayhan. His disapproval etched into the scowl on his face, Al Abdul glared back at them and waited. *I could bolt and find Donnie.* Again, Rayhan touched her arm. "Please," he begged. "I know this is crazy, but it is the only way. You must meet them. I will understand if it doesn't work. Just try." He stepped closer and took her hands in his, blocking his actions from his uncle's steely view. "Don't deny it."

I can't. I'm standing here trying to make sense of it. Denial, no. Disbelief, yes. "How am I supposed to explain we're suddenly engaged?"

"Just honor the custom," Rayhan pleaded. "Give me a chance."

A lifetime passed before she moved from in front of Rayhan to his side. She knew nothing about him, his family didn't approve, and she teetered on the edge, about to take an action without knowing the outcome or the consequences—something she never did.

Twenty steps lay between where she stood and her destiny. Over the initial shock of Rayhan's announcement, her stomach reeled. She could not refute his magnetic pull. His genuine desire to help her, the importance of his church, and the enormity of his burden to follow his customs were qualities which she admired.

As the distance closed, she grew calmer. If she chose to follow her heart, she'd give up her life as she knew it. Her family had been scattered along both coasts since her parent's retirement. Her mother and father had moved to her dad's family home in Morehead City on the Atlantic Coast. Ben and Joshua followed them, but fled back to the West Coast where she had stayed, the winters too cold and the summers too short.

Her inseparable twin brothers settled in Southern California until Ben met his future wife, an Aussie, and now they lived in Brisbane. Liz knew her family stayed heart-close, if not distance-close. Her last tie to the States would have been her job, and the director had all but told her it wouldn't be there when she returned.

The scowl on Al Abdul's face unnerved her. The hard lines drew into a frown, his eyes burned with fury. Liz forced herself to smile. She wanted—no needed—more time, but the luxury of slow decisions no longer existed. If she waited, her conclusion might be altered. *Did Addie think of how her vacation would end when she woke up six days ago? What decision might Addie have put off?* The thought sobered Liz, and in that moment, she sealed her future.

The gap closed and Rayhan introduced them. "Uncle, this is Liz McCran, the American I told you about."

Al Abdul nodded and bowed. The traditional flowing tunic and billowing, white pants did little to hide his massive bulk. "Please." He gestured to the entry. They followed him, leaving their shoes at the door. Liz glanced down at her bright, pink socks, and from the heat growing on her cheeks, she knew her face was the same color.

The thick-walled room they entered offered relief from the mounting heat, but the calm coolness did not ease her agitation. Sunlight filtered through woven shades and played on cream-colored walls. A large, wooden cabinet sat against one side. The dark wood intersected with oversized brass hinges and pulls reflecting local craftsmanship. The slightest hint of jasmine tickled her nose. Agitation grew, and she glanced around, nerves on edge. Her apprehension, a knot at the pit of her stomach.

A woven, Egyptian wall hanging caught her eye. The brown and white design took up the entire expanse on the opposing wall. The neat row of tassels at the bottom rested just above a beige, leather couch. Geometrically patterned tiles brought the entire room into a blend of old Egyptian and contemporary living. Liz concluded Al Abdul had more means than the average Egyptian. She recognized the touch of a woman's hand, and wondered where Rayhan's aunt might be.

They sat across from Al Abdul on caramel-colored rattan chairs near a low table and Liz braced herself for the conversation which could change her life. She smiled at him as he studied her. She refused to let him have the upper hand.

"My nephew tells me that he wants to announce his engagement. I must tell you I do not approve. You are neither Egyptian or aware of our religious background."

Al Abdul, undeniably the master of his household, shifted his hardened eyes to Rayhan. Liz fought to find her inner strength. She knew he cared for Rayhan, traveling thousands of miles to bring him back to their beloved Egypt. "I have studied your country for many years and I am aware of your customs. No one was more surprised than I when Rayhan asked me to come here to meet you. We do things quite differently in America, as I am sure you are aware. We meet someone and get to know them over time. Amongst your people, dating is unusual. I will discover who Rayhan is while I am here and he will get to know me—with or without a betrothal."

She paused, her mind mired in confusion. She wanted this, perhaps more than she wanted anything short of finding Addie. "We are all Christians. We worship in different ways, but we believe the same." Liz shot a quick sideways glance at Rayhan and found dread filled his face. Had she said too much? Been too bold for a woman in this culture?

The words were out of her mouth. Her heart called out and she had spoken from a place she did not know existed. Unruffled, she continued, "With your permission, I would like to accept Rayhan's proposal. I am not of your culture, but Rayhan has asked me to give him a chance, and I am willing."

"Where would you live? America?" Al Abdul continued his harsh investigation.

Liz squared her shoulders. "Here in the country we both love."

"You'd give up your life and your customs?"

"One thing at a time, Uncle Abdul," Rayhan barked and surprised Liz with his sudden outburst. "Could we just consider a courtship?"

Al Abdul studied the young couple. "Then this is not an engagement, but a request for a courtship?"

"Yes," they said in unison.

Al Abdul thought for a moment as he stroked his bearded chin. He glanced up at the doorway then back to Rayhan. Finally, with great hesitation, Al Abdul spoke. Liz held her back rigid and waited as he struggled to say the words, his voice low. "I will not approve of a courtship."

"I touched her," Rayhan blurted out into the silent room, and the force of his words echoed back to her ears. A deafening stillness filled the room

Al Abdul's lips grew thin. "Then, it must be an engagement."

Liz turned to see Rayhan's face and fear-filled eyes met hers. She quivered and jammed her clinched hands into her lap. An older woman stood near the entrance of an adjoining room. Dressed in dark, shapeless clothes, her face and head covered, only her bright, twinkling eyes were visible. She observed Liz from a distance.

Rayhan dipped his head to Al Abdul. "Thank you, Uncle."

Al Abdul shifted in his seat. "We will speak of this later." He turned to the woman. "Yalla, Yalla," he called. "Ghadaa."

"I'm sorry. We do not have time for lunch, but perhaps a small snack before we return to the Giza." Liz spoke in Arabic, not wanting to offend his offer of food.

"You speak Arabic?"

"You speak perfect English."

"I teach at the University of Cairo. Let my wife bring food to the Sofra table." His hard expression lingered, unchanged. "I realize you must go, and the urgency in the need to find your friends, but let us bless this...err...engagement with a quick meal."

The woman turned at his command and brought plates of food to the table in front of them. She rested her gaze on Rayhan, then nodded at Liz. *The woman approved, at least.*

Al Abdul appeared to have accepted this declaration, if only temporarily, and in a strained voice he announced, "This is my wife, Amisi, and my son, Jahi, is here somewhere." Al Abdul rose from the table and called out several times, "Jahi. Jahi."

Liz reached over to touch Rayhan's arm when Amisi left the room. He had spoken very little since his outburst. "It went okay. Didn't it?"

He smiled, but shook his head. "Do not be so sure all went well. You no doubt impressed him, but once my uncle says no, he isn't easily swayed." Rayhan let out a slow pent-up breath. "I was confused and hurt when I returned to Cairo. Uncle Al Abdul would oftentimes give in to my requests to prove a lesson. He used it to teach me if I begged for something and it turned out to be a bad choice."

"I thought I helped you convince him," Liz whispered. "He agreed, didn't he?"

Rayhan grew thoughtful. "I don't think so. He was so angry with me before you arrived." Rayhan moved uncomfortably in his seat and ran his hands through his hair. "They do not believe I should marry outside our culture, and I forced him into giving his consent. My aunt is not as strong in her disapproval, but my uncle has the last word, and has been known to change his mind."

A pang of guilt stabbed at Liz's heart. She wanted to please Rayhan, follow his customs, and if it was meant to be, go beyond this arrangement they'd stepped into. "Rayhan," she whispered quietly, "let's see what happens. I believe we have a chance. We could go back to the States."

Al Abdul and Amisi walked through the doorway. Liz wondered if they had heard any of her conversation with Rayhan. The little boy, whom she'd given the dollar to earlier, peered around the corner from the other room. "This is Jahi?" Liz asked. "We've met."

"Where?" Rayhan asked.

"In the marketplace while we waited for you."

Jahi vanished for moment and returned with something under his arm. He approached Liz with caution, then handed her a book.

Al Abdul chastised the boy sternly. "Ta'ala."

"No. It is all right," Liz said and motioned for the boy to approach her. She laughed when he turned over the cover. Peter Pan swung from the vines and had just landed on the deck of Captain Hook's boat and neatly printed below, in Arabic, the title and J.M. Barrie. She understood he wanted her to open the book. Together they examined the pictures.

Al Abdul spoke. "I hope my son did not trouble you. Jahi Mark can be a handful."

"Jahi Mark?"

"Jahi means dignified. Mark was a great man of God." Al Abdul beamed lovingly at his son. "He goes by Jahi, but unlike many of my kinsmen, I added a Christian name. It isn't on his birth certificate, but a good name nonetheless."

"Yes," Liz said, "a very good name." She smiled at Rayhan, taking direction from his nod. They'd eaten enough of the celebration meal to show respect to his family. "We should leave for the necropolis."

"Yaiebu an athhaba al ann," Jahi said, pulling on Rayhan's arm.

"Laa," Rayhan said, telling him no. "He wants to go with us."

"I don't mind." Liz glanced between Al Abdul and Amisi, then back to Rayhan.

Al Abdul took Jahi aside and spoke to him quietly, then indicated in Arabic he must stay with Rayhan. Their goodbyes said, the three of them left to find Donnie.

Liz spotted him where she'd left him at the end of the street. Donnie had several bags in his hand and waved to Liz. She walked closer, noting he seemed far from pleased. "You were gone a long time, and who's the kid?"

"He's Rayhan's cousin. He's going with us to the vanishing point. I didn't see any harm in it," Liz said to Donnie's back as he walked ahead. "What did you buy?"

"Just a few things I needed," he answered. "I'm going to pay one of the vendors to have this stuff delivered to the hotel." Donnie proceeded to the end of the strip, making no further attempt to speak with Liz.

They walked in silence the short distance from the marketplace, and the four boarded a shuttle bus to the Giza, buying their tickets from the driver. They positioned themselves at the rear of the sightseers, and as the guide directed them to enter the Great Pyramid on the northern end of the plaza, they hung back, moved to the eastern wall, and then south toward the Pyramid of Menakure, the smallest of the three. Rayhan proceeded to the center of the south wall and moved his right hand above his eyes to shield them from the afternoon sun. He motioned to Donnie, who aligned his binoculars against Rayhan's left arm, which he'd extended toward the horizon. His face told Liz he'd seen what they came for.

"Liz, come here." Donnie offered her the high-powered lenses. "We've found it."

She took the glasses and placed them against her brow, and with a slight adjustment, focused on the white building gleaming in the sun. The next piece of the riddle lay ahead of them, a half mile to the south.

Her three companions faced her, and in their various expressions, she witnessed the same question. They wanted her to give the command. "Yalla," she spoke to Jahi and pointed in the direction of the horizon. He ran out in front of her, his footprints hollowing the sand as his sandals hit the ground. Donnie, Rayhan, and Liz, at a markedly slower pace, followed. Each step caused the anticipation to heighten beneath her skin. The sand tugged at her feet and legs. The very earth itself held her down, kept her from her purpose. *Could this be where they'd taken Addie and Gary? Then why all the secrecy?* Liz feared this could be another part of the puzzle, and not the answer she wanted.

HER PULSE QUICKENED as they covered the distance. Jahi stood very still on the edge of the makeshift yard. He turned his face up to Rayhan, and in the slightest whisper, said, "Jereon."

Donnie's quizzical expression caught Liz's attention. "Holy man," she said.

Just inside the door, visible to Jahi, and now to the rest of them, an elderly man spread a crimson runner across the length of an old, wooden table. Dressed in a black galabayas, an ordinary length of rope tied at his waist accentuated his humble servitude.

Rayhan turned to Liz, pointed to her scarf and motioned for her to cover her head, then pulled her aside. "Whatever we find out, just remember, I'm here." He stepped forward and walked to the entrance of the building and engaged in a low conversation, which Liz couldn't hear. He returned and guided her toward the door. "Talmar would like to speak to you. He has news."

Jahi advanced a step forward, but Rayhan shook his head. Donnie removed the binoculars from his neck and took the boy's hand. As he handed the lenses to Jahi, Donnie spoke to him in English, and they walked away from the dwelling. He gave instructions on using the instrument to see far off across the desert sands. To Liz's surprise, the boy understood and followed Donnie.

Her heart fell to the pit of her stomach as Rayhan fixed his eyes on her. Without saying a word, he told her the news she'd so badly wanted from this priest wouldn't be heard today. Rayhan led her to the doorway of the plain, white building. The holy man held out his hand in welcome and motioned for them to sit on a low bench against the wall. The rudimentary furnishings helped her understand the last line of the riddle. *He knows of many things, of God's whispered breath and angel's wings*. The walls were covered with religious artifacts and paintings. His ceremonial garment, a white robe trimmed in gold hung, spread flat in a glass case. To the left of it, a small shelf held a round, dome-shaped head covering. Liz stared at the formal adornments. The long sleeves ballooned out, resembling angel's wings.

Rayhan spoke with him in hushed tones, then turned to Liz. "He was the one who sent the ankh. It is his and he asks for you to bring it back to him after your trip."

Her trip? She couldn't comprehend what Rayhan said. *Send it back from America? What about Addie and Gary?* "Rayhan, does he know where they are?"

"Yes. You must travel to El Kudish. They have been taken there to heal." Talmar spoke in Arabic. He had either anticipated her question or understood English.

"Heal!" She spoke too loudly and brought her hand to cover her mouth. She lowered it, as well as her voice. "What happened? How badly are they hurt? Can you take me to them?"

"They have been removed from danger. The transportation of your friends to a southern settlement was of the most secrecy. No one knew." Rayhan repeated what Talmar had said in Arabic, even though he knew Liz understood.

This explained why Moustafa didn't know whether or not they'd been rescued. Liz had to follow her instincts and trust Talmar and the men who had saved her friends. She had no other choice. "But why weren't they brought back to the hotel? How can I be certain they're in El Kudish?" Her heart fluttered. Miles of desert now separated them.

Rayhan's dark brown eyes clouded over as he assessed her with something she couldn't determine...pity, sorrow, both? He turned his gaze to Talmar and they quietly spoke again.

Talmar crossed the room to stand over Liz, and his soulful expression made her shudder. He kept his eyes locked on her face while he spoke to her directly, no longer using Rayhan to translate. He said in Arabic, "Did Moustafa tell you of the attempt to kidnap them?"

"Yes," she moaned in utter disbelief. "But why?"

"Any number of reasons. First they are American and carrying something to an Egyptian national who is under scrutiny."

"What do you mean?" Her skin prickled and she set her jaw, a bad habit she had when stress overrode her sensibilities.

Rayhan faced her. "Behavior deviant from the norm makes us stand out, even though we try with the utmost care to blend in. Moustafa is often times too bold."

"But Addie and Gary weren't doing anything wrong," she interrupted.

Talmar's face softened. "They carried documents to be given to Moustafa," he said. "That alone may have put them in jeopardy."

"How could delivering a message be so dangerous?"

Rayhan's eyes drilled into her. "Do you think they knew what was in the letter?"

"Pastor Waterford told Donnie the envelope was sealed and Addie and Gary were to give it to Moustafa." She glanced nervously back and forth between the two men. She would tell Rayhan later what Pastor Mike had told her about the shipments.

Rayhan took her hand. "Even the arrangement of this meeting with Moustafa was enough to cause trouble for your friends."

Talmar's wide-eyed expression, waiting for Rayhan to explain why her hand now rested in his, unnerved her. "Hayete," Rayhan said to Talmar.

Surprised, she turned and glared at Rayhan. He had just told the priest she was Rayhan's life, but the Egyptian meaning went deeper. The love of his life had been what he meant. She'd never heard those words from anyone. Liz saw a flicker of disapproval float across Talmar's face, but he said nothing.

"Do you know what happened? Moustafa called me to meet him at the Giza." Liz brushed an errant tear from her cheek. Too many emotions charged through her. Rayhan had just declared his undying love for her in one Arabic word—and in front of a priest—but she had to find out what happened to Addie and Gary. *Has God also brought me here to find my soul mate?*

"Moustafa found your friends beaten and bound in an alleyway behind the El Dar. Moustafa heard a conversation going on just inside the doorway. Someone was waiting for a car to arrive to take the captors and the Americans away from the city."

"Why didn't he involve the police?" Liz questioned.

Talmar made quick eye contact with Rayhan, then spoke again, not answering Liz's question. "Moustafa placed them into a cart at the back of the building, one used to carry trash from the restaurant. He then removed his suit coat and covered his head with his traditional klaft and wheeled the cart to the end of the street. Moustafa's driver, who had waited while he searched, drove them away."

"The kidnappers didn't notice?" She found herself in the middle of something she didn't want to know about.

"We have learned to be...how do you say it?" Rayhan creased his brow in thought. "Stealth."

"I appreciate Moustafa's help, the help I've received from all of you, but why did he go out of his way and take such risks?"

"He probably felt responsible." Rayhan lowered his eyes. "He isn't careful. We have both told you how he endangers himself and others. I don't think it is intentional, but he takes risks."

Liz didn't want to find herself caught up in anything which involved Moustafa's secretive background. They had to figure out how to get to El Kudish. Would Mr. Aston help them? Her mind numbed with the details. "Who attempted to kidnapped Addie and Gary?"

"We are not certain." Talmar sighed. "There are many militant factions throughout our country."

"Why El Kudish? It's miles from here."

Rayhan tightened his grip on her hand. "Our people were afraid for them. We don't know if your friends still had the envelope. The men were only trying to help them, and El Kudish is a refuge for our people, and away from the city and ah—"

"How can I be sure?" she questioned, placing a three foot space in between them. She did not want to face either one of them for fear she'd break into tears.

Talmar went to a small wooden desk at the edge of the room near the front door. He opened a drawer and an eerie creak split the silence of the still, dark room. He brought something toward Liz, curled in his large, brown hand.

She searched his saddened expression. He moved nearer and motioned for her to take what he held. He dropped a gold key into her outstretched palm. The key to the empty metal box Donnie had found in a cave in Texas. He had given Addie the key as a wedding present. It represented other things to her—the key to her family and the key to her faith. Addie later told Liz she had given it to Gary. Neither one of them would be without it, and now it lay in her hand, covered in blood.

Gasping for fresh air, she raced out of the door and left the two of them behind. Once outside, she clung against the cool limestone and inhaled, air not reaching her lungs, in an attempt to calm her nerves and uneasy stomach. The twenty-third Psalm spilled from her lips. *"Yea though I walk through the valley of the shadow of death...."* She slumped down against the side of the building. The sand in front of her blurred and her limbs grew weak. *God, let me find Addie and Gary and let us get home safely. Please.*

Rayhan appeared in the entrance.

"I needed some air. Give my apologies to Talmar. Let him know I appreciate his message."

Rayhan nodded his head and retreated. He reappeared and offered Liz his hand. She took it and allowed him to pull her into him. He reached for her face and she moved her cheek into his quick caress, but shook her head and nodded toward Jahi and Donnie. Rayhan put his fingers to his lips and released a shrill whistle into the crisp morning air. Jahi turned and ran to his cousin.

Liz stood braced against the building while she waited for Donnie. "What's wrong?" he asked.

"They were hurt." Liz opened her hand and showed Donnie the key.

"How bad, and why did the holy man have Addie's key?"

"I don't know. The riddle has left me with more questions than answers." She glanced at Rayhan, who waited with Jahi. "Could you take Jahi and let me talk with Rayhan?"

"About what?" Donnie questioned her. "Anything I should know?"

"It was something he said." Liz grew impatient as she waited for Donnie to leave. "I just need to talk to him."

Donnie motioned for Rayhan to join Liz for the walk back to the plaza. Donnie took the boy's hand and Liz waited until they had walked ahead.

She glared at him, confused, as she searched for the right words. "Hayete?" Liz shook her head. "Why? Especially in front of Talmar?"

Rayhan took her hand. "It is true. You are my life, my love. I know we just met, but when I saw you at the airport, I felt it here." He grabbed his shirt and his eyes glistened.

Her temples pounded. Too much had happened and far too quickly. "You forced your uncles' hand to allow an engagement, now you just declared your undying love for me to a holy man. You might as well have let him marry us on the spot."

Rayhan stopped walking and turned to face her. "Would that have been so bad?"

Liz couldn't answer him.

CHAPTER FIVE

JAHI SKIPPED ALONG in front of the adults, making small whirlwinds of dust. Life at the Giza continued to blossom as the unforgiving sun seared Liz's fair skin. She wrapped the scarf around her head and shoulders and surveyed the horses, cars, carriages, and buses loaded with tourists. Soldiers carrying AK-47's mingled together with the visitors and locals. Egyptian women in black, their heads, and bodies covered, clung together in clustered groups. The younger women wore western clothing and blended in with the American sightseers, and always the vendors everywhere one turned, forcing their wares.

They approached the parking lot where salesmen offering papyrus and trinkets mingled with the crowds. The aroma from fast food restaurants mixed with the smell of camels and horses met her nostrils. She could taste bile as it rose in her throat. Liz stared out into the desert while they waited for the next shuttle bus. Her spirits withered with the heat, but a new hope centered on the key clutched in her hand. A dead horse lay on the banks of the Nile, bloated in the sweltering sun. Further out, the sands were strewn with shells of old cars, wires, cables, plastic bottles, and debris. Desolation edged into her heart, and the hope Talmar had given her drained away. She questioned their ability to find Addie and Gary. Sparks from a smoldering ember grew in her heart, too. A storm raged within her, two equally strong sources opponents—fear and love.

Her brain numbed from the numerous things which had to fall into place. She couldn't remember the exact location of El Kudish, but it would be at least a two-hundred mile trip. They needed a vehicle and a guide, if Rayhan didn't know his way around southern Egypt. She tried to remember the conversation with Talmar, but she couldn't move past Rayhan's one word: *hayete*.

They said their goodbyes once they were deposited at the Mena House. Jahi could not be persuaded to leave and stopped twice to stare back at her before he disappeared around the corner near the marketplace with Rayhan. Each time they stopped, Rayhan placed his hand over his heart—a gesture meant only for Liz.

Donnie pushed Liz for answers before they reached the lobby. "Do you know where El Kudish is?"

"It is in southern Egypt. Exactly, no, but it won't be hard to find." Liz paused a moment, then hesitated before she told Donnie more. Maybe he'd go along with her idea, but most likely not. "I'm calling Mr. Aston."

"Why? It's obvious he isn't going to help us," Donnie grumbled.

"He told me twice to call him, which I haven't done." Liz studied Donnie's expression and tried to measure his reaction. "I'm calling him and then Rayhan. We need a vehicle, too, and I doubt if anyone but Mr. Aston could secure one for us."

"What about Rayhan's uncle?" Donnie glared. "Does he have something we might borrow?"

"I don't think so, and if he does, I wouldn't feel comfortable asking."

"That reminds me. Why did you take so long when you went back with Rayhan?"

"We weren't discussing their vehicles, believe me." Liz froze. She didn't want to tell him about the engagement. He'd never understand the tradition, or how she'd lost her heart so fast to someone she barely knew, but what Donnie thought about the subject didn't concern her. "We were following a custom, a blessing of sorts." She glanced over at him and the answer halted his questions.

"We've lost another day. When do you think Aston will be home?"

Liz checked her watch. "Soon. It's almost four. I'll call when I'm back in my room. Perhaps we can go there this evening."

"I still don't think he'll be so willing to help us," Donnie complained.

"At this point, what have we got to lose?"

Liz considered herself victorious when he didn't argue. Addie had told her Donnie had been quite different when she had first found him after years of searching, following a disagreement between their fathers. Donnie's parent's untimely death had split the family. He had been living on the street and spent some time in a detention facility. His experiences had left him angry and broken. Since then, he had turned his life over to God, but Donnie didn't back down easily.

"WHY ARE YOU different?" Jahi asked Rayhan as they walked back home through the marketplace.

"I'm not different," he laughed. "I'm still Rayhan."

"No, not like that. You are happy, and I know I would not be happy if Father was mad at me like he is mad at you." Jahi stopped and gazed up at his cousin. "Are you glad Father is angry?"

Rayhan bent down, rested his knee on the ground, and came closer to Jahi. He missed very little in his six-year-old world, but Rayhan couldn't be sure Jahi had caught on about Liz. "Do you like Miss McCran?"

"Yes. She is a nice lady, and she let me go to Talmar's house with you. I like Mr. Donnie, too. He showed me the far-away eyes." Jahi made circles with his thumbs and index fingers and brought them to his brow.

"I have told your father Miss McCran and I are engaged. It is why I brought her to the house this morning."

"Oh!" Jahi grinned. "I think it is very good...but Father is angry."

"Yes." Rayhan placed his hand on Jahi's shoulder. "I'm afraid he is. Miss McCran is not an Egyptian or of our culture, and those things worry your father."

"She is a very pretty lady. Is she why you are happy?"

"Yes, but it makes me sad your father is upset with me."

Jahi thought for a moment and drew on his youthful wisdom. "Father may change his mind. If I am very, very good, Father lets me have my way, sometimes."

Rayhan smiled at Jahi and rose to continue their walk home. Rayhan would be the best nephew possible if being good could change Al Abdul's mind, but he knew it would take more—much more. Certain of what he wanted and the risks involved, he would marry the dark-haired, feisty American who had come in search of her friends. He would go to America and find her if he could not persuade his uncle, but part of him knew he had to convince her, too.

Rayhan's cell phone rang and jolted him out of his thoughts. He smiled to see Liz's number on the screen. "Yes?" he answered.

"I just spoke with Mr. Aston. Donnie and I are visiting his home tonight. Do you want to go with us, and do you have a car we can use?" Liz spoke in a quick, breathless whisper. Her voice quickened his pulse and he thought about her smile in the moonlight.

"No. My uncle walks everywhere, and I only use the Embassy car while I'm at work. I'm afraid we'll need a cab." He checked his watch. Had they only been separated less than an hour? He wondered if he could find a way, tonight, to hold her in his arms.

DONNIE AND LIZ CROSSED the lobby and she glanced at the main desk. Ini must have the night off. A brief tightness caught in her chest as she thought no one would know where they were, but the fear vanished as quickly as it had come.

Three cabs lined the circular drive in front of the Mena House. They took the first in line. Donnie held the rear door open for her then talked to the driver while they waited for Rayhan. She grew restless and turned her face to the window, impatient for him to come into view. What did he find so interesting about her? Why did he think she was the one? Those were questions only he could answer and she intended to ask him as soon as they were alone.

Rayhan rounded the corner at the end of the drive. He jogged across the pavement to shake Donnie's hand. Donnie took the front passenger side while Rayhan joined Liz in the back.

She reached over the seat and handed the driver the address for Richard's home located on Al Ashur Road. He turned and studied her with an expression somewhere between quizzical and awe. "The American Ambassador?" He spoke in practiced English.

She nodded, assuming he hadn't been requested to drive there often. The car moved into traffic and Liz shot a quick glance at Rayhan as she felt the warmth of his hand over hers. He caressed her fingers and massaged his thumb in tiny circles on the back of her hand. A warm tingle moved up her spine and her cheeks warmed. Liz removed her hand and brought it to her face, where she felt the heat his touch had generated. Rayhan's smile caused her to blush even more. She kept her eyes fixed on the rolling landscape outside the window and fought the impulse to return her hand to his.

The short ride took no longer than twenty minutes. The driver maneuvered the car out of the crowded streets of Cairo into a subdivision of larger homes. The Ambassador's residence and the others in the area were large, single dwellings, a vast difference from those in town where small quarters and tiny apartments were the norm.

Donnie thanked the driver and paid him. Liz paused for a moment and took in the two-story, traditional Egyptian-style house. Palm trees grew in the back, cresting above the dome-shape of one of the sections, and reached into the red and gold evening sky. The wall adjoining the hemispherical roof stood another several feet taller and squared off. Below it, a window with a small balcony created a terrace, set apart with an iron railing.

A stairway, which divided the house into triangular sections, bisected the structure. They had gathered at the foot of the steps when Mr. Aston appeared on the first landing. "Welcome. I heard the cab. Did you have any trouble getting here?"

"No, not at all, Mr. Aston." Liz reached up and shook his hand as they met near the middle of the staircase. "The driver knew right where to go, even though I think it shocked him a bit to bring us here."

"Please call me Richard. I think we've moved beyond the formal correctness here." He smiled down at her. "I see you've brought Rayhan. Come in. Inez has made us some nibbles. Rayhan told me your friends might be at El Kudish. I've made a few inquiries and planned a route." Richard Aston, out of his business suit and in khaki shorts and a polo shirt, appeared to be far less rigid than he had been at the Embassy. Gratitude washed over Liz and her trepidation eased away.

Richard ushered them into the house where Liz noticed the furnishings were more Egyptian than American. Through a large, undraped window, Liz gazed beyond the structure and into the yard. Surrounded by a three-foot, rustic brick wall in the same brownish-orange color of the house, the property opened onto a field filled with some type of vegetation blooming in tiny, white flowers.

The large dome ceilings arched twenty feet above their heads and the window encasements were the same type she'd seen at the El Dar. The aperture came to a slow, curving point at the top with glass panes set at least two feet away from the opening. The eighteen-inch thick walls created a deep ledge.

Mrs. Aston waited for them in the living room. The rattan furniture, arranged into a circular formation for their visit, rested on burgundy-colored tile. The muted floral design on the coverlet matched the pillows scattered across the couch and chairs. The only hint Liz had seen of anything westernized was a long, low table centered in the middle of the circle of chairs.

Would Mrs. Aston exclude herself from their conversation? *She must have experienced the same anguish, despair, and guilt as churns beneath my skin.* Did Richard's wife still hold on to the hope her daughter would be found? Liz knew she'd never let go of the hope of finding Addie and Gary, or their memory, if it came to that.

Richard crossed the room in several long strides and stood beside his wife. He put his arm around her with care, in what Liz thought of as an act of protection, then introduced them. "Inez, this is Liz McCran and Donnie Barnes. I briefed you on their situation."

His use of words, as well as the beauty of his wife, made Liz smile. She extended her hand to Inez, but when their eyes met, Liz saw what words could not say, and she lowered her head before the familiar sting sprang into a full force of tears.

They settled in around the low table, Rayhan and Liz on one side, Donnie and Richard on the other. Inez poured coffee from an ornate, silver coffee urn and served a plate of interesting sweets. Liz recognized the fresh date and ground nut mixture dusted in powdered sugar and cut into squares, as well as another tasty treat—flaky baklava dripping in honey syrup.

Liz reached to take her plate and looked past Inez to the shelf area of the window seat nearby. Neatly arranged in tidy rows, a series of family photos, including the one of the grandchildren she'd seen in Richard's office, and several others of the young family who had their mother stolen from them too soon. In the center of the shelf stood a beautiful, silver-framed picture of their daughter. She possessed the same build and features as Inez, but the photographer had captured her boldness and assurance.

Inez stepped back to leave the room and Liz called to her, "No. Stay. You've been in this situation. You may have some insight I don't have. Please? Unless it is too painful for you." Inez smiled with understanding reflected in her deep blue eyes. She moved a chair into the circle and they intently listened as Richard explained his plan.

"Rayhan, could you fetch my maps for me?" Richard asked. "They're in the study."

Rayhan rose and walked to the end of the room, his heels striking out a sharp clink against the tile. Donnie and Inez had their backs to him, but Liz saw Rayhan remove a long, tubular document from a leather carrying case. She observed his every movement. He released the leather strap, which held the circular case closed, with one swift motion of his hand. A shock of black hair fell over his eyes. He reached up, pushed it back, and smiled at Liz.

She found herself reliving the meeting with his family. She had been amazed at her own behavior, speaking so bluntly and forcefully to his uncle, especially in a culture where women did not speak their minds. Liz feared his uncle would never approve, but Amisi's smile brought Liz an ally in Al Abdul's camp.

Should she have ventured into the relationship in the first place? She didn't know Rayhan, and now they were engaged. She sensed an urgency to learn more about him, his childhood, his family, and his life before her. What would he be like as a husband?

He crossed the room while Liz and Inez cleared the remaining dishes from the coffee table as he spread out a map. Richard had taken the time to mark their destination and deciphered it would take five hours to reach El Kudish.

"I see you've done some planning here, Richard," Donnie said. "I have some plans of my own."

"Well, maybe we can work together on this. I simply mapped out the area. I'm not exactly sure how you'll work out all the details. You'll have to travel under some sort of ruse."

"Yes. I've thought of that," Donnie said.

Liz let herself drift away from the conversation. Emptiness and grief festered under her skin and their cold fingers clutched her heart as she thought of her friends, hidden somewhere in the desert. Traveling to El Kudish would be difficult. They didn't have a vehicle, and there would be certain provisions they'd require. She didn't know what Donnie had bought this afternoon, but they needed food and emergency supplies. Her hope dwindled as fear tightened its grip. Her lips moved in a silent plea. *Please, God, hear my prayer, know our plight, and guide our way. Let us find Addie and Gary, and somehow let them know to stay steadfast and not give up.* She felt Rayhan's eyes on her.

Richard broke into her thoughts. "I have borrowed an old jeep for you. It belongs to my handyman, Habi. It is reliable, but has spent many years in the desert sun. It will be perfect for your journey. It looks like all the other vehicles here."

"Good," Donnie said. "I had something like that in mind. Should we be traveling alone?"

"I thought of that, too." Richard shifted to face him. "I will send Habi with you. He knows the way, and if you're stopped for any reason, he can handle it."

Richard turned his attention to Liz. "You haven't said much. Is there something wrong?"

"What about papers? When I've been here before, I needed clearance to go out that far."

"Habi won't need them." Richard drummed his fingers on his knee. "I'll figure out something for you and Donnie. Maybe you could pose as a married couple."

The very last thing I want—a romantic connection, even a false one, to Donnie. "I don't mean to sound ungrateful, but I have some thoughts on this, if you think they might work." She reached down and picked up the map.

"Go on." Richard's expression reflected his interest and she hoped she hadn't been too intrusive.

"You said Rayhan is at our disposal. I would like him to go with us. We don't have the time to obtain the right paperwork for Donnie and me. Rayhan could pose as my husband. Wouldn't that make it easier for us to travel?" Liz glanced up at Rayhan. She knew he would understand what she meant.

Rayhan smiled and brought his hand over his mouth. Richard didn't catch the gesture, but Donnie, on the other hand, glared at Liz, questions painted visibly on his face.

"I follow you." Richard thought for a moment. "Rayhan will have no trouble and I'll grant you a marriage visa, but I'm really hesitant for any of you to travel the two hundred miles south of here." Richard rubbed his long fingers against his chin.

"A marriage visa?" Donnie asked.

"If there is a relationship or engagement between an Egyptian and an American, I have the authority to draw up the document."

Little did he know. "Then that part is settled," Liz said

"What about Donnie? Where does he fit in?"

"Oh, he definitely needs to come." Liz nodded to Donnie and remembered the black bag he'd laid out on his bed at the Mena House. Donnie's colored past would come in handy. "He has some ideas of his own, and he will be quite useful. He is Addie's cousin, and he can pose as mine."

"It could work." Richard nodded.

"There are others who have helped us—Rayhan's friend, Ini, and Talmar the priest."

"Wait. They can't all go with you. You need to be covert, so to speak."

"I know, but each one of them has something to offer. I need all of their resources."

"Can you have everyone together tomorrow, say early morning? You should get started." He turned to Inez. His eyes begged her to say something.

"Don't wait too long. Don't let the trail become cold." Inez reached over and took Liz's hand. "Every minute is precious. Don't waste it."

Liz examined Inez's deep set eyes and pondered what might have happened when her daughter had been kidnapped. Had they failed to start soon enough? Had they done all they could? Would she be haunted with those questions the rest of her life, too?

"Richard," Donnie interjected, "don't you think we've lost enough time? We've been here two days. It makes six since they've went missing. I feel helpless here. Addie is very important to me. I can't explain it to you. She's Liz's friend, but she's my relative." Donnie drew his hand through his hair. Liz knew he wanted to be in control, they all did, and every moment made the chances of finding Addie and Gary grow smaller.

"Talmar has assured us Addie and Gary are in the care of the men from our church. I don't think we have to worry about their safety. We just need to find them," Rayhan offered.

Donnie shot daggers at Rayhan. "That may be true, but there's something wrong here. There is too much secrecy: riddles, notes, symbols. Why aren't we just taken to where they are and be done with it?"

Rayhan opened his mouth to speak, but Richard raised his hand. "There are a lot of things you don't understand. I'm the no-holes-barred, full-steam-ahead type, like you are, Donnie, but this is a different culture than ours. Liz is aware of many things you do not know about the Egyptians, and how they view a situation. Rayhan is a good resource, too. His concern for his people and their culture is invaluable." Richard cleared his throat. "I know you're having trouble with my part in this, but I truly intend to help you. I just can't as the ambassador. You three will make a good team. I wish you God's speed."

Liz hugged Inez goodbye and Richard led them outside to a small shed near the side of the house. The burning sun had set and the fleeting light painted the evening sky in shades of orange and bronze. Richard carried a flashlight and shined the beam on a large, covered object. He bent down and removed a canvas tarp. A weather-beaten vehicle built around the time Liz was born sat in front of them. The condition of the jeep made Liz question its ability to make it back to Cairo, let alone to El Kudish. Richard gave Donnie the keys, and turned to Liz. "Where will we meet tomorrow?"

"The church near the marketplace," Rayhan offered. "Do you remember where it is?"

"I do. About eight then?" He extended his hand and helped Liz climb into the jeep.

"Yes. Eight." Richard held onto his grip long after she'd taken her seat. "Thank you." She smiled.

As Rayhan climbed onto a wooden bench behind him, Donnie reached across the seat and shook Richard's hand. "I'm sorry I doubted you. There is a lot I don't understand." Donnie put the key into the ignition, and after a couple of long, grinding turns, the old engine started.

He drove to the Mena House without instruction, his sense of direction another of his irritating talents. The night air remained warm and the pale yellow sliver of moon guided their path and gave a luminescent glow to the desert sand around them. Liz turned to him. "How did you know which way to go?"

"I just paid attention. It wasn't hard." He drove into the circular drive and handed the keys to the valet, who gave a huff of disgust.

"Park the car, will you old man?" Donnie said in his best British accent, and she tried hard not to laugh.

Liz spotted Ini at the desk when the threesome entered the lobby. "Good evening, Miss McCran."

"Hello, Ini," she said. "I have a favor."

He grabbed a pencil and notepad. "Anything you wish. The Mena House is at your service."

"I want you to arrange a meeting for us tomorrow at eight at the church in the marketplace."

Rayhan moved closer. "I can do that for you."

"I know, but I want you to convince your uncle and Talmar to come to the church, too."

"That may not be easy. My uncle is not happy," Rayhan said, turning to see if Donnie heard him, "about the situation, and Talmar may not leave his compound."

"Try." She reached to take his hand, but stopped. She remained hesitant to show her feelings for him in public. "For me?" she finally said.

Rayhan smiled. "Okay. I will try to have everyone at the church." He moved closer and pressed his hand into hers. Ini didn't see the gesture and Liz worried his open affection would only bring him trouble, but their fingers interlocked.

"Thank you, Ini." Liz turned away from the desk and focused on Donnie. "You go on up. I need to talk to Rayhan."

Donnie waved goodbye and took his time as he crossed the lobby to the elevator. He cast a glance over his shoulder at Liz and questioned her with his eyes, but she ignored him as she and Rayhan walked through the main doors of the hotel and out onto the veranda.

"Take me to the church," Liz said.

"Now?"

"Is it open? I need to talk to you, somewhere safe and private. Where could we go other than the church?"

Rayhan ushered Liz down the driveway and to the corner. They followed the path bathed in clear, opalescent moonlight, needing no other light. The vendor's stands were closed for the evening, either draped with tenting, or folded against the building. Liz saw a dim light at the end of the walkway and assumed the glow came from the church.

Midway between the corner and the chapel, she spotted a small recess made where two buildings joined together. Secluded and just large enough for the two of them to stand together, Rayhan pulled her inside.

"Let us not love with words or tongue, but with actions and in truth. There is no fear in love; but perfect love casteth out fear," he quoted from John.

"You're risking too much by loving me. Your uncle does not approve. I see the troubling glances from people like Talmar. Why me? Why am I so special to you?"

Rayhan stroked her chin. He brought his hand to her lips and traced the outline of her mouth. Her heart raced at the sight of him bathed in the half-light of the all-knowing moon. They were close enough to embrace, but she kept her back rigid against the wall. He moved closer and brought his hand to the nape of her neck. His warm breath caressed her cheek and she couldn't resist him any longer.

"Rayhan, are you certain?"

"I don't know how else to convince you."

"Why me? You said there had been others."

"Yes, but none like you."

She melted into him and invited him to kiss her. For a brief, incredible moment, her worries flew on the wings of hope. They'd find Addie and Gary, and Al Abdul would be dealt with. Three things will last forever: faith, hope, and love, but the greatest of them all is love.

CHAPTER SIX

L<small>IZ SPENT MOST</small> of the night curled into a big, overstuffed chair near the window. The moon cast a pale, yellow light on the balcony, and the pyramids glimmered in the illumination. How could she enjoy the beauty before her while the lives of her friends remained uncertain? A sense of foreboding crept into the corner of her thoughts, but she held it there and wouldn't allow it to take over. Liz couldn't let herself be afraid. She wrestled to turn it all over to God, needing to pray for His will in finding Addie and Gary, and the outcome of her engagement to Rayhan. She remembered a poem her minister had once given where he told the congregation they must trust in God and His perfect timing. Somewhere near dawn, she climbed into bed and closed her eyes.

Early morning dreams troubled her with scenes of Addie and Gary. They called her, stretching their hands in desperation, but when she approached, they disappeared. The same sequence of images appeared over and over with the same outcome. Liz slept fitfully and awoke with a start when a scuffle erupted in the hallway outside her room.

She grabbed her robe and, cautiously opening the door, found Donnie holding Jahi a good three feet off the ground. Hissing like a cat who had just been dunked into a tub of water, Jahi kicked and punched the air in the distance between them.

"Donnie, put him down." Jahi ran behind her as soon as Donnie released him. "He doesn't speak much English. You probably terrified him. Shh, both of you. Come into my room."

"He tried to bite me." Donnie grumbled and shut the door. "I thought he liked me yesterday."

"What would you do if someone twice your size picked you up by the scruff of the neck?" She reached over and rubbed Jahi's shoulder and he crumpled into her arms, sobbing.

"He was hanging around your door. How was I to know what he wanted?" Donnie walked over and squatted down in front of Jahi. "Sorry, little man. You okay?" Jahi held back a sob while Liz patted his back. "I wouldn't hurt you. Do you understand?"

Jahi nodded. Donnie held his mysterious black bag in his hands and from it he pulled a chocolate bar and gave it to the boy. The language issue evaporated as Jahi's fingers wrapped around the candy and tucked it into a hidden pocket in his tunic. His hand immediately reappeared with a note. He handed it to Liz. She glanced at Donnie as she unfolded the paper. Her heart sank—another riddle.

The trusted one is no more.
The prize he brought is at death's door.
The dwindling sands cannot be stopped.
Before the waning doth begin.
They will be moved, yet again.

Search as you might, you may not find
Use the ankh to find the sign.

Donnie stood by Liz's side and read the note. "Where did this come from?" he said to Jahi.

"Jereon," the boy answered.

"Talmar?" she asked.

"What?" Donnie interrupted. "Who is Jereon?"

"Not who, what. Jereon means holy man. Remember I told you yesterday? It could have been any priest. Maybe Rayhan or Jahi's father can tell us when we meet at the church. He was obviously sent here by someone to give us the message."

"Jaddah." Jahi searched back and forth between them. "Jaddah."

"Your grandmother?" she questioned. "This gets more and more complicated." Liz whispered to Donnie, "There's a donut shop on the veranda. Buy him something and make friends again."

"Do you have time to solve another riddle?" A sober expression crossed his face.

"I don't need to solve it. I know." This riddle, unlike the first, did not guide them to a mysterious priest who held the answer to where her friends had been taken. The riddle had been clear, and she didn't want to think about it. *God give me the strength to voice my fears.* Her throat constricted as she said the words. "Something has happened to Moustafa. Addie and Gary are near death, and whoever has them will be moving them before the quarter moon. I hope they're still headed for El Kudish."

"Near death? What does that mean?"

"Don't panic. It's a metaphor. I've seen it used in Egyptian writings. It means their time is running out. Whoever sent this wants us to hurry." Liz trusted she had guessed what the author of the note meant, but she shivered, remembering the blood on the key.

"We're leaving this afternoon. No matter what you find out at the church today, we're going." He reached to put his arm around her shoulders, but she backed away. "Change your clothes and Jahi and I will meet you downstairs." He stared at her for a moment and Liz couldn't read the message on his face. He took Jahi by the hand and they moved toward the large, carved wooden door of Liz's room. Donnie turned in her direction. "Lock this behind me."

Liz walked to the balcony window and focused on the outline of the pyramids, radiant in the morning sun. She'd talked so much about Egypt and how much she loved it that she'd convinced Gary to give Addie a trip as a gift. Liz had helped him plan the whole thing as a surprise, and now his anniversary present had turned into a nightmare, and a pang of guilt stabbed at her. Maybe she could have prevented all of this if she'd only known. Liz brought her hand to her neck and fingered the chain. *Use the ankh to find the sign.*

Liz yanked the pendant over her head and reread at the inscription. *Talmar.* Talmar's ankh. *What did it mean?* She walked to the dressing area and placed it on a table. She put her overnight bag on the bed and dressed in blue jeans, a cotton top and tennis shoes, pushed her short curls into place, and picked up her scarf.

She had run out of time and she didn't want to keep Donnie and the others waiting. Liz glanced at the blinking clock on her nightstand—7:30. She thought about the meaning of the ankh. It might be a key. *Maybe it opened something.* She dumped her purse on the bed and searched for the small travel map. Nothing. 7:40. She jammed her hand into one of the side pockets and found it. Perfect.

The verse and Talmar's name still didn't mean anything. She turned to the dressing table and picked up the ankh and the note.

She flipped the paper over in her hand. A tightness rose in her chest. She didn't have time for another guessing game. Addie and Gary's lives hung in the balance.

She sat down at the large, wooden table near the center of her room, the ankh in one hand, the note in the other. Liz took a fresh piece of hotel stationery. In large bold print, she wrote Talmar's name. Then she wrote out the letters in reverse order: *Ramlat.* Liz immediately thought of the Empty Quarter, Ramlat Al-Sab'atayn, and the mythical home of the Queen of Sheba. She examined the map. Yemen, too far away. She couldn't make a connection if one even existed.

Maybe Rayhan knew something. She hurried to the nightstand and picked up the phone. Liz dialed his number and glanced at the time: 7:50. *Had he already left for the church?*

"Hello?" he answered, surprise in his voice.

"This is Liz. Are you at the church?"

"No. I was about to leave. It isn't that far from here."

The sound of his voice reassured her. She wished they had time to talk, a moment to find out who they were and what they meant to each other. She tucked away her wish to know him better. "Rayhan, are you familiar with the legend of the Queen of Sheba? She bore Solomon's child, a son, who became the ruler of Ethiopia. Her home was Ramlat Al-Sab'atayn."

"There is a book translated in 1932, Kebra Nagast, The Glory of the Kings. The book was compiled by a 6th century priest. It is a combination of myth and legend. The boy, Menyelek, would also have been from the House of David." Rayhan sighed. "Ramlat is in Yemen, Liz. I thought you needed to go to El Kudish."

"I received another riddle. Jahi said your grandmother told him to bring it to me."

"What?" Rayhan said. "My grandmother?"

"Why would she have been given a note for me?" Liz questioned.

"She goes to church early then stops by to see my aunt. Maybe someone gave it to her at the services. I don't have time to find out." He hesitated. "What did the riddle say?"

"The last line says I'll find the answer in the ankh. The inscription on it is Talmar. Ramlat spelled backwards."

"What's the name of the church in El Kudish?"

"Church of the Angels or something with a similar meaning. Why?" After she had voiced the question, she understood the House of David had to be the clue. "I need to find a church with a name like, Son of God or Holy Redeemer, don't I?"

"I guess you figured it out. I'll see you in a few minutes." Rayhan lowered his voice and whispered, "I love you." He hung up the phone without another word.

Liz remembered the stolen moments the night before. Her mind had been tangled with the events of today, and she'd almost forgotten he had kissed her. She smiled. They had lingered in the alcove and Rayhan's kisses left her breathless, trembling in his arms.

Her past relationships left her wanting. Her college boyfriend had been a dreamer. Fortunes were made from songs warning women to be careful who they loved. She found truth in those words. She dated a few of the young interns once she joined the museum, always dissatisfied with their desire to commercialize history and their findings. She had almost given up, until now. Liz and Rayhan never made it to the church and she never spoke with him about her troubled heart. Their kisses sealed their fate. They were meant to be together. She would find another time to voice her concerns, but not today. She quickly inspected her room, locked the door, and left to find Donnie.

Liz reached the lobby where Donnie used Ini as a translator. "Did you find out who gave Jahi the note?" she asked as the boy ran to a nearby table.

"Yes. His grandmother did give it to him. Evidently she went to mass early this morning and the priest asked her to see that the message was taken to you. Jahi doesn't know anything else." Donnie nodded a thank you to Ini.

"Rayhan said his grandmother goes to the church each morning, which confirms Jahi's story."

"You talked to him?" Donnie asked.

"Yes," Liz answered. "We can find out more when we're at the church."

"I'm leaving now," Ini said. He pointed Liz in the direction of a table in the lobby where Jahi sat waiting patiently to devour the chocolate donut in front of him.

Donnie sat opposite her as she slid into her chair. "I may know where we should go."

"What did you figure out?" Donnie picked up his maple bar, which Jahi took as the sign to attack his breakfast.

"I need to find a church that has some reference to the Son of God or the Redeemer. Something. There should be a map of the churches in a room that adjoins the chapel. I'll see if I can locate it when we're there."

"How did you come to that conclusion?" Donnie took a sip of his coffee.

"It is a common practice. Maybe there will be other clues, too. There are sometimes references to other churches or a string of churches. You know—like the California missions were built so many miles apart, or so many days' ride."

Donnie nodded his head as Liz ignored the sweet roll they'd bought her and drank her cup of strong, Egyptian coffee. Jahi eyed her plate and she passed it over to him. She tapped the crystal on her watch. It was almost eight. "Let's go."

They walked the distance from the Mena House to the marketplace. Jahi ran ahead. The merchant's clamoring voices punctuated the air. Each vendor, louder than the next, shouted out as they bartered with their customers. An unusual blast of hot air ruffled the brightly colored canopies of their stalls, and a hush fell over the market. A woman near Liz drew in a quick, short breath, indicating the gust had frightened her. Spring could bring sudden sandstorms, and the fruit, vegetables and other wares were quickly covered. A small child cried somewhere down the street, but not even a minute had passed before the haggling started again. God's grace had prevailed. There would be no evil wind today.

Jahi stopped at several stalls and talked with the proprietors. He pointed back in their direction as Donnie and Liz approached. She covered her head and face with the scarf. She hoped Jahi hadn't told too much of their tale. They were greeted with nods and smiles. Whatever the boy said met with their approval.

Jahi scurried past his father and Rayhan, who stood near the front of the chapel, and disappeared behind the large, wooden entrance. Liz and Donnie joined them and introductions were made. "Are the others here yet?" she asked.

"Yes." Rayhan gestured toward the door. "Ini and Mr. Aston are inside, but Talmar did not come."

"We're all here, then." Liz glanced up at Al Abdul, but saw nothing revealed in his face. He showed her neither approval nor contempt. *How will I convince him that I'm worthy of his nephew?*

Single file, the four of them entered in reverence. Jahi, comfortable with his surroundings, had made his way to the front of the church and sat in one of the pews next to a large, wicker basket covered with a woven Egyptian cotton cloth. The pale honey and cinnamon colors muted together in a soft, swirl design. Bars of gold thread dissected the pattern. Neatly tucked in at the edges, the fabric covered the contents of the vessel. The woven design reminded Liz of the wall hanging in Al Abdul's home. She assumed Amisi had designed them both.

Liz's eyes grew accustomed to the gray interior of the darkened room, and she noticed an altar boy attended the candles. The only electric lighting came from a row of small globes placed with care into an added crown molding encircling the room just below ceiling level.

They had arrived at the church an hour after morning prayers, and the smell of incense was strong. Sweet and pungent, the aroma made Liz lightheaded. She wavered and put her hand against the cool, rough wall.

"Steady," Rayhan spoke quietly from behind her.

A shiver ran up her spine and she pulled the shawl from her head and covered her shoulders. The thin covering didn't halt the chill. Her nerves played a larger part than she wanted to acknowledge, but she managed to smile.

"You okay?" He extended his hand to support her.

"I'm freezing. I probably should have eaten the pastry Donnie bought. I think my blood sugar just went through the floor."

Donnie, who stood within earshot, pulled a small, green package from the remarkable black bag, his constant companion. He unfolded the object and shook it out into a nylon parka. "Here. This might help." He draped it around Liz's shoulders.

"What all do you have in there?" she questioned in disbelief. "You're amazing."

Donnie smiled but didn't answer, and Rayhan's eyes ignited and he moved closer to Liz.

The priest, dressed in a black robe, asked them to remove their shoes and directed the group to the front of the chapel near where Jahi had found a seat. Rayhan, Al Abdul, and Ini followed the priest in making their signation and sat on the left side of the church directly behind Jahi.

Liz walked across the stone tiled floor in front of the podium and turned to face the men. She clasped her hands together to control her nervousness as a lump grew in her throat. Her resolve crumbled, but she had to explain their plan. She thought for a moment. *Donnie should be the one to deliver the information.* Rayhan appeared hopeful, but a scowl had settled on Al Abdul's face, and Jahi sat swinging his feet underneath the pew.

Liz swallowed her fears and cleared her throat, wondering if she could talk without crying, but the priest raised his hand. Her eyes scanned the back of the church where the young altar boy, not much older than Jahi, bolted the door and dimmed the rim of lights. Liz's eyes widened as Talmar appeared from a side door. The priest bowed and offered Talmar his seat on the platform at the head of the church, but Talmar declined and sat, instead, beside Jahi.

Talmar brought with him a certain serenity. The soft candlelight from the altar mixed with the filtered sunlight from the windows wrapped her in familiarity. A mixture of protection and security blanketed her. She didn't want to step away from the feeling and embark on a journey which might change everyone's life. Even though she anticipated no harm would come to any of them, she feared Moustafa had given his life doing his part in this unbelievable story, but prayed this wasn't the case. Her friends were sheltered and cared for by strangers. Her only desire—to find them—would be her goal, no matter the odds.

She thought of Rayhan, who she would not have met under any other circumstances. Their relationship had been tested from the beginning. They had been brought together by tragedy, and fought adversity for a chance to discover if their love could bloom. Her heart flooded with emotions, but above all, her hope had returned. *But the needy will not always be forgotten, nor the hope of the afflicted ever perish*—Psalms 9:18.

She scoured the faces of the strange assemblage of men bisected by the center aisle of the sanctuary. They were from all over the world, and they'd come to a small church in an otherwise unnoticed place in Cairo. The thought astonished her. She briefly scrutinized her collaborators. Three Egyptian men sat behind Talmar, the much revered Jereon of their district. She turned to Al Abdul, whose looming presence had worried her when they'd met yesterday. He spoke in quick, short sentences, often accentuated with hand gestures and loud tones. Liz could not decide if he had been a willing participant, or if he did so out of love for his nephew and his son.

She thought of Ini, who had been friendly from the first. He went out of his way to help her. Then her gaze came to rest on Rayhan. He filled her heart, and just to look at him made every inch of her skin come alive with the sensation of his touch. Her affection for him would carry Liz through the ordeal.

On the left side of the room sat Richard Aston, who had so boldly met this challenge. He had his own reasons for helping her. He didn't want to see another loved one lost, another heart broken. She fixed her eyes on Donnie, whose mysterious past and love for his cousin made him an essential component.

Liz's voice quivered. "Rayhan." She made a hesitant turn in the direction of the man she had chosen to be her husband for this mission and perhaps the rest of their lives. "Could you join me here to translate?" Rayhan stepped beside her and nodded. His presence bolstered her strength. Liz spoke in English. "I'm sure you all know my friends, Addie and Gary, have disappeared. I've received notes concerning their whereabouts, and the information from Talmar confirmed they are on their way to El Kudish." She paused and scanned their faces. "Additional news this morning urges us to leave before they are moved again."

Eyes riveted to Rayhan as she waited for him to translate. Liz gathered the courage to tell them about Moustafa. "I'm afraid Mr. Moustafa, who so valiantly rescued Addie and Gary, is no longer with them. I fear the worst, but we can pray that is not the case."

Al Abdul appeared stricken. He spoke perfect English, but he chose to speak to Rayhan in Arabic. Rayhan turned to her.

"No. I do not know what happened," she said, answering Al Abdul's question. "The riddle said the trusted one was no more. He had secured safe passage for Addie and Gary to El Kudish. Something went wrong." Guilt flooded over her. *Have I asked too much of these people who are fearful for their own lives?*

Al Abdul stood and walked directly in front of Rayhan, but turned to her, concern creasing his brow. "Do you realize what you're getting yourself into?" he shouted. "You could be killed and bring vast harm to all of us, even our entire community." Al Abudl turned and spanned the room in a few exaggerated steps then leaned against the far wall. His white, cotton tunic swirled into place above his knees. "You have come here and brought great trouble with you. You might not return from El Kudish. You're going several hundred kilometers into the desert. Most Egyptians don't go there unless they have just cause."

"My friends need me." She asked God for strength. She didn't want to offend those who risked so much to help her, but she had to make Al Abdul listen. "Our cultures are different. You must understand. Addie is my best friend and she's Donnie's cousin." Liz squared her shoulders as she continued to speak. "We cannot leave them, hoping they'll somehow find their way back here safely. We're going. I know we're in a perilous situation, but my mind is made up. I have no choice. Would you not try to find Jahi or Rayhan if you were in my shoes?"

Al Abdul's hard features softened. "I, too, would go." He spoke in English, but turned and left the church. Liz choked back tears and shifted toward Rayhan, who shook his head and lowered his eyes. A hush fell over the room.

Richard broke the awkward silence. "Did the note mention anything else?"

Liz closed her eyes. She had likely offended Al Abdul and may have, in the process, caused Rayhan undo grief. She blinked away tears and mumbled, "Use the ankh to find the sign." Talmar stood and approached Rayhan.

He turned to Liz after a hushed conversation with Talmar. "Give him the ankh."

She removed the cross from her neck and dropped it into the weathered, brown hand of the old priest. He moved down the aisle of the chapel and into a small, adjoining room. He motioned for them to enter and indicated for the chapel priest to close the door. Talmar spoke to him in rapid, staccato dialect, which she didn't understand. The wide-eyed priest shook his head.

"Rayhan," Liz said in a hushed tone. "What's going on?"

"He wants the priest to show us something, but he isn't sure he should. Talmar is convincing him it's all right."

The priest bowed to Talmar, walked to the side of the room, and opened a small, red velvet curtain on the wall. Behind it sat a roughhewn, wooden box. The hinges and door pull were old and made of black cast iron. Talmar opened the small cabinet with the key tied to the bottom of a gold cord, which secured his robe. Inside, carved into the wall, an ankh-shaped depression. Talmar took the cross he'd given Liz and placed it into the opening. She gasped. It fit into the carving. The tumblers clicked once the symbol fell in place. Talmar rested his hand on the wall, and placed his shoulder against the solid wood block. He pushed the door as it groaned and slid it aside. A small, cell-like room was revealed. Her eyes widened. Both Talmar and the priest made the sign of the cross, blessing the room.

"The hidden room," she gasped. "I've read about them in legends. They do exist. I can't believe it." Her pulse quickened. "The sign was carved in churches built in the fifth century. The priest's ankhs were cast from those early carvings, but everyone thought they'd been destroyed over time and disappeared."

She reverently entered the chamber and glanced back at the wall to locate the map of the other churches. She noticed some of the chapels boasted the sign of the cruciform, while others did not. "Does this mean those marked churches are fifth century? Do they all have hidden rooms?"

"Yes," the priest spoke up. "But only someone who has studied our religion, or those who are very devout know this." Uneasy, he cleared his throat. "You must not ask to see the sign. It is well-guarded. We cannot have it destroyed. Or have anyone know the rooms exist. So much of our faith and beliefs have been dashed by others."

A tear slid from her cheek. They lived in fear and secrecy, yet they dared to endanger themselves for others.

"Your friends will be in such a room. Even if they are moved from El Kudish," Talmar said. "The rooms were made to hide and protect our people. Now, not our own, but two of God's children wait for you there."

Liz reviewed the map a second time. The church at El Kudish had such a sign, but something bothered her. She had been confused about the directions in the riddle. *Were they looking in the wrong place?* She finished with her explanation of their plan as they huddled in the room built for no more than two inhabitants. "The sketchy information I've received indicates they have been hurt. I know they were beaten at the restaurant where Moustafa rescued them." She waited for Rayhan to translate.

"Talmar confirmed what Moustafa told me earlier. Addie and Gary were removed from Cairo. The papers they carried were of more importance to someone than we realized. The people who have befriended them cannot bring them back, or they will jeopardize themselves." Even as she forced herself to form the words, the task ahead of them took on such an enormity she shuddered.

She glanced at Donnie before she began speaking, "Donnie gave Addie a golden key for a wedding gift. She would have kept it with her." Liz thought of the blood-covered key and shuddered again. "It was far too important to Addie to willingly give up. By the key being returned to Talmar, I believe Addie and Gary are trying to contact us. We're running out of time." She paused again, anticipating the translation. "Each one of you has played a valuable part in this, either by your knowledge, understanding the logistics, or just by being my confidant. I can't express to you how important you've all been getting us to this point." Casting a glance at Jahi, she smiled. Even the gapped-toothed boy had a hand in this.

"Donnie, Rayhan, and I will be leaving this afternoon." She hesitated, and focused her eyes and thoughts on Rayhan. "We should only be gone a few days. I don't think they'll be at El Kudish much longer. The last piece of information I was given specified they'd be moved before the moon wanes."

Rayhan glanced in Talmar's direction, but addressed the entire group. "It will make it much easier to explain why she is out in the desert if she is married to a National."

Liz believed this untimely match of two hearts could be right for both of them. "Rayhan and I will pose as a couple. I discussed this with Richard and we came to the conclusion it would be safer for us to travel that way. Donnie will assume the role of my cousin."

Talmar glimpsed between Liz and Rayhan. She couldn't sense his feelings by the expression on his face. Finally, he nodded his approval.

"Liz." Richard Aston approached them. "I drew these papers up this morning for you and Donnie. They aren't official, but no one will know without a highly trained eye. They will be sufficient when needed to cross any road blocks, or pass most of the military police."

She gave Richard a quick hug. "Thank you. You have no idea how much your help means to me. This couldn't have been done without you."

They made their way out of the small room into the foyer. Talmar bowed, patted Liz's hand gently, and smiled. He made his way up the aisle and vanished behind the curtain.

"It will be all right, Liz. You'll find them," Richard said. "If you're in any danger, send a message to me." He turned and left through the narthex.

Donnie moved closer to Rayhan. "Come to the Mena House by noon. Liz and I will be ready."

"I still feel something is wrong," she broke in. "What about the name of the church? The reference to Ramlat?"

"Christ is our redeemer, Liz," Rayhan said. "It could be all the reference meant. Or maybe it meant nothing. Talmar's name is on the ankh; he showed you how it should be used."

"I guess," she said, still unsure and fraught with uncertainty. The last line of the riddle bothered her. She couldn't decipher it. *Use the ankh to find the sign. What sign? The sign of the church? Ramlat? What? Should she run after Talmar and ask him? Perhaps he wrote the note, or did he even know?*

Ini, who had briefly left them, stood by her side with the basket. "From all of us, Liz, for your journey." He had tears in his eyes as he handed it to her.

"How kind." She smiled. "What's in here?"

"Food, maps, things we thought you'd need." Jahi pulled at his arm. "Jahi and his mother bought dates and nuts for you at the market."

Liz handed the basket to Donnie, bent down, and kissed Jahi goodbye. "Please thank the priest for me." The absence of Al Abdul and his blessing on the journey saddened Liz. She prayed she and Rayhan could change Al Abdul's mind.

Have I asked too much of God and His people? She had questioned her faith before. Yet, God's grace surrounded her and brought her to Him once again. It would be His grace that would lead them to Addie and Gary, and His wisdom would open an old man's heart.

CHAPTER SEVEN

LIZ GLANCED AT her watch when she and Donnie reached the veranda of the Mena House. "It's eleven." He shouldered the basket and carried it through the lobby. "Do you want lunch?"

"There's probably enough in here for a small army." He glanced up toward the hamper. "We could eat on the road."

"No." She moved toward the stairs then to the elevator so Donnie wouldn't have to haul the parcel any further. "I'll order something from room service. We should probably save whatever is in there for when we really need it."

"Okay." He groaned as they waited for the next lift. "I'll dump this off in your room and pick up my bag. I'm packed." He set the carrier on the floor in front of him.

"Me, too. Do you think the jeep is ready?"

"Ini made the arrangements for someone to check out the mechanics. He told me they'd bring it to the hotel before noon. It could be earlier. I'll call him from your room."

"Anything special for your last meal?" she joked.

"Hamburger, fries, and a chocolate shake." He winked at her and grinned. "I don't think we'll get much of that where we're going." The bell over their heads clanged and Donnie pushed the basket in ahead of them with one foot. "You know, this thing is really heavy."

"Do you want me to carry it?" She gave him a sidelong glance. "I brought you over here for a reason, you know. The last camel had been taken."

"Not for my quick wittiness and wily ways?" he teased.

"Please. Don't try to impress me. Just pick up the basket." She then remembered she'd seen Donnie in deep conversation with Richard before he left the church. "What were you talking to Richard about?"

"We exchanged cell phone numbers. I wasn't venturing off to who-knows-where without some sort of backup."

"You told me not to use my cell phone—it can be traced. It's okay for you?" She hadn't mentioned she had used hers to call Rayhan.

He made a face and answered her in a sing-song voice. "No. It's not okay for me. I bought a throw-away type. I'll ditch it if I think someone's on to us."

"It's going to work over here?"

"Liz. You decipher the documents and the riddles. Leave the other stuff to me. I paid extra, and it will work. The only thing is I hope I can hit the Loral satellite. The Iridium one stinks."

"You're talking Greek to me, you know," she laughed.

He placed the basket on her bed next to her bag and was crossing to the door when the phone rang. Bewildered, she turned to Donnie. "Who would be calling me? We saw everyone at the church." She picked up the receiver.

"You have a call from a Pastor Michael Waterford," the switchboard operator announced.

"Yes. Put him through." Liz turned to Donnie. "It's Pastor Mike. Maybe something has developed on his end." Liz waited an eternity and then the connection clicked in her ear. "Pastor Waterford. Do you have some news for us?"

From the other side of the world, Michael Waterford cleared his throat, then his voice quivered from the depths of his anguish. "I'm so sorry. You have to forgive me. I didn't know."

"Pastor? What are you talking about? Forgive you for what?"

He didn't speak for a moment and Liz listened intently, thinking they had become disconnected. After a long pause, he continued. "I did some checking on Mr. Hamaka. He's in trouble with the authorities in the States, all the way to the NSA and the CIA. I think he's wanted in Egypt, too."

"No." She grappled with this new information and motioned to Donnie. "How could this happen?"

"I didn't know. Please believe me, I didn't know."

Her legs buckled and she clutched for the nearest chair as her strength drained away. She handed Donnie the phone.

"This is Donnie. Why didn't you call me? What were you telling Liz?" Donnie eyed her and shook his head as the pastor repeated his information. "Well, that certainly explains this situation in a new light, doesn't it? When did you find out? Who told you?" She couldn't hear what Pastor Mike told him, and Donnie turned his back. "Okay. Okay. No. It isn't your fault. It changes nothing for us except to confirm the danger we suspected. We were about to leave." Donnie pulled out a chair and sat down. "Ask for the desk clerk, Ini, if you have any further messages for us. It will get to us somehow." He reached over and patted Liz's hand. He'd read her thoughts.

Liz observed him as he hung up. "D-Donnie? What else did he say?" A new surge of fear rushed through her. How did they get into this? She stopped for a moment and asked for God's help. Talmar and the priest blessed their journey, but she wished, now, they would have all prayed together.

"Not much more than he told you. He called here because I wasn't in my room, but this is bad, very bad, especially if Addie and Gary still have the note. We need to leave as soon as Rayhan brings the jeep and take advantage of all the daylight we can. You know this is going to be more dangerous than we thought, don't you?"

"Maybe we should just turn this over to the police. Even though you worry we shouldn't, the whole thing is too..." Her voice quivered and she attempted to remain in control.

"Let me take care of it, Liz. I've been in and out of more jams than you can imagine. We would implicate too many people—Richard, Rayhan, Ini, and the group of men from the church—if we bring in the authorities now, and I don't trust the police or anyone else here. Do you realize how easily they're bought off?"

"I know. Seriously, I don't think Richard can help us. He's in a tough spot. Ini's an innocent bystander, but Rayhan is into this as deep as we are." She forced the corners of her mouth into a smile. "Four days, Donnie. We've been here four days, and it's more involved every minute."

"Come on. Take a deep breath. Where's your sense of adventure? Do you know how much I ran from the law when I was a kid? I'm sure I can outsmart this Hamaka and whoever his contacts are over here." Donnie rubbed her shoulders and tried to relieve her tension. She stiffened and he removed his hands. "We'll have to find a place to stay once the sun sets, in case of robbers. I hope there's not a Kashmin while we're out there."

"How do you know about the Kashmin winds?" She recognized his maneuver to diffuse the situation and respected the gesture.

"I read a lot on the plane." He smiled. "Semper paratus. That's my motto."

"Always be prepared," Liz repeated. She prayed they were.

"Liz," he said, lowering his voice, "when this is all over and Addie and Gary are home, do you think…" He paused. "I come to California often. I know long distance relationships don't often work, but it did for them."

Liz felt her face blaze and drew her mouth into a tight line. "Donnie. I'm terribly flattered, but I'm involved." His sudden attention unsettled her. She'd met him a couple of times at Addie's, but had no idea he wished to be more than casual friends. She didn't want that, but he did have some redeeming qualities.

"Oh. You haven't made any phone calls or anything back home. Where is the lucky guy?" Donnie questioned.

"He's here in Egypt," she said, her voice calm and steady.

"You've seen him since we arrived? I've been with you almost every moment."

Liz knew she had to tell him. It would make their trip easier. He had a right to know. "Donnie, I'm engaged to Rayhan. For real."

"What?" He glared at her, mouth open. "Did you know him before? You didn't act like you were engaged at the airport."

"Donnie, you aren't going to appreciate this. We've all been telling you things are different here. Rayhan was interested in me. We wanted a courtship, but to honor his customs and his beliefs, it has to be an engagement." She refused to tell him all of it.

"This is nuts. Is that why you went to his home? Al Abdul doesn't approve, does he? That's why he left this morning."

"That's right. I won't ask you to understand. I'm not sure I understand everything myself. It all happened so fast." Liz let her thoughts drift to last night, when Rayhan walked her back to the veranda. They spoke very little, and he held her hand even as he turned away to go. Her fingers slipped through his until just their fingertips touched. Such electricity charged between them, she still felt its pulsating tingle.

Donnie ran his hand through his hair. "Well, I guess it won't be hard for you two to pull off your charade. No wonder you made the request." He shook his head. "I hope this doesn't complicate things." He walked to her door then stopped mid-way. A glint of sorrow burdened his eyes.

Though she suspected his attraction, she had no idea he cared for her so much. She hadn't meant to hurt him, but she never saw this coming. Not from him. Had she been so blind? If anything, she'd been blinded by Rayhan.

"Do you even know how crazy this all is? Don't you have enough going on? Trying to find Addie and Gary, all these riddles and all this other nonsense, and you two decide on an engagement in the middle of it."

"Please…" she began, but he put his hand up and continued toward the door.

Her heart pounded as Donnie removed the security chain and slid the deadbolt. He never turned around, and when he slammed the door, the vibration shook her. She hadn't planned on falling for Rayhan, but she had failed to convince Donnie. She'd talk to him later, if he would be willing to listen.

Liz called room service and asked them to pack a picnic. It took a while to explain what she wanted them to do, but eventually they understood—three lunches "to go."

She jumped when the phone rang again and a chill crept through her. She reached for the receiver and relief flooded over her at Donnie's voice on the other end.

"Ini just called, the jeep is ready. He's having Rayhan pick it up, and we'll meet in the foyer." Donnie coughed nervously. "I'm sorry about earlier. I was just suffering from a little ego bruising. Are you ready for this, Liz?"

"I think so." She didn't intend to create any animosity between them and felt relieved he'd backed off. *Men.*

Liz picked up the lunch box left outside her door, shouldered her bag, and glanced around the room. She kept a constant prayer in her heart this trip would be easy and Addie and Gary would be found safe, but again her hope faltered.

God be with us. She remembered Moustafa said those exact words. *Be of good comfort, be of one mind, live in peace; and the God of love and peace will be with you.* Had Moustafa given his life to save Addie and Gary? What had happened? Or could he still be alive? Maybe he sent the messages.

She joined Donnie and Rayhan in the lobby and they walked to the waiting jeep parked in the circular drive. Rayhan climbed into the back and positioned himself on a wooden plank, which replaced the original bench seat.

"Are you going to be comfortable?" Liz asked him, gesturing to the splintery boards.

"I'm fine for now. I can cover it later on with blankets if need be." He smiled at her and continued. "Don't worry about me. I've learned to make do." He leaned back against the Egyptian basket.

Liz swung her leg into the front of the jeep and a quick flash of white materialized behind them. She turned and searched beyond Rayhan to the open back end of the vehicle, finding nothing. Liz decided she hadn't really seen anything. She'd lived on coffee and little else for the past few days, and it had made her edgy. *But I saw something. Or did I?*

Donnie pulled the car away from the Mena House, maneuvered around the waiting taxis, and out into the street filled with other vehicles and donkey carts. She seized the opportunity to lose herself in the observance of the people-infused streets. The rising mid-afternoon heat only disadvantaged the tourists. They sat at roadside coffee bars under awnings or umbrellas as the locals continued on in the elements, not giving a second thought to the scorching sun.

The jeep Richard had borrowed from Habi had no top or sides. She reached down into her bag and pulled out a baseball cap. Where they were going, her head and face didn't need to be covered. The hat kept her eyes shaded and her short, wispy curls confined, but there would be no reprieve from the heat. April's temperatures were on the mild side, but high pressure had caused a three-digit rise. The heat rose from the pavement and stagnated the air, making it difficult to breathe.

"Okay, Rayhan," Donnie spoke over his shoulder. "Which way do I go?"

"This road will lead us to the highway. Drive straight ahead, then we will travel along the western shore of the Nile." Rayhan pointed between the two front seats, brushing Liz's shoulder. "Have you driven here much?"

"No, just back from Richard's last night. The traffic wasn't like it is now."

"People drive differently here than they do in the States. They ignore the traffic lights and pedestrians walk in among the cars, not on the side of the streets. It's pretty much every man for himself."

They turned onto the main road where the two marked lanes had been expanded into four by the motorists. Carts mixed in with the vehicles and bicyclists who darted in between. They pulled up next to an old diesel bus and the fetid exhaust furthered their discomfort.

"I see what you mean." Donnie shook his head.

"Trade me places until we're out of the city. This could take hours if you don't know what you're up against." Rayhan had already removed himself from the wooden seat, hopped out, and stood at the driver's side of the car.

Rayhan and Donnie exchanged seats while the stalled traffic stayed cemented to the asphalt. "Hang on," Rayhan shouted as they jerked through the cars, wagons, and those on foot, while he held his hand on the horn. He drove over the edge of the sidewalk when they reached the intersection and shot across oncoming traffic and onto a side street. "There. I think I just saved us a couple of hours. You want to drive now?" he asked Donnie.

"No. Go ahead," Donnie laughed appreciatively. "You know what you're doing."

Rayhan used narrow, nearly nonexistent roads. Liz thought they'd be better described as bicycle paths. They reached the banks of the Nile after a few quick shortcuts. She took the opportunity to relax, something she hadn't done since Rayhan's call days ago. She shared a quick smile with him and settled in to enjoy the scenery. The smell of the Nile waters spurred her memory of her first trip to Egypt.

Her father, a career Army Officer, brought the family to England for the duration of his tour. Seventeen-year-old Liz had been in her senior year of Aberdour when she had the opportunity to visit Egypt with her class. When her dad retired from the military and joined the normal workforce, they settled in the San Francisco area, and while in college she had an opportunity to serve as an assistant on a summer archaeological expedition in the Valley of the Kings.

She had never known anything so foreign and as exciting as Egypt. As an army brat, she'd visited several different countries, but the moment the plane landed in Cairo even the air felt different. The blue, almost cloudless sky stretched out in a vibrant blue arch. The warm breezes peeled away the shrouded winter chill of England, and the moment her feet touched solid ground she had come home. Home to a place she'd never been, but still felt so right. The pyramids, the history, and the people left a lasting impression, and she continued coming back year after year.

A breeze drifted across the road from the wide, blue river and small boats strained against the current. A larger cruise vessel made lazy ripples in the waterway. A group of passengers sunbathed on the uppermost deck.

The tributary had allowed this civilization to flourish for thousands of years. The papyrus she categorized for the museum would have been written by the hands of a person whose eyes rested on these same sights many, many years ago. Fat, lazy crocodiles sunned themselves on the banks, and if a fisher eagle flew too close with its catch, hungry jaws snapped at their talons. She didn't notice Rayhan as he downshifted, slowing the jeep until they were almost at a standstill. He approached a check point.

Two men stood in the roadway as the jeep approached the barricade. Rayhan spoke with them in brisk Arabic. "Your papers?" He put out his hand and glimpsed in Liz's direction, but his dark, smoldering eyes revealed little. She dug out the documents Richard had prepared, handed them to Rayhan, and pulled the cap further down over her eyes.

One of the guards touched his beret and whispered something. Rayhan responded, and she caught the word American. The three men laughed and the guard waved them on.

"What did you say to them?" Liz asked as she replaced the papers in her bag. Their dialect, thick with local phrases, didn't allow her to follow the conversation.

"I told them my wife was an American and very fond of baseball," he chuckled. "It worked." He grinned. "They let us go."

She smiled. *My wife.* He stepped into his role so easily. He knew what he wanted. His straightforward assurance impressed her. He had defended her when she spoke her mind to Al Abdul. *This could work.* Rayhan reached for her hand and held it, caressing her fingers. He had said he turned sixteen right before he came back. What had he learned in America about women? Had his parents assimilated so well into the American culture that Rayhan wanted what they had? Al Abdul and Amisi were steeped in their traditions and practices. It had become obvious to Liz that Rayhan wanted something else, but he held onto his cultural obligations. Their relationship could be a bumpy ride.

Liz glanced over her shoulder at Donnie, who had his eyes locked on the horizon. How quickly all their lives had changed. A few days ago, she worked in San Francisco and he in Arizona. *What had Rayhan been doing two days ago, last week, last year? Had he had other girlfriends? What did he want to do with his life? Stay at the Embassy or work in the archaeological field?* Somehow Liz felt all the unanswered questions only brought her to one conclusion—the answers would lead her to adore him more.

She shifted her gaze to the miles and miles of shimmering, sun-kissed sand, and let her mind drift. Liz couldn't shake the thought they should search somewhere other than El Kudish. Her concern grew as she feared more time would be wasted, but she couldn't decipher the part of the riddle which told her where they would be taken if they were moved. The rough translation of Ramlat meant desert, which described a large portion of this part of the world. Dangerous, uncaring, shifting mounds of—

Rayhan jerked the wheel to avoid an oncoming vehicle and the jeep lurched in the air. Their equipment in the rear of the jeep resettled with a loud thud and a very small yelp from a stowaway.

"Rayhan!" Donnie shouted from his perch on the wooden plank. "Pull over."

Rayhan shook his head. "I was afraid this might happen. He begged his father and me to let him come along. Jahi is going to find himself in a lot of trouble this time."

"Jahi?" Liz blurted out, surprised. His tunic had been the flash of white she'd seen at the Mena House. He'd climbed into the back.

Rayhan jumped out, walked to the rear of the vehicle, and threw back the canvas tarp covering their supplies. Jahi had crouched down among them in a space far too small behind the basket they'd been given at the church. He squatted, holding his knees. "Jahi Mark." Rayhan exploded in an Arabic tongue lashing too clipped and quick to follow.

His anger expelled, Rayhan reached in and lifted the boy to the ground. Jahi sniffled. "We should take him back," Rayhan said as Liz stroked Jahi's head. "We can start again in the morning."

"There isn't time," Donnie interjected. "We've wasted most of today. It took far too much time to plan the trip. The afternoon is almost gone."

Liz's tolerance grew thin. She'd already argued with Donnie once today. Pure reasoning told her they shouldn't take a child with them, but they raced against some unknown clock that could cost her friends their lives. She had to weigh out a fight with Rayhan and what it could do to the early stages of their relationship. She had to stand her ground, and the sudden change in his demeanor intrigued her. Rayhan would get to know her on this trip, whether he liked the outcome or not. "No. Donnie's right. Make room for Jahi in the back. We'll take him. He might be able to help us somehow. Let's go."

"Liz." Rayhan turned to her, his jaw set, taut and stern. "It's too dangerous."

"The whole thing is risky. There may be gun shipments involved…" She stopped. "Donnie told you about the note, didn't he?"

"Yes. It's far too perilous to take a child." Rayhan touched Jahi's shoulder. "I can't jeopardize his life."

"We're leaving, Rayhan. I need you to come with us. Climb in."

"I can't…"

"She's right," Donnie broke in. "It has been six days since Addie and Gary's disappearance. They could be anywhere. We can leave Jahi at a church or with a priest if necessary. We'll come back for him, but right now, we need to go."

"All right," Rayhan conceded. "There will be a small store when we stop for gas, in Bani Suwayf. I want to buy him a shirt and trousers. He should be dressed in Western clothing."

"Why?" Liz glared at him.

"It will be easier to explain if we are stopped. Al Abdul insists Jahi dress in his traditional tunic. I will need to pass him off as our child if we are questioned by the authorities." Fingering the collar on his denim shirt, Rayhan went on. "Jahi looks out of place."

"How are you going to explain him?" Donnie asked. "He has no papers."

"He doesn't need any. A child of an Egyptian father is considered an Egyptian." Rayhan said something over his shoulder to Jahi. The wide-eyed child nodded his head in understanding.

"Jahi is to stay with me when we go into the store or around other people. He may stand by you, but do not hold his hand."

"I know." Liz smiled at Jahi. "He's a very affectionate child. Does he know what he should do?"

"I'll speak to him. He's used to being with family. It is our culture for a child approaching his age to be cared for by his father. Back in Cairo, he isn't old enough to go to school or outside the marketplace. Out here..." Rayhan paused and stretched his hand out to the skyline. "It's different."

Liz tilted her head back to view the afternoon sun, then glanced at her watch, confirming the time—two o'clock. Another delay, but they couldn't return to Cairo and start again tomorrow. She had to agree with Donnie and hoped Rayhan could explain the situation to his uncle. She remembered they'd never eaten their lunches from the hotel and reached down to the box at her feet. She handed Rayhan and Donnie a sandwich wrapped in waxed paper and offered hers to Jahi. He declined. Not knowing how long it had been since he'd eaten, she spoke to Rayhan. "Do you think you should tell him to eat something?"

"No. He isn't bashful about eating. He saw me take my sandwich, so he knows it isn't something forbidden. He's okay."

Her nurturing awakened as she handed the boy three almond cookies. He grabbed them with his brown, slender fingers and grinned. She couldn't help but smile at him, but she prayed they weren't putting him in danger.

The sun, relentless in its barrage, sat unmoving in the afternoon sky as they continued skimming the artery parallel to the Nile. Rayhan drove on toward Bani Suwayf as Liz became mesmerized by the rolling desert dunes. She thought of the story of Cambyses' army being swallowed by the great Sea of Sand near the Siwa Oasis. Addie and Gary had just vanished. Had they, too, been devoured by the desert? She went over the scene at the El Dar and forced herself to invoke a mental picture of the kidnapping, her thoughts clouded. She couldn't shake the feeling she had about the riddle. Both Rayhan and Donnie thought she had the answers, but as the miles grew between them and Cairo, so did her uncertainty.

"Lizzz." Jahi tugged on her shoulder. He jolted her out of her dismal thoughts and brought a smile to her lips at his attempt to pronounce her name.

"Jahi!" Rayhan scolded him. A scowl knitted his eyebrows. He continued with a string of Arabic.

Jahi hung his head and Liz reached over and lifted his chin in her hand. "What is it, little one? What did you want to tell me?"

Jahi scrambled out of his makeshift seat and crouched down near the gearshift knob. "Umm, look." Jahi pointed across the desert to a row of camels on the horizon. "Bani Suwayf."

Liz turned to Rayhan. "Don't be so hard on him. He's just a little boy."

"He shouldn't be here." Rayhan glowered. "I must protect him, and if he is to act as our son, he can't call you Liz."

"I know. I feel responsible for him, too. Nothing will happen to him. I promise."

"You can't promise that." He turned toward the small settlement and pulled the jeep into second gear. "Not now."

"We agreed we couldn't take him back. This didn't exactly turn out like I'd planned either. What do you want me to do?" Liz felt Rayhan's displeasure with her. She had strong ideas and she didn't mind expressing her opinion. Maybe she was too much for him.

"Be subservient. You must act like an Egyptian wife, even though you are an American. Just follow my lead and we'll be fine. Don't question my authority and if I tell you to do something, do it."

"Well, good luck with that one," Donnie interjected and a smile crossed Rayhan's otherwise troubled face.

"We don't want to draw any attention to ourselves." Rayhan slid his hand from the gearshift and took her fingers in his. With a light squeeze, she sensed his indication that he understood. *Did he?*

She didn't have much choice other than to do as he said. She wouldn't do anything to jeopardize their chances of finding Addie and Gary, or hurting Jahi. *Please, God, let us find them*, tumbled unheard from her lips and repeated constantly in her thoughts.

Rayhan stopped the car and checked around him. He jogged in the direction of the market, pulling Jahi along. Rayhan stopped for a second and called over his shoulder. "Hurry, Liz. I'll pick him out some clothes. We must get back on the road."

She tossed her baseball cap on to the seat and covered her head with the thin scarf she had in her purse. Now, she wished she'd brought a shawl. She decided she should follow Donnie's model and be more prepared. Liz glanced over at him as he fiddled with something from his black gadget bag. "You coming?"

"Nah. I have to see if something works. You two lovebirds run along. I'll wait here and protect the jeep."

She surveyed the endless rolling dunes. "From what?"

"Go on," he said. "Rayhan's waiting." Donnie grinned. "Subservient? He doesn't know what he's gotten himself into, does he?"

Liz didn't answer and scanned the short distance to where Rayhan stood. Although they'd disagreed, he smiled at her. His hand rested on Jahi's shoulder, and they portrayed the image of the father and son they pretended to be. *A glimpse into her own future?* Rayhan turned and continued toward the compound.

She caught up with them as they entered the store. She said nothing and hovered behind Rayhan as he picked out an outfit and paid for the clothing.

She glanced across the shop where several venues converged under one roof, and she waited as her eyes drifted across a small deli, café tables and rows and rows of snack-sized packaged goods. She recognized several American products, their familiar logos written in Arabic. The store reminded her of the mini-market around the corner from her apartment.

Near a window in the back, two men stood. One pointed toward the crest of a sand dune beyond the rear of the building. He turned to deposit his bottled drink on a nearby table and she froze. The dark, scar-faced man, who threatened her with the meat cleaver at the El Dar, turned toward her. A chill ran through her as she spun around to find Rayhan. She had to avoid the man who had returned to the window, but her legs remained motionless, anchoring her feet to the floor. She opened her mouth to call out to Rayhan, but the action would thwart their charade. She strained to hear the men's whispers as Rayhan, unknowing, moved away from her. The clerk behind the counter turned a stoic face to Liz, expecting her to fall in line with Rayhan, and she lowered her head and walked in the direction of the door.

She rushed to Rayhan as he cleared the store's entrance. He and Jahi ambled toward the vehicle as Liz ran to catch up. "Hurry. Run to the jeep. I think those men back there were involved in the kidnapping."

"Who?"

"The two men standing next to the window." Liz climbed into her seat. She placed Jahi on the floor where he crouched at her feet. "Just drive out of here, and when you reach the highway, put some distance between us." She turned to include Donnie in the conversation and noticed the empty seat behind her. Fresh fear washed over her. *Why had he chosen to go exploring now?* Her hands shook as she removed the scarf from her head. "Where did Donnie go?"

Rayhan started the engine and pointed toward the road. "He's up there."

Did the man see me? What happenstance could have brought him here other than for the same reason I have?

Then maybe they were looking in the right place. Or worse yet, somehow the news of their trip had leaked out.

Liz felt a hard tug at her heart for the child clutching her leg.

Rayhan pulled near the stretch of blacktop. "Come on," he yelled as he slowed the vehicle for Donnie.

He had no more than sat down when a cell phone chirped from his pocket. "Hello? Yes, Ini. Apa Bane? Okay. Okay. I'll tell him. Bye."

"Rayhan. Do you know where Apa Bane is?" Donnie questioned, ignoring Liz's puzzled glare.

"Yes. It lies ahead of us, maybe one hundred and twenty kilometers. What did Ini tell you?"

"He told me we should go there."

"Deir al-Salib is in ruins. No one lives there. Who contacted Ini?"

"The communication came from Al Abdul. The priest at the chapel received a message this afternoon after we left. We are to spend the night there." Donnie paused. "Your uncle knows we have Jahi."

Has my future with Rayhan already begun to unravel?

"Is he furious?" Rayhan asked, lips pressed tight with worry.

"Most likely, but Ini didn't say. Once your uncle figured out Jahi had disappeared, he knew he was with us."

Rayhan's gaze fell on the boy. The smile turning up the corners of his mouth belied the stern expression in Rayhan's eyes. "Jahi seems to get himself into a little trouble now and then."

"Your family is very close, isn't it?" Donnie asked.

"Yes. My uncle is the head of our family since the death of my father. You, too, are close with Addie and Gary, no? You came halfway around the world to find them. It's all the same."

"Addie and I hardly knew each other two years ago. People drift apart and forget what is important to them."

Rayhan shifted in his seat. "It is the very core of our culture to regard one another with the deepest respect. I'd lose honor with Al Abdul if anything happened to Jahi."

Rayhan's deep conviction to family and his young charge warmed her heart. His gentleness of spirit flowed through him, yet she'd seen him turn that same moral fiber into a force of strength. Good qualities in a father, and better yet, in a husband. He reached over to the boy, who now sat on Liz's lap, and tousled his hair. "I must care for the little one God has given us to protect."

"That's why I'm here, too, Rayhan. We realize how important we are to each other, and Addie and Gary…" Donnie trailed off.

Is Donnie worried we won't find them? He'd been so sure. She moved Jahi over, pulled her knees up into the seat, and rested her chin between them. She needed strength. She reached deep down within herself, closing her eyes to pray. She couldn't let her apprehension rage, and fought to control her emotions.

Donnie interrupted her deep thoughts. "Who are we running from, Liz? Who did you see in the store?"

"One of those men back there was at the El Dar where Addie and Gary were last seen. He threatened me when I tried to pass through the kitchen to the back door alleyway. He's implicated in this. Why else would he be at Bani Suwayf, too?"

Rayhan jammed the jeep into four-wheel drive and they lurched off the highway and out into the open desert.

"What are you doing?"

"Cutting as many miles as possible off this trip. Did you hear me call Apa Bane Deir al-Salib?" He took his eyes off the vast sand spreading before them and rested them on her. "Do you know what that means?"

"Monastery of the Cross. It's another clue, isn't it? Why else would we be sent there?" Liz asked.

The wind picked up and gathered sand in soft swirls on the horizon and then into more biting blows against their unprotected skin.

"Kashmin?" Donnie asked of Rayhan.

The spring sandstorms were brutal, and they would need to find shelter, but Rayhan eased their fears. "I don't think so. The winds are coming from the wrong direction, perhaps just a small storm. We still have about a forty-five minute drive. I'll lose my way if the winds prevail."

Donnie's large hand extended from the back seat. "Here." He handed Liz a black leather case. "Use this."

Opening the compass, she showed it to Rayhan. "Just slightly southeast, is that right?" He nodded, but said nothing, concentrating on the horizon.

The blowing dirt and sand grew stronger until they choked on the air they breathed. Liz took the napkins from their lunch and moistened them with bottled water. She offered them to each of the others to cover their nose and mouth. Rayhan sped across the forsaken landscape, glancing at the compass. A dark form loomed in front of them and he slammed on his brakes. The jeep slid in almost a complete circle, and Liz grabbed Jahi. An odd grunting sound trailed off in the distance.

"What was that?" she yelled over the roar of the blowing sand.

"Probably a camel." Rayhan rubbed his eyes. "They do that—just rise up out of nowhere."

"Did we hit it?" she asked.

"No." Rayhan shook his head. "It would have been like hitting a brick wall. He must have strayed from somewhere. It isn't unusual."

Donnie climbed out of the jeep and stood near the rear. "Maybe we should stop while this thing blows over." He lifted the large basket out of the back. "I'll make an awning from this blanket and we can just sit it out."

Rayhan turned off the ignition. "Not a bad idea."

Donnie spread a tarp from the floor of the jeep's storage compartment on the ground, then dropped the heavy basket onto the middle to hold it down. He pulled a roll of silver duct tape from his bag and fashioned a lean-to to the side of the jeep and the four of them crawled underneath.

Rayhan checked his watch. "It's four now. If the winds don't die down soon, they will near sunset, and we'll have to wait until then. There's enough daylight to make it to Apa Bane." He pulled Jahi into his lap.

Rayhan's constant attention to Jahi warmed Liz's heart. The cousins shared a profound commitment. Had Rayhan been close to Jahi's siblings as they grew up? How had he reacted to the loss of his parents? Did anyone comfort him?

Donnie burrowed through the basket they'd been given at the church. Along with additional blankets, fruit, nuts and other food items, he found a large book with a soft, leather cover. The book, bound by a golden, knotted cord, appeared otherwise plain and ordinary.

"The Agpeya," Rayhan murmured.

"What?" Donnie asked.

"The Book of Hours. It's the seven prayers of the church."

"Why did they send us a prayer book?" Donnie untied the cord and placed the book on his lap. "Wow. There are maps to several of the old churches and layouts of the monasteries."

Rayhan shifted Jahi off his lap and moved closer to Donnie. "These are the plans for the fifth century churches. They're sacred. No commoner has ever seen them. No one is for sure the secret rooms even existed. I didn't believe it myself until Talmar showed us today."

Donnie leaned into the diagram. "Where are the hidden rooms?"

"I can't tell," Rayhan said. "I'll need to look at it further. The diagram of El Kudish is confusing. There might be more than one secluded area."

Liz surveyed them and thought out loud. "Talmar said Addie and Gary would be in such a room. Remember?" Why did Talmar send all of the layouts if Addie and Gary were taken to El Kudish? Did he think they were somewhere else, too? She noticed it had grown quiet. The sandstorm had stopped. The sun filtered through the blanket, but a shadowy silhouette appeared outside the lean-to and cast a shadow over them.

CHAPTER EIGHT

FILLED WITH SHEER horror, Liz turned to Rayhan. Her mouth went dry. "Did they find us?"

"Not unless they're ten feet tall," he laughed. "I think our camel has come back." Rayhan yanked the blanket back from the side of the jeep, freeing the duct tape from what had become their fortress.

Everyone shared the joke at her expense and laughed. It felt good to think about something else for a while. Jahi, who had absolutely no fear, made immediate friends with the animal. He pulled on its harness and made circles around the jeep while the rest of them packed their gear and scooped out drifts of sand.

Liz spotted a cardboard box in the back storage compartment she hadn't seen before and called Donnie over to the rear of the vehicle. "Do you know what's in there? It wasn't in the jeep when we borrowed it from Richard."

"It's just a few things I needed that wouldn't fit in my bag. I paid the mechanic a little extra to pack some additional necessities."

"What?"

"They wouldn't make any sense to you, Liz. Don't worry. Nothing out of the ordinary." Donnie smiled.

What had he been up to? Maybe she didn't want to know. Liz turned her attention to Jahi and his newfound pet. "Should Jahi be so friendly with the camel?"

"He's been around them all of his life. He knows to stay out of its way if he needs to." Rayhan raised his hand to shade his eyes and grinned at Jahi. "I can have him stop if it's upsetting you."

"We need to go anyway." She turned to the two odd companions, a large, brown lump of fur and a small boy who hardly reached the beast's knee joint. "Come, Jahi. It's time to go." Jahi reached as far up the animal's side as he could and scratched deep into its hide, then spun around and ran back toward the jeep.

"Will the camel be all right just left here?" The dromedary trudged toward the open desert under the watchful eye of Jahi.

"He should be fine. He has a fat hump. His owner will come looking for him soon enough," Rayhan said. He slid behind the wheel. "Everyone in? Let's go."

"Where's Donnie?" Liz asked. "Is he gone again?"

Rayhan paused and searched for him, then pointed in the direction of a rising sand dune. Donnie stood on top and used binoculars to study the shifting landscape. "He's looking for something. He's been acting strange all afternoon." Rayhan put his index finger to his lips as he indicated to Jahi to keep their secret and moved closer to Liz. He brushed his lips against hers. "Are you okay?"

"I think so. I'm just afraid I've gotten you into trouble with your uncle. He and your aunt must be terribly worried about Jahi."

"I was upset Jahi followed us. I didn't mean to be angry with you. This is no place for a child."

"I agree, but there isn't much we can do about it." Liz moved closer into Rayhan's arms and rested her head on his shoulder. He pulled away from her after a brief moment. "Donnie's coming," he whispered into her ear.

Liz shifted to see Rayhan's face. "He knows. I told him this morning."

"What did he say?"

"He thinks we're crazy."

Rayhan whispered, "Maybe we are." He pulled her into a long, slow kiss. He held her and rested his chin on her head. "I'm glad he knows."

"Me, too." She sat up in her seat. "Here he comes."

Rayhan turned the key in the ignition once Donnie had climbed into the jeep. Rayhan maneuvered through the sand dunes, which left Liz to wonder why Donnie had kept to himself since they'd left Bani Suwayf. Liz sensed he'd been on edge, but he would adapt and, with his box of secrets, hopefully keep them out of trouble. Her mind drifted to the riddle. She had the knowledge to solve the puzzle, but still it wouldn't come to her.

Rayhan brushed her hand as he reached for the gear shift. The sweetness of Rayhan's lips lingered on hers. His determination to have her in his life concerned her. He didn't care if his uncle didn't approve, yet Rayhan had been so upset when he found Jahi, worried Al Abdul would not be pleased. Rayhan turned out to be an enigma. The night before, they'd never made it to the church as she had planned. In the alcove, wrapped in his arms, nothing else mattered. A shy smile formed on her lips. Every day, she learned more and her affection grew.

"There," Rayhan shouted and pointed toward a shimmering structure over the next dune, jarring Liz from her thoughts. "Apa Bane."

They drove closer to the monastery, which time had turned into ruins, partial buildings and tattered walls. The empty shell of the tower wall cast eerie shadows on the floor of the desert.

"Donnie." Liz turned in her seat. "Are you sure this is the place?" They were far from civilization. How could this be where they were supposed to spend the night? Would someone come to greet them?

They neared the barrier surrounding the church and Donnie tapped her shoulder. "Liz," he said in a whisper, "the wall."

The crumbling brick had a cross painted on it to welcome the weary travelers. A Christian cross with a red banner draped on the horizontal bar. It had been done decades ago, perhaps when the monastery had been in use, but the dyes and tinting couldn't have been more than thirty years old.

Rayhan cut the engine and they sat for a moment. Her eyes darted in his direction. Targets if they didn't move, Rayhan met her gaze and shifted his scope to include a small arched opening in the wall. A man dressed similar to Talmar stood in the entry. "The priest," Rayhan reverently whispered.

Liz spoke quietly. "I thought this place was deserted."

"It is. He probably came from El Minya. He'll know what to do." Rayhan swung his leg over the side of the jeep, reached for Jahi, lifted him to the ground, and scrambled up the rocky path toward the priest. Donnie and Liz followed to the aperture. Rayhan turned to face her after a brief exchange. "I'm to move the jeep where it won't be easily spotted. We'll spend the night in the chapel, but we must leave early tomorrow."

"Is he staying here with us?" Donnie nodded his head in the direction of the holy man.

"No. He brought us provisions and bedding, but it is too dangerous for him to stay. He's sure no one will find us."

"No one will find us!" Liz repeated. "Is someone else looking?"

"The desert has eyes and ears, Liz. We were spotted at Bani Suwayf. Two men stopped at the church in El Minya. They were asking questions."

The two men she'd seen earlier? The courage she had bolstered into a small amount of pensive confidence drained out of her. "What if they show up here and find us alone? What then?"

The clergyman noticed the exchange between Liz and Rayhan. The holy man beckoned to them. She and Rayhan trailed behind the aging gentleman as he picked his way over the rocky terrain and stopped at the furthermost wall surrounding the chapel. She shifted her gaze to where he pointed to a row of dunes. "Allah alim."

Liz's questioning glance found Rayhan. The priest had said, "God knows best."

"What does he mean?"

"We're being protected," Rayhan said. "There's an encampment of men just beyond the hill. We will be gone before light. We're safe here."

She didn't feel safe. She'd never felt further away from her comfort zone. The different dialects of Arabic often left her puzzled and confused. She shook her head, exhausted. Her optimism had grown thin. Too much had happened since Rayhan's phone call days ago. She needed something to rejuvenate her.

Liz, on autopilot, along with Donnie and Rayhan, carried their belongings into the large area the priest had prepared. In several places, the ceiling had caved-in and rubble and debris which had been swept aside filled the corners, but they'd make do. Flat bread and ground chick peas were set out on a carved wooden tray and a large container of coffee. *Ah, caffeine.*

The long shadows crept away and night closed in as she helped Rayhan settle Jahi down for the evening. She then crossed the barren, cold floor to the side of the room Donnie had claimed for himself. He leafed through the Book of Hours, but rose to his feet as she approached.

"Find out anything interesting?" she asked.

"I think this place has a secret room. Want to go find out?"

"I'm beat, but I doubt if I could sleep. We might as well."

"Rayhan, Liz and I are going to walk around. You'll be okay here?"

Rayhan placed Jahi on a stack of thick blankets and indicated with a wave for Liz and Donnie to go ahead.

She followed Donnie to the back of the sanctuary. The partial moon created an unnatural glow and streamed in from the uppermost portion of the monastery dome. It bathed the building in a surreal half-light. They entered from the north side and walked to a pillar in the center of the floor. Five columns flanked it on both sides. The eleventh shaft separated the aisles and marked the western most end of the church. He opened the book to the floor plan of Apa Bane. "There are three small cubicles at the front of the sanctuary." Donnie traced his finger over the layout.

"This is a triconch design. It was built between the fifth and seventh century. It was an evolutionary development from the basic basilica with a nave and two side aisles. There are three semi-circular rooms forming a clover pattern." Liz hurried up the aisle to the front of the church. "The hidden room must be back there among the cloverleaf."

"Wait." Donnie called. "I have a flashlight." He pulled a sleek, micro-beam light from his black bag and narrowed it down to pinpoint the path in front of them.

"What you don't think of?" She laughed. He could certainly take care of himself. Even with their constant battles, he had become an essential ingredient in her quest.

There were fine niches and small columns in the main portion of the sanctuary. Liz would have loved to examine every one and record what she'd found, but she didn't have time. Urgency enveloped her to find the hidden room in this church and see if what Talmar had shown them held true in each chapel. If the ankh opened the lock at Apa Bane, then it would open the door to the room in El Kudish. Liz thought about the riddle. Where were the men taking them if Liz didn't make it there before the moon waned? Where was Moustafa?

Donnie and Liz reached the back of the sanctuary. She counted the rooms off as they circled around the main section. Numbness grew in her fingers as she groped the walls for an opening. One by one, she touched the smooth surface—nothing. No hidden doors or secret passages.

"Liz. Come over here." Donnie summoned her from a dark corner of a fourth room. "I think I have something."

She found him with the beam of the flashlight, honed down on a small alcove near the back of the chamber. The area narrowed to a small entryway, and in a carved-out nook, a painting of a cross glowed, radiant. The reds, blues, and golden colors had not faded as there was no natural light in the passageway. The small mural measured about eight inches wide by ten inches high. Liz brushed her hands over the surface. "It's beautiful, isn't it?"

"There's an opening at the bottom." He intensified the beam. "Slide the ankh in there."

"It isn't the right shape. It isn't the same as the lock at the Cairo chapel."

"They might not be alike. These people had to be astute. They struggled for their existence and still do. Consider it another mystery to be solved. "

Liz couldn't argue with his reasoning and removed the cross from her neck. She slid it into the opening, the long end first. She groaned when nothing happened. Liz took it off the chain and put the looped end in the slot. The familiar shift of the metal tongue met their ears and the door scraped open. Donnie rushed past her and she jerked at his arm.

"Wait. This room hasn't been opened in centuries. There will be a certain amount of gaseous buildup from the paints. Let it air out a second."

"What did they use?"

"Hematite. It could make you sick. Haven't you ever heard of the mummy's curse? You know...in the old movies?" she questioned.

"What are you talking about?"

"There were two authors in the mid-1800's, one of them being Louisa May Alcott, which referred to the mummy curse. Then there's the curse of the pharaoh, and the opening of the tomb of Tutankhamen, and the mysterious death of Lord Carnarvon and others."

"Well, that's just great," Donnie grumbled.

"Everything can be explained away," she said. "The breakdown of the chemicals in the paints along with centuries of closed quarters could cause death, but bacteria or tomb toxins forming in the enclosed atmosphere were the real culprits." She let go of his arm and waited several minutes before her eyes adjusted. A small shaft of light pierced the darkness. Liz took Donnie's hand and pointed the flashlight toward a small portal window near the roofline. "This room has an air source. It's okay, come on."

A dark, dank odor filled the air. Donnie panned their surroundings with his flashlight. A small cot sat on one side of the room and a shelf with a few jugs and bowls were on the opposing wall. The floor shifted beneath their feet and the items on the shelf rattled.

"What was that?" Donnie said. He steadied himself against the wall.

"The earth plates moving." Liz didn't want to tell him Cleopatra's entire temple lay at the bottom of the bay in Alexandra due to such movement. "It's common here. It happens at home, too. Don't worry."

"You mean an earthquake, don't you? You Californians make light of it, but it makes me jumpy." He laughed, but she noticed his nervousness. "Make it quick. We need to get out of here."

Liz surveyed the beautifully painted room of greens, golds, and reds with scenes depicting the birth, life, and crucifixion of Christ, and the ceiling had been painted with the ascension. She observed the cot in a dark corner. A folded blanket lay neatly at the foot. This wasn't the first time the room had been opened in centuries. A pad and pencil lay on a small shelf near the bed. Liz reached for the notebook when the earth shifted again, and one of the bowls winged past her hand as the vessel careened and smashed to the floor.

"Let's go. We need to get back to Rayhan and Jahi." She tucked the pad inside her jacket and zipped it. Donnie pulled the door shut and she removed the key from the lock. The bolt settled into place.

Liz and Donnie hurried to the end of the cloverleaf formation and walked down the narrow hallway to their sleeping quarters. Rayhan stood, ashen faced, over Jahi's bed.

"I must have fallen asleep after you left. I checked to see if Jahi was all right when the tremor hit." He stared at them, fear glistened in his eyes. "He's disappeared."

"He can't be far. We weren't gone more than twenty minutes," Liz said. "Maybe he went out to the jeep."

"I gave him strict orders not to leave my sight." Rayhan rubbed his forehead. "I told him to wake me if he needed anything. His stubbornness exasperates me."

"Rayhan, you and Liz stay here. I'll go out to the vehicle and see if he's there." Donnie made his way toward a side door, then paused. "He could be in the funerary or the bakery. The old buildings are still attached to the chapel. Maybe he was awakened by the tremor and stumbled off in confusion." Donnie handed her the Book of Hours. "Here. Use the floor plan. It's easy enough to follow."

"Okay." She placed the book into the pocket of her jacket and felt the sharp corner of the writing tablet against the back of her hand, but Liz didn't have time for it now. As Rayhan went toward the sanctuary, she worried it might not be the safest plan for each of them to search on their own. The acoustics of the monastery allowed their voices to carry, but loud noises could bring unwanted attention.

Liz exited the chapel on Donnie's heels. He went out into the open courtyard toward the jeep and she took the opposite direction toward the bakery. The roof in this area had partially collapsed, too, and the starlight filtered through in a blue-tinged haze. The night air cooled her skin and she shook off a chill. She'd walked about ten feet when she came to a partition. Liz took a second to examine the layout of the rooms. The food preparation area for the monastery should be on the other side. Meals would have been cooked and even served in the area when the church had been in use. Much of the pottery and other artifacts were gone, either pillaged or removed by archeologists. She wondered what Jahi thought he could find?

Liz rounded the corner of the wall and saw the boy at the end of the building. He crouched down against the sandstone slab, motionless.

She quickened her step to reach him and didn't see what kept Jahi pinned to the wall. His small, horror-filled voice split the silence of the desert night. "Naja haje!"

The Egyptian phrase and the sight of the deadly snake registered at the same split-second. Six feet in front of him, fanned and arched in a menacing pre-strike stance, a cobra swayed slowly from side to side. Her resolution not to make any loud noises would not be kept as a scream escaped her throat.

Donnie appeared at the edge of the dividing wall. "Do something. We have to save Jahi," she called.

Jahi, frightened and small, whimpered. Why hadn't he listened to Rayhan? He shouldn't have wandered off and she would scold him when they were out of this predicament, even if Rayhan disapproved. Then, she thought of her own agitated speech to Rayhan this afternoon when she admonished him for being upset with Jahi. He hadn't known what he had done then, nor did he understand any disturbance on their part could bring half the town of El Minya over the dunes toward them. Liz feared they'd heard her outcry. She glanced around and saw half of a large pottery bowl and picked it up. "Dear God," she murmured, "please let me reach him."

"What are you going to do, Liz?" Rayhan called as he ran to join them in the center of the culinary floor. "You can't kill it. They're protected."

"I don't care." She fought, one-handed with the earthenware, hoisting it over her head. "I'm going to throw this pot at it."

"Don't." Donnie stopped her. "It will strike. I'll distract it and when I do, get Jahi."

"How are you going to do that?" she questioned, but should have known Donnie would have some trick.

Rayhan took the pottery jug from her hands and put his arms around her. "Don't make any sudden moves." He brushed a stray tendril from her forehead. "Stand perfectly still and let me help rescue Jahi."

"While the snake has its hood up, it's partially blind. I'll approach it from behind, get it to move to the left, and you go to the right. Go—now!"

Donnie, who held a small baton-like object in his right hand, ran toward the back of the cobra. With one swift motion he produced from the staff a rod which tapped the snake behind the hood. Donnie hurled an object to their left that made a quick, loud pop. The snake, confused by the two motions, turned its attention to Donnie as Rayhan rushed to Jahi and swept him up.

Donnie waved the cane back and forth in front of the cobra while he slowly backed away.

Rayhan ran to Liz and placed the child in her arms. "Back up slowly and then return to our sleeping area. We'll be right behind you."

Rayhan took off his jacket as he, too, approached the snake from behind. He made eye contact with Donnie and, at his nod, Rayhan threw his coat over the cobra and they hurried back to the chapel.

"It must be late," Donnie said when they returned to their cots. "What time is it?" He looked in her direction for an answer, but Jahi had his arms twisted so tightly around her neck, Liz couldn't see her watch and support his weight.

"Midnight," Rayhan offered. "We should sleep."

Donnie wrinkled his forehead. "Sleep? We've had an earthquake, and that little thing back there with the snake, and you can talk about sleeping?" He shook his head. "Go ahead. I'll stand watch."

Liz's biggest concern centered around Jahi, and after a quick check of the area for another snake or other unwanted creature, she put Jahi down and studied his face. "Keef Halek?" she said. She bent over him and stroked his hair. Liz reached for the water jug and held it out to him. "Moya?"

Jahi's small hands stretched to reach for the container. "Taieb," came in a whisper from his lips. His small hands shook as he touched the vessel. He returned to his pallet after a quick drink from the canteen and patted the mat, indicating he wanted Liz to stay.

She wouldn't let him lie on the ground and searched for something higher they could sit on. Liz spotted a stone box against the wall across from Donnie's lookout post, picked up the blanket and took Jahi by the hand. "Hennak." She pointed and walked across the room. Jahi obediently followed. The carvings on the large, stone container on which they were about to spend the rest of their evening depicted the age old ceremony of partaking the consecrated bread and wine.

"Wait!" Rayhan called. He made sure there weren't any places behind or underneath it that anything could crawl or hide in. He took Jahi's hand and helped him up on the box. Rayhan turned to face Liz. He pulled her into his arms and she felt a tense rigidity as she laid her head on his chest. The comfortable silence lingered and an unmistakable change flowed from him into her. She loosened herself from his arms and searched his face.

"That was close," Rayhan said when he finally spoke. He continued to watch her and she swallowed hard as she tried to read his thoughts.

"You forgot your jacket," she managed.

"It isn't important." He let out a pent-up breath and inhaled again. With a weighted thoughtfulness, he stood rigid and several seconds passed before he spoke. "I'm going to take him back to Cairo. You and Donnie will have to go on without me."

Her heart dropped. Rayhan's sense of responsibility for Jahi grew, but they had agreed they couldn't take him back. "Rayhan?" She reached out to him, but he backed away.

"I have put the desires of my heart before everything. I'm sorry, Liz. I have gone against God and put Jahi in danger. Tomorrow, I will take you and Donnie within walking distance of El Kudish. It is off the main road, and we would have to abandon the jeep at that point anyway. Jahi and I will go." Rayhan averted his eyes and would not meet hers. He turned to walk to where he'd made a place for his cot. "I hope you find your friends and you all return to America safely."

"What about us?"

"I should not have let this happen. I put myself first. I told you my uncle would often let me have what I wanted to prove a lesson. I understand that now. I wanted you—" He stopped and cleared his throat and her heart ached as his eyes clouded over. "I never asked permission. I never prayed that God would allow you to be mine. I forced His hand just as I did Uncle Al Abdul's." His shoulders slumped as he delivered his final words. "It was wrong, and Jahi almost paid for it with his life. I must take him home."

Liz sat on the edge of the carved box and slid back against the wall. She reached out to Jahi and pulled him up into her lap. "Al Ann," she said to him as he settled in and curled against her. Like Donnie, she could not sleep. Rayhan rested his head on his knees and sat close to a fire Donnie and he had built in the middle of the floor, his back touching the far wall.

Peacefulness settled over Jahi and the taut lines of his face slowly relaxed into sleep. Her eyes stung and a single tear slid down her cheek as she observed Rayhan. He wouldn't face her and it broke her heart. She remembered the jacket he threw over the cobra and thought it had been such a noble gesture. Now it lay unclaimed and forgotten. A hollow emptiness crept over her. *Had she been as unimportant to him as his discarded coat?* He acted as if what had happened between them could be erased.

Rayhan's help had been an added bonus, one they had not anticipated, and she had not expected to fall in love with him. Somehow, she had. She wondered if she could change his mind and talk him out of his resolution. *How could one incident just change everything?* Rayhan told her what he wanted—an equal, not a submissive mate. He had wished for an American woman. What had he experienced in his young life that lead him there? Had she disappointed him? She might never find out. His decision had been made.

The night grew quiet and the coolness of the desert evening crept into the old building. Liz observed the clear, bright night through a missing section of the roof. Constellations displayed themselves in an open panorama with no ambient light to steal their luster. In awe, she considered why she'd never been aware of them before. Liz moved her eyes to Rayhan, who had followed her gaze.

She craved his touch, his breath against her cheek as he held her, and the sweet taste of him. She would have savored their last kiss and held him close if she would have known their romance would end as it had. She wanted time to talk and at least to let her heart find closure, but Rayhan remained stilted. At last, Rayhan managed to search her out from across the room. The sorrow in his eyes touched her soul. She yearned to imprint his every feature into her mind, the gentle touch of his fingers in her hair, the light brush of his whiskers on her cheek and his gentle, yet protective caress.

"Liz, let's go." Donnie nudged her shoulder. "It's after six. We need to head out."

Liz forced her eyes open. She had fallen asleep. The sun had not yet risen, but they had to leave. She shook Jahi. "It's another day, little one. Come on."

It became apparent to Liz the memory of the previous evening had been forgotten when Jahi bounced out of her lap and ran to Rayhan. Liz smiled at the boy's resiliency and her heart ached. She questioned her ability to rebound from Rayhan's rejection. He pointed to the basket and Jahi grabbed a handful of fruit. They left the chapel through the easternmost doors and made their way to the jeep.

Donnie and Rayhan had packed up their camp while she slept. Liz rummaged through the wicker container and found a crust of bread. She ran her fingers through her hair. She yearned for a hot shower and a bed with clean, white sheets, but the delight in comfort would have to wait until they returned. They would be in El Kudish by noon. She braced herself against the disappointment. There might be some additional clues at El Kudish, but if she didn't figure something out soon, another six hours would be wasted.

Rayhan did not speak to her all morning. He stood not far from her in an unheard conversation with Donnie and when they finally shook hands, she assumed Rayhan had told Donnie of his plans to take Jahi back to Cairo. A sea of tumultuous emotions crested within her and she admonished herself because she had let her own desires get in the way of her mission, just as Rayhan claimed he had done. Maybe he had a point. They shouldn't have gone against his customs and forced his uncle to approve.

Liz tried to put aside her own situation, but a verse from Psalms kept running through her thoughts: *Delight yourself in the Lord; And He will give you the desires of your heart.* God would not punish Rayhan or her. Could she make him understand that?

CHAPTER NINE

JAHI HAD SEATED himself firmly in the passenger seat before Donnie and Liz reached the jeep. "Jahi," Rayhan spoke in a quiet whisper of Arabic. "Move to the back so Liz can sit up here."

"No," she said. She swung her foot over the back panel and settled in next to Donnie. "I'll be fine."

Rayhan nodded his head and buckled his seatbelt. He placed his hands on the wheel and drove from behind the protective cover of the monastery walls. Lined on the crest of the dunes above the building were at least sixty men, some on horseback, who observed as they drove away.

"That's pretty incredible," Donnie declared. "They protected us all night. They would have been down here in an instant if we needed them. I doubt many people in the States would put themselves at risk for someone else."

It amazed Liz how they'd been accepted, without condition or question. The entire community came forward to offer their help.

She didn't agree with Donnie's prospective. There were many people the world over who would welcome a stranger in need.

"I well imagine you were in their daily prayers, too." Rayhan maneuvered the car through the dunes and back toward the main road. "We pray for our country, the Nile, the government, and the army, but above all, for the people of Egypt. You are considered one of us."

Liz had kept her heart in check all morning, but now, from the back seat, she took in Rayan's profile, and she could no longer control her thoughts. She respected him for what he believed and without regret, she would have moved to Egypt to be with him. His adamant conviction in taking the blame for Jahi's incident didn't make sense. How could Rayhan dismiss their relationship? She admired his devotion to his family and Jahi, but the finality of his abrupt rejection stung.

Maybe it worked out as it should, she reasoned, *if he can't stand by me now...* She couldn't think about it anymore. She'd rushed into this arrangement and it had been a mistake. He needed to take Jahi home, and she needed to finish what she'd started.

Liz reached to unzip her jacket and felt the small tablet she'd tucked inside and pulled it out. The markings on the page were deep, and Liz remembered when Donnie found the address to the El Dar with a rubbing, but she didn't have a pencil. She had another question for him first. "What made that little explosion last night?" She turned to him.

"What little explosion?" he said, with an arguable display of innocence.

Exasperated, she shifted in her seat toward him. "The popping noise with the s-n-a-k-e," she spelled out the word so Jahi, even with his limited English, wouldn't understand.

"G-u-n-p-o-w-d-e-r," he spelled back.

"Donald!"

"Little bits wrapped in tissue paper with flint, nothing worse than a cap going off." He smiled. "Don't worry."

"How did you clear security at the airport?"

"I didn't. I bought it here. They have all kinds of stuff in that marketplace over by our hotel. I picked up a few other things, too."

"I don't want to know." Liz sat back in her seat. "Do you have a pencil?"

"Mechanical or number two, standard schoolhouse?"

"Either one will do," she said, her voice laced with sarcasm as she took a bright, yellow wooden pencil from his hand, one of the two types he offered.

Liz positioned the pad on her lap and stroked the point of the pencil against the page. The words began to appear, and she continued to the bottom before she began to read it.

I don't know where they've taken you. Separating us for the trip to El Kudish might not have been the best idea .The beating was worse than I thought and I'm afraid I may not see you again. I've asked the people I'm with to deliver this note to you if I don't make it out of here.

I love you, Addie. The last two years were the best of my life. I gave the gold key to Moustafa's driver just in case someone comes looking for us. – Gary

A large, invisible hand came down with a severe blow that further bruised her spirit. Liz crumpled. She drew her legs up, clasped her hands around them, and lowered her head to her knees. Every emotion she'd held back for the past few days gushed out into one uncontrollable sob. Her body shook as she cried from the depth of her heart. Gary's note indicated they'd taken separate routes to El Kudish. Liz felt a pang of selfishness cross her heart, too, crying out for her own loss.

Donnie moved his hand to her shoulders and patted her back. "Liz?"

She handed the note over and his face darkened with concern as he read. "Then Addie isn't with Gary?"

"Talmar told me they were rescued together at the El Dar, and they were being taken to El Kudish." Liz glanced from Donnie to Rayhan. "Isn't that what he said, Rayhan?"

Rayhan nodded his head. "Talmar said Moustafa saved them both."

"Gary wrote it while he stayed in the hidden room at Apa Bane." She managed a smile. "They're alive."

A weight lifted from Liz's heart as she thanked God, but up until now, she had concentrated on finding them together. Did they need to split up and make separate searches? El Kudish remained the constant factor. The angles of the earth, moon, and sun revealed the waning stage in the previous night's sky. Maybe the men hadn't moved them, but she couldn't shake the gnawing undertow that Addie and Gary weren't there. Liz went back to the last line of the riddle: *use the ankh to find the sign.* It burned in her brain.

Donnie nudged her arm. "There's more. Here on this second page."

He showed her a group of drawings, and beneath them, Gary's handwriting. An eye, several rows of the number three written in a tight sequence, and the phrase: *dark is the night, walk in the light.*

"Does any of it mean anything to you?" Donnie questioned.

"Gary had begun to study Egyptology and compared it to Christianity. It was a hobby of sorts, based on Addie's own interests. The phrase is common. I've heard Addie's minister use it. Maybe Gary was just doodling to pass the time." Liz reached for the tablet Donnie held is his hand. "Let me see."

The eye Gary had drawn on the page hadn't been just any eye, but the Eye of Horus, son of Osiris, the king of the dead, and Isis, the eternal mother and High Priestess. The two Egyptian symbols which made up the ankh.

THE REMAINDER OF the trip on the main road proved uneventful. Jahi's head bobbled back and forth as he warded off the lure of sleep. She reached forward and pulled him into her arms. Careful not to disturb him, she handed him to Donnie, who held the boy while Liz crawled to the front.

"Here," Liz said as she turned in her seat. "I'll take him."

"He's fine." Donnie smoothed out the gold and honey colored blanket. "He's having trouble staying awake. I'll put him down next to me."

Rayhan hadn't spoken since they'd found Gary's note and he hadn't said much at all since they'd left the monastery. He took his eyes off the road for a moment, sweeping his eyes over Liz. "You'll find your friends. The men they are with will keep them from harm." His lips jerked into a quick, terse smile, but he returned his gaze to the stretch of blacktop.

"Rayhan." She spoke in a hushed whisper. "How much do you believe in Egyptian mythology?"

"It is very much part of our history. It is woven into our culture and it forms our lives."

"How does that affect you and your Christian beliefs?"

"It doesn't. I believe in the one, true God, but the mythology is there. It is one of the threads in the fabric of each Egyptian. Our cross, for instance, is an ancient symbol."

"Do you see other symbolism, too?"

"Yes. Some of the mythology parallels Christianity to a point."

"That's what I'm saying. I see that, too, and I believe Gary was following that same course."

"Wasn't there something you believed in and then learned it wasn't true?" he asked. "Like Santa Claus? Something so magical and mystical you wanted to believe in it with all your heart?"

A lump grew in her throat and tears welled in her eyes. She lowered her voice so Donnie couldn't hear. "I believed in us," she said to Rayhan as she gazed into his eyes. She yearned for some sort of affirmation.

"Liz. Don't. I told you it can't happen. I have gone against custom, angered God with my desires, and I've endangered Jahi all for my own benefit," Rayhan replied.

Liz turned to see Donnie, who had pulled his hat down over his eyes. He either decided to give them some privacy and ignore her conversation with Rayhan, or he'd fallen asleep. "It is hard to separate the myth from the true history and culture because the ancients believed in those traditions. Evidence is everywhere—and before this rescue trip, it was the very reason I'd come to Egypt."

"Where are you going with this?" Rayhan asked.

"I'm not sure, just thinking out loud. Maybe I'm trying too hard to solve the riddles." She sighed. "I'm making them complicated when I should be looking for a simple answer. I think we should find a simple answer too, Rayhan. I believe you are wrong."

Donnie stirred and raised his finger to his lips. "Shh. Listen."

Liz strained to hear a distant siren, far away over the dunes, but it grew closer. The isolated signal reached them across the wide expanse of the desert, muffled by the sand dunes.

"Rayhan? Do you hear that?"

Pallid, he turned to her. "I'm afraid I do."

The blood drained from his face and increased the nauseating knot which grew in her stomach. It became an immediate concern that the men who attempted to kidnap Addie and Gary may have tipped them off to the police, or even bribed them, in order to track her down. She remembered she'd been warned not to go to the authorities. She had been too trustworthy. She should have realized not everyone was on the right side of justice. Now, what if they'd been reported for some made-up infraction and couldn't explain what they were doing in the middle of the desert? They were in deep trouble if the police were on the take, or if the guns were for them. The sound grew closer. *Think, Liz. Think.*

"Stop!"

"What are you doing, Liz?" Donnie yelled.

"Out," she ordered, "and bring everything in the jeep with you."

"This is crazy."

"No. Trying to out-run whoever they are is crazy."

"You're right. If they're looking for you and me, let Rayhan ditch us here. He wants to take Jahi back to Cairo anyway."

Rayhan didn't move from behind the wheel. He turned his face toward Donnie, but remained frozen.

"Donnie, take the plates off the jeep and put Jahi in front. Rayhan can drive back toward them. They won't expect anything from an Egyptian man and a little boy. We'll find our way to El Kudish."

"You're right. He'd be the one they'd least suspect."

"Okay, okay. Then let's do it." The wail grew louder. "They're coming closer. We don't have much time. Take the basket and the prayer book and anything else suspicious. Leave the rest of it."

Liz walked to the side of the vehicle and touched Rayhan on the shoulder. "I'm sorry. I shouldn't have gotten you into this mess. Any of you." Liz saw the pain in Rayhan's eyes. "I—" She choked. "I love you, Rayhan. I hope someday you'll change your mind."

"I will not lie to you. I wanted so much for us, but it is wrong, and God is punishing me for my desires."

"I know how hard it is for you to make this decision, but it wasn't your fault. Do you really think that your self-imposed exile from me will solve this?"

He scanned her face and didn't answer. "I need to protect Jahi. I'm certain once you reach El Kudish, the people who took your friends there will help you. I don't know what to do, Liz. Try to understand."

"Rayhan..." Liz stopped. She had to let him go. "Promise me one thing."

"What?"

"You'll try to find me if you change your mind."

Donnie walked up to the side of the jeep. "You need to go. You're putting yourself and the boy in more danger."

"Donnie's right," Rayhan said. He made a U-turn in the road and then stopped. "God be with you, Liz."

"And with you," she called as he disappeared over the next rise.

"WHAT'S YOUR PLAN, Liz?" Donnie came up behind her. Their feet were swallowed by shifting sand off the paved road and they found cover behind a row of dunes.

"At this point, I don't exactly have one." She stopped and waited for him to catch up. The sand swirled around her feet and reminded her of drifts of snow. She kept an eye on the moonscape in front of them.

"We're going to walk to El Kudish? It's obvious you didn't think this one through, did you? How would it look? Two Americans on a stroll in the desert?"

"Well, I was just a little pressed for time. I didn't see you coming up with a plan. Let me know if you have a better idea," she barked.

They trudged away from the main road and into the desert in silence for over an hour, until Donnie stopped and put down the basket. "We're going to stop here for a while. I want to check a few things and find my bearings." The rise of the dune kept them out of view from the road, miles and miles of undulating sand surrounded them.

A lone palm tree stood fifty feet from where they'd stopped. "We're going to need shade." She pulled the Egyptian blanket out on the sand. They built an A-framed hut to provide shelter after Donnie made several trips to the palm tree. "So, MacGyver, how did you pull the palm fronds down?" she asked as they settled into their temporary dwelling.

"I threw a rope up into the tree and pulled them loose. It doesn't take much to yank them down, once they've died off from the main cluster of growth near the top." Donnie sat down beside her and reached into the basket for the prayer book. "Don't you have any palm trees in San Francisco?"

"Of course we do. They have thorns. I keep my distance."

"Those are Mexican Fan or California Palms. These don't have the stickers. They're nice and smooth."

"Is there anything you don't know?"

"Funny." He grinned over in her direction. "I don't know how far it is to El Kudish. I was hoping the prayer book might give me a clue."

She eased herself into a half-reclining position and tried to read his face, but he remained stoic. Did he know what had happened between her and Rayhan? "What did Rayhan tell you back at the monastery?"

"That he would take us to the road to El Kudish, then he was going to take Jahi back to Cairo."

"Did he say anything else?"

"No. Should he have?"

Liz decided Donnie either didn't know what happened, or he chose not to pry into her private life. "Do you think they'll be okay?"

"Well, Rayhan and Jahi have a better chance in a vehicle than you and I do out here, but we'll all be fine." Donnie glanced up from the book and studied the horizon in the distance. "I'm hungry," he said. He dug around in the remainder of their supplies and opened the neat, paper-wrapped packages. "We have dates, nuts, bread, and water." Liz didn't waste any time before she joined him.

"It's been too long, hasn't it?" Her voice cracked as she spoke and the familiar sting formed behind her eyes.

"It's been what now since you heard? Six or seven days? We know several things, though—they're alive and on the move." Donnie stopped and drew his hand across his face. "I just wish we knew something about Addison."

"You call her Addison?"

"Yeah. It annoys her to no end when I do. It was our grandfather's name, but it always got her attention." He smiled. "Out of all of us grandkids, she measured up to what he wanted from us. His name fits her well."

"She's okay, Donnie. I know she is. We just need to trust in God." She reached over and took the Book of Hours from his hands. "Allah alim."

"What?"

"God knows best."

"We'll need to start out soon. I've been looking at the maps in the prayer book. The monasteries were built at somewhat equal distances apart. We have several miles to go, and if we don't go before long, we might not reach El Kudish by nightfall."

Liz glanced at her watch. Rayhan had been gone an hour. "We should go now."

Donnie nodded in agreement and it took him less than fifteen minutes to tear down the hut and make a sled from the palm fronds. Donnie came up with a piece of rope, then tied everything together. Liz had given up asking him where he kept all of his secrets. She peered around the row of dunes as they walked toward El Kudish. The wind, which hailed small needles into her skin, had not subsided with the oncoming sunset, but the gusts wound down into a steady, constant force. She searched the road for Rayhan and wished he'd changed his mind, but Rayhan wouldn't be coming back.

The sirens stopped not long after they'd made their shelter. She prayed he and Jahi made it to Cairo, safe within the walls of the community they knew and drew protection from. She felt a trickle of sweat run down her spine. The sun perched at somewhere around six o'clock, but she glanced at her watch to confirm it. They had a couple of hours of daylight left.

Donnie, who walked beside her in silence, reached into his pocket and held out an Egyptian Piaster. "A penny for your thoughts," he said.

"That's not a penny." Liz took the coin from his hand and examined it. "Do I have to tell?"

"No. You've been quiet." He smiled. "Rather out of character."

"You haven't said a whole lot either." She kicked at the sand. "I'm just concerned where we'd go if we were confronted. There's nowhere to take cover."

"We'll need to stay near the main road if we're going to find our way." Donnie checked the surrounding area. "We'll be fine. Trust me."

"I do, but I'm worried. We're pretty vulnerable out here, and we can't explain our way out of this. We better hope we find where were going soon. Any ideas?"

"It should take about two hours. It won't be long before we'll turn away from the road. There will be a small oasis and a dirt trail or path leading to El Kudish, if the maps in the prayer book are still correct. An hour at the most to that point, I'm sure of it."

Liz removed the canteen from her belt and took a long pull on the lukewarm water, then offered it to Donnie. He took it from her, but before he put the bottle to his lips, he paused. "Can I ask you some questions?"

"Sure."

"Talk to me about the note from Gary. The one with the Egyptian symbols. You're the Egyptologist." He stopped and drank from the container. "What did he mean?"

Liz, thankful he did not ask about Rayhan, didn't know where to start. She tried to remember when Gary became interested in symbolism. "After Addie and Gary were married, they took a class at church on the Christian use of symbols. They studied the different crosses that were used by different religions, or even different Protestant and Catholic churches. The Signs of the Early Christians was the name of the course. Then she received a trade paper with an article about an archeologist finding mines that slaves were kept in before the exodus from Egypt. It included the location where the first time the name of God was thought to be written down. That's when Gary began looking into Egyptian symbols."

"Go on," Donnie urged.

"The further he dug into it, the more excited he became about her work. He saw parallels in the Egyptian myths with the stories from the Bible. He viewed the mythology as them retelling things in their own way, because they couldn't explain it."

"How do you know all of this?

"The three of us discussed this in depth. Gary immersed himself in it, and of course it was Addie's job as a restoration expert. We talked way into the night more than once on the subject."

"Do you think he's trying to tell us something with this Eye of Horus thing?"

"He may be, but I think he's using the phrase about walking in the light to convey a message. It will all come together. I just have to sort it out."

They continued along for a moment and Liz wished she could use some mental power to contact Addie and Gary. She needed to think about Gary's clues—the drawings and the note. Were they doodles, or a real message? He didn't mention the ankh.

"There." Donnie interrupted her thoughts as he indicated to a crude sign post which pointed south and toward the tops of several palm trees in the distance just over the rise.

The path to the oasis had become not much more than a rut. The shifting terrain and sand storms covered most of the indentation and trudging through the sand reminded her of walking on the beach not far from her home on the California coast. The sun held steady on the horizon, and the heat lingered, stifling the air. Liz glanced towards the oasis, which never moved any closer. She thought about Rayhan and wished he could be with her. She tried to convince herself to forget him. He had chosen his path.

"Do I need to offer you the penny again?" Donnie turned to Liz.

"No. What did you need to know now?" She smiled, tears moistened her eyes, and her voice betrayed her heart.

"What happened to you and Rayhan?" Donnie stopped. "I thought you were betrothed or something."

Liz began to cry. She'd been a fool. She fell in love with someone she didn't know, and now she stood in the unrelenting sun explaining it all to someone else she'd only seen a couple of times and didn't particularly care for. "He dumped me."

"I thought you were following his customs and doing what he wanted by rushing into this marriage deal." Donnie placed his hands on her shoulders. "I told you that I thought it was crazy."

"Rayhan felt he forced God's hand and put Jahi in harm's way."

"That doesn't make sense. How were we to know that Jahi had climbed into the back of the jeep? Does Rayhan feel he's being punished?" Donnie reached into his pocket and gave her a white handkerchief folded into a neat square. "I thought he was a Christian. He should know that isn't how it works."

"I know, but as I said, customs and beliefs are entangled here. Between the quake and then the snake…for him, those were serious warnings." Liz smiled up at Donnie through her tears. She wiped her face and slipped the handkerchief into her back pocket.

"Do you want me to talk to him when we get back in Cairo? If I can't have the girl, then one of us should." Donnie reached over and lifted her chin. "I'm not good with crying women. I'm going to walk on ahead a bit. Is that okay?"

Liz nodded. She appreciated his insight, but wanted to be alone. Donnie stepped in front of her and quickened his pace. Her mind wandered back to the clues from Gary, and the unknown writer of the riddles. She slowed down to comprehend their secretive meaning, and the distance between her and Donnie grew.

Liz walked with a measured gate, thoughts churning through her head, until everything became crystal clear. She knew where Addie and Gary were, and it wasn't at El Kudish. With the realization, her heart skipped a beat and she stopped on the path. She had deciphered the part of the riddle centered around the ankh. Everything made sense. Liz placed her hand near her mouth to call Donnie, when a searing pain tore through her right upper arm, and everything went black.

RAYHAN FOCUSED ON the road ahead and tried to forget Liz. His last memory of her would forever haunt him. The sight of her in his rearview mirror made him miserable. She'd stood in the middle of the road, her shoulders slumped in defeat.

He had to protect Jahi. Liz knew that too. She didn't argue with him. He could not deny he loved her, but why couldn't he tell her that before he left? She asked one thing of him: to find her if he changed his mind. He couldn't even give her that much. He glanced over at the boy asleep in the seat next to him. Rayhan put both hands on the wheel and pulled his cap down to cover his eyes from the glare on the pavement.

He had never met anyone like her, alive and fearless and ready to take on the world. She believed in him, too, and would have been willing to make Egypt her home and take up his customs, but he had been carried along like a raging inferno, not stopping to ask nor pray for a blessing. He had rendered his own punishment—separation from Liz.

He would take Jahi back to Cairo, and then what? Would his uncle let him live in the house, or tell him to leave? Or worse yet, marry him off to one of the many waiting young women who appeared out of nowhere at family gatherings. Maybe he'd quit his job at the Embassy and go with the University on an archaeological expedition. Out in the desert doing research, making rubbings and cleaning artifacts, the months of solitude would help him stop thinking about her. The curve of her lips, the sweet taste of them on his, and the way she blushed every time they kissed. Could he ever forget Liz?

Jahi stirred and sat up as the siren grew closer. "Why did you leave Liz and Mr. Donnie back there?"

"I needed to take you home. Uncle Al Abdul and Aunt Amisi will be worried."

The boy didn't respond and turned in his seat toward Rayhan. "Your face is not happy."

"No. Jahi, I'm afraid we may have a little problem up here with whoever is using the siren. They may be looking for us."

"Because I ran away and hid in the back of the jeep?"

"No. We may have to stop soon. Be a good boy and don't say anything."

The vehicle bore down on them. Rayhan gripped the wheel and hoped they'd just drive on, continuing south. Donnie and Liz had plenty of time to be on the trail to El Kudish by now. Rayhan saw the flashing red lights. He slammed on his brakes to avoid being broadsided as the other driver made a hard turn into the jeep. Six armed gunmen jumped out of the other vehicle before the dust settled. Each shouldered a high-powered rifle, and waited for Rayhan to make an untimely move.

"Take him to Ahmad at El Kudish," the leader said as he pushed Rayhan into their vehicle.

Jahi squirmed to free himself from a second assailant, who hoisted him over the side of the jeep and dropped him into the front seat. Rayhan grimaced as the driver slapped Jahi's face.

CHAPTER TEN

LIZ WOKE ON a stiff bed constructed of hard, dirty mattresses, the vinegary taste of Egyptian lentil soup on her lips. Her arm throbbed, and her head pulsated with waves of nauseating pain. She glanced down at bloodied strips of the gold and brown blanket, torn into bandages, which were wrapped around her arm and shoulder.

What were her last conscious thoughts? She'd been on the dunes, Donnie a few passes ahead. She solved the riddle, then men dressed in white, hands dragged her into a blanket, she was carried, and darkness enveloped her.

Her blurry eyes focused on a group of priests huddled in an arched doorway. They were held back by a dark figure dressed in a linen-colored tunic, dingy white, baggy pants, and army boots. A sash-like cloth hung from one shoulder to his waist, held by a leather bandoleer. The first belt bisected crosswise with a second, both bands with long, brass bullets, ends directed skyward. Her vision came into clearer focus as they settled on Rayhan and

Donnie, who sat across from Liz on the floor, bound and gagged. Jahi was seated between them. His uncontrolled cries touched her heart. He sat, untied, closer to Rayhan than Donnie. A bright red handprint flamed across the boy's left cheek, and he wiped his nose on his sleeve.

A second Arabic nomad loomed, large and ominous, as he stood over them, his knife close to Rayhan's face. Each time Jahi cried, the man lurched toward them. A loud sob escaped from Jahi's lips, and Donnie battled against his ropes. A maternal instinct she didn't know she possessed urged her to protect the boy. When the assailant turned his back, Liz yelled, "Jahi!" The child scrambled to her side.

She winced, relieved the boy had crossed the floor without incident, but the man turned, his face white with anger, and with one swift movement, he threw the knife. It traveled end over end, swooshing as it cut the air, until it landed less than three feet from her head. The point embedded into the old, dirt floor of the church at El Kudish. Liz drew in a quick breath, but suppressed a scream. Well practiced with the weapon, if he had wanted to kill her, he would have, but he needed her and they both knew it. She glanced over and shook her head at Rayhan, who attempted to crawl to his feet.

The man walked across the room with three long steps and stood at her side. "Miss McCran." He spoke English, although thick with his Arabic accent. "Where are your friends?"

"I do not know," she lied. She ignored her pounding head and the nausea as she balanced on her good arm. "I thought they were here."

"We have been here for hours." He jerked his head in Rayhan's direction. "We were able to capture him, and he was eager to trade this location for the boy's life." Rayhan looked at her briefly, his eyes solemn, then he hung his head.

"My name is Ahmad, and your friends have something I want." He bent and pulled his knife from the ground. "Do you know what it is?"

"They had a letter to give to a Mr. Moustafa. They succeeded as far as I know."

"Then why were you at the restaurant? If they completed their mission, then you wouldn't have come looking for them, would you?"

Liz couldn't think fast enough. She did not intend to tell him where she thought Addie and Gary were, and since she and Ahmad had both searched for them, it was clear they weren't in El Kudish. They were left to a battle of wits. "I don't know where my friends are. Do you think I would have come all this way if I hadn't thought they were here?" Liz glared at Ahmad. "Now they clearly aren't, and I can't help you. I can't help either of us." Ahmad raised his knife and someone gasped from the doorway. She pulled the ankh from beneath her blouse and placed it where Ahmad could see it and hoped the significance of it in this holy place would discourage his actions. The arm he'd drawn back over his head hesitated. Her face twisted with pain as she ground her elbows into the dirt floor and waited for the blow.

Without a word, Ahmad turned, and his defiant stare fell on the man who had denied the priests entrance to the room. With a rapid hail of Arabic from Ahmad, the guard moved aside.

One of the priests rushed to comfort Liz. His eyes widened with fear, but he proceeded to change her bandages. With a great deal of care, he wrapped a folded paper against the final turn of the cloth. He held her in his gaze for a brief moment, then backed away.

Ahmad launched across the room toward Donnie and Rayhan, but stopped short, and in an aggravated gesture, twisted back to Liz and added, "We will talk further. I'll leave Ismar to guard you and the boy. They," he said, pointing the blade at Donnie and Rayhan, "will come with me." With proficient skill, Ahmad slashed through the ropes that bound his captives.

Pain marred his handsome features when Rayhan turned to face Liz. His soulful eyes burned into her spirit. The attempt to protect the boy had only augmented their danger. She smiled at Rayhan and placed her hand over her heart, but Ahmad jerked Rayhan by the arm and forced him to stand beside Donnie. Had Rayhan seen her? Would he have returned her gesture?

After they had been escorted from the room at gunpoint, Liz gathered Jahi in her arms. She felt a flood of emotions ripple through his tiny body as he erupted in fresh tears. She cradled him against her and hummed a lullaby. The words were long forgotten, but she remembered her mother singing it. Not since meeting Rayhan had she felt so lost and alone. Tears slipped down her cheeks as she rested her head on Jahi's and rocked him back and forth until she could no longer suffer the agony and shifted him down on the mat. He whimpered once and fell into a deep, peaceful sleep.

Ismar, who sat between them and the doorway, dozed as he warded off the sleep that beckoned him. Liz stroked Jahi's back and continued the song, but kept a watchful eye on Ismar, and he, too, nodded. Liz unbound her upper arm when restless breathing turned into rhythmic snores. The bullet had torn through. It cut straight across the muscle nearest the shoulder, but the profuse flow of blood had stopped. Liz fumbled with the bandage to find the note the young priest had wrapped inside. When she opened it, one word had been printed in English: Keystone.

Liz had a few solitary moments to sort out her thoughts while Jahi and Ismar slept. Although she grew concerned for Donnie and Rayhan, she knew Donnie could take care of himself. She had observed his concealment bag wasn't around his waist, but his ever tucked-in shirt had been pulled free. Certainly he still had the pouch; she suspected he must have it hidden under the loose fitting garment.

Her thoughts drifted to Rayhan. She'd lost hope the minute the anguish in his dark, brooding eyes found her heart. He treasured his people and their culture, but did he value her, too? She wanted to make him understand Jahi's adventure with the snake hadn't been Rayhan's fault, nor did it represent punishment for his failure to ask God's blessing on their relationship. It would be harder to persuade Rayhan, now, since their situation had been altered from seekers to prisoners. Their love did not break God's law. He forced his uncle's hand, but it did not warrant such severe consequences. Her heart ached to assure Rayhan. *Do I understand him and his upbringing well enough to convince him we were meant to be together? I thought I knew about his customs. But what I know comes from book knowledge and a few vacation trips.*

Maybe you don't really know a person until… you fall in love with them.

He had taken that first step and she had, without forethought, followed. Now could she try to change his mind and not let him dismiss what they both felt, or should she just let him go?

She couldn't answer her own question and turned her thoughts to Ismar. Eyes closed, his head rested on his chest. She pulled Gary's note and drawings from her hip pocket and placed them in order between Jahi's back and her leg so she could hide them if necessary. She added the last clue: keystone.

Liz went over Gary's note: a series of the number three, written together in tight sequence, and the phrase *dark is the night, walk in the light.* So far, she knew the number referred to two things: the Egyptian mythological legend of Isis, Osiris and Horus, and to the Holy Family who fled to Egypt. Gary's interest in the parallel meanings of Egyptology and Christianity and his archeological background drove him to investigate the various digs and research projects Addie worked on. They'd made several trips to the museum to visit Liz where he'd copied hieroglyphics. Had the note she found only hours ago been more than random doodling Gary's part?

Liz recalled in 332 BC, Alexander allowed the Egyptians to build a temple to Isis in Alexandria. Later, the Apostle Mark established the Church there. The Egyptians were able to embrace Christianity as it paralleled and gave meaning to their own mythology. Gary's phrase referred to Christ being the light of the world and, she deduced, to the Light House at Alexandria—she'd caught the reference to both.

Jahi whimpered and Ismar jerked awake. He appeared annoyed at his failure, and an angry scowl distorted his features. He scrambled to his feet. Liz rolled the child onto his back, covering the notes, and patted him on his stomach, he drifted back to sleep. Ismar walked toward her. Liz's heartbeat untamed within her chest, and she leaned over Jahi to protect him. When Ismar reached them, he moved his foot, readying it to kick the boy.

"No," she screamed, reaching out toward Ismar with her one good arm. He grabbed it, pinning it against her. Liz kicked at his legs, causing him to drop his rifle. The butt hit the floor and the gun went off, sending a shower of broken bricks hailing down on them from the ceiling. Awakened, Jahi cried out and began to move from his makeshift bed. With all the energy Liz had left, she covered his small body with hers. Ismar had rendered her powerless, and the burning pain from the twisted muscle and skin left her weak.

Ahmad returned to the room and, with a quick staccato phrase in Arabic, Ismar released Liz. She stayed crumpled against Jahi and waited for another assault. A hand reached down and lifted her.

"What happened?" She fixed her eyes on Rayhan, who was unexplainably free.

He smiled. "Magic."

Ismar, who held her in a dark, satirical stare, reached for his gun and walked toward the doorway as Ahmad barked orders to another priest. Liz retrieved the notes and tucked them back into her pocket when Rayhan bent down to help Jahi. Even though Rayhan had a fresh cut on his face, he seemed relieved.

"What is going on with you two?" she whispered and reached up to touch his cheek.

He didn't have time to answer before they were ordered to move across the sanctuary to a small room much like the one at the monastery where Gary had spent the night. There were four cots against the walls, and the priests busied themselves as they delivered food and water. Their Egyptian basket and its contents sat on the floor under a long, wooden table. Liz wondered who had the keys to the jeep, and knew their captors wouldn't have been so generous to leave those with them, too.

Ahmad and his men, whom Liz had earlier counted to number no more than six, stood outside the door. His eyes were defiant as he observed her walk in front of him, but he said nothing more as they entered the room. The door locked behind them.

Once they were alone, she broke the silence. "What happened? How did he just let you go?"

"Ahmad questioned us and when we refused to tell him anything, the jerk drew his blade across his face." Donnie gestured to Rayhan.

"But you're okay?" Liz asked.

"Of course," Rayhan said as he brought his hand to the wound. She feared he'd paid too great a price for his silence. He reached out to her moments earlier when Ismar had been told to leave her alone. *Had Rayhan changed his mind?*

He came to her side and took her hand in his and brought it to his lips, then brushed her palm with a tender kiss. "You risked your life for Jahi." He gazed into her eyes. "You protected him."

"I wouldn't have thought of doing anything less. He's a little boy."

"My uncle will be very pleased."

That's all? Did he just thank me for doing what I would have done anyway? She didn't seek his uncle's favor.

She turned her attention to Donnie. He cleared his throat and walked to the table, poured a cup of water and brought it to her. "Ahmad realized we didn't know anything more, and when one of the priests insisted he leave us alone, Ahmad obliged. I had Rayhan ask the priest to bring some boiling water so I could cleanse Rayhan's face."

Donnie reached under his shirt and brought out a small bottle of white pills. "When the priest came back with the water, I threw baking soda into it. It boiled over and achieved the exact outcome I'd anticipated." Donnie shook two of the tablets out into his hand and returned the bottle to his pouch. "I had Rayhan tell Ahmad I had magical powers, and being naïve to the chemical reaction, he bought it." Donnie handed her the pills. "Here. Take these and try to sleep."

"What are they?"

"Don't worry. I won't poison you." Donnie pointed to the water. "Take them."

Liz swallowed the tablets, but found it hard to relax. Her thoughts returned to the riddle about using the ankh to find the sign. She had been successful in using it to open the secret rooms and in warding off Ahmad. Liz planned to use his superstitious nature to her advantage. The inscription on the ankh, Talmar, meant more than the holy man's name. She had one more clue to lead her to Addie and Gary's whereabouts. If she had arrived at El Kudish before they had been moved, it wouldn't have been necessary to use the final puzzle piece.

Liz reclined on her cot with her face against the wall and rolled over to observe the others. Donnie worked on something in his lap, and Rayhan read to Jahi out of the Book of Hours. Rayhan demonstrated the fruits of the spirit—kindness, love, peacefulness, self-control—the very traits that drew her to him, but he couldn't move beyond the rift he thought he had created between himself and God. She could not condemn Rayhan when she had faults of her own, but she could help him grow.

Jahi's eyes were wide with wonderment, and Rayhan used his hands to point around the room and gestured toward the back wall as he unraveled a story from the prayer book. Liz wondered if Rayhan had figured out what she already knew.

"Donnie," Liz called out. "Borrow the prayer book from Rayhan."

"You're supposed to be resting," he said, but did as she asked.

Liz smiled as she took the book from his hand. "Why aren't you trying to figure out how to get us out of here?"

"If I remember correctly, we're locked in," he answered ruefully. "I didn't bring any dynamite."

"You don't know where we are, do you?" Liz groaned as she stood. The medication didn't quell the pain.

"Stay put." He walked toward Liz to block her, but when she reached out for him with her good arm, he pulled her to her feet.

"We're in the secret room." She grinned. "Rayhan, did you figure out where the door is?"

Rayhan left Jahi and rose from his mat. "It should be in this back wall, here." He pointed. "I was looking at the floor plans while I told Jahi the Egyptian proverb: *the only thing that is humiliating is helplessness*. I explained to him we are far from helpless, and there is no reason for sorrow." He locked his gaze on Liz.

She tried to read his thoughts. If he meant for her to understand, she didn't. The fracture in her heart grew wider. "You're right." She walked to the rear of the room. Liz felt along the brick wall and dug her fingers into the crevices between the stones. "Where is it?"

"You're standing on it," Donnie chuckled.

"I thought you said you didn't know."

Donnie gave her a pained expression. "I didn't. Check out the floor. The bricks have a wider groove around that four-by-four square. The door's right below it."

Liz knelt down and brushed the dirt and sand away from the bricks. In the middle of the square, the mark of the ankh lay recessed into the surface. Donnie dislodged the brick with the mark and under it, a wooden door, an indentation in the center with a visible impression of the key.

"There still may not be a way out," he said and brushed the dirt from his hands.

"If it isn't, it will be a good hiding place." Liz grimaced as a pain shot through her shoulder. Donnie pointed her back in the direction of her cot.

"Why do we need to hide?" Donnie gestured to the door. "They're standing right outside. They'll know we didn't just vanish." He paused and rubbed the two-day-old stubble on his chin. "You know where Addie and Gary are, don't you?"

"Yes. I figured out the clues he left me, and I think the final piece of the puzzle."

"And…" Donnie waited.

I knew it wasn't just a coincidence that Talmar spelled backwards was Ramlat. From my Middle Eastern studies, Ramlat Al-Sab'atayn is one of the kingdoms involved in the story of the Incense Road, where the riches were carried to Solomon as mentioned in Chronicles 9. "The Sabaeans, as other Yemenite kingdoms, were involved in traveling caravans of the Spice Trade and brought frankincense and myrrh to Egypt." She paused to see if Donnie followed her ramblings.

"Those were two of the gifts brought to the Christ Child, but you're missing the third element—the gold." He adjusted his Stetson and leaned against the wall. "Where is it?"

"Gold was plentiful in Egypt, and Ptolemy commissioned the streets of Alexandria to be paved with it." *I had determined Addie and Gary were in Alexandria when we were on the trail to El Kudish, but the note from the young priest—keystone—confirmed what I believed.* "Alexandria is where the start—or keystone—of Christianity began. Addie and Gary are being kept at The Church of Alexandria."

"You're sure of this?" His eyes met hers and she thought he didn't quite believe her.

"Positive."

"Then we need to find a way out of here and move on to Alexandria."

"What we need is a little of your magic for that to happen. What's the date?"

"The twelfth. Why?"

"Gary left me one other clue, too, one more reference to light—the Eye of Horus. I had lost track of the days, but I knew a total eclipse of the sun would occur soon in this hemisphere. If I have figured correctly, with a little help from you, we could use the eclipse to plan our escape. This will happen on the thirteenth, which is tomorrow. You can spook Ahmad with one of your tricks, and we can crawl down into that room." Liz glanced over at Donnie just in time to see him roll his eyes. She let out a long, slow breath in aggravation. "Well, do you have a better idea?"

"We don't know that door leads to anywhere. It could just be a hole in the ground." He took off his cowboy hat and drew his hand through his hair. "I don't know, Liz. If they find us, it might mean—"

"They won't. We have to believe that. Your job is to think up a distraction. My job is to remember the Egyptian mythology that surrounds the Eye of Horus." She stole a quick glance at him. "Another little job I have for you is to crawl down in there and see if it goes anywhere."

Donnie's expression soured. "We don't know what's down there. How did I get the short straw?"

"It's our only way out. Open the door and check it out. Or I will," she said.

"No." Rayhan came and stood between them. "I'll go."

"You stay with her." Donnie jutted his chin toward Liz.

Rayhan glared at Donnie. "You're always trying to prove yourself, and so far, I've made allowances for you. Or is it that you don't think I'm man enough or have enough bravado or whatever it is that drives you?"

"If I'm not back in twenty minutes, send Rayhan to find me." Donnie repositioned his Stetson, and without a word, crossed over to the back of the room, opened the door and disappeared down the steps.

Jahi had fallen asleep and Rayhan sat engrossed in the prayer book. He gazed at the page and then closed his eyes. With his head bowed, he moved his lips in silent prayer. Liz smiled at the two of them and Rayhan's devotion, and her heart swelled that he stood up to Donnie. So she wasn't the only one put off by his testosterone-charged attitude.

The sun had disappeared below the horizon, but none of them had taken the time to light the candles the priests had left. The room grew still. Liz lay coiled against the unknown, her blanket pulled to her throat. Her inner turmoil gnawed at her soul and drove away the hope of sleep.

She rose and moved to the window. *The stars are so brilliant out here. Why didn't I notice them before? Too busy? Not in love?*

"They're beautiful, aren't they? I used to sit at my window when I was a kid and dream about following the stars, letting them navigate my journey." Rayhan broke into her thoughts. "I never dreamed I'd be here under these circumstances and with a beautiful woman."

She said nothing and remained motionless as he came to stand beside her. "Liz, I need to apologize. I—"

"Don't worry. It's about time someone stood up to Donnie." She smiled. "Your people are gentle and quiet. I admire that characteristic in you. He needed to be taken down a notch."

"It isn't that. I didn't willingly surrender your position to save Jahi. I'm not a coward. They overpowered me and threatened to kill you. Ahmad was already here. But I told them nothing."

Liz had never believed Rayhan had easily given over their hiding place. The guilt in his eyes tore into her. She wrapped her arms around herself and rocked on her heels.

"It was a mistake for Jahi to come. I should have faced the situation earlier. Maybe I shouldn't have come either."

"No," she interrupted. "I understand. It's partially my fault. I can't..."

He turned, his voice acquiescent. "You can't what?"

"Let you go against your customs." She shook her head as she answered. "We'd both be hurt."

"I won't hurt you, Liz, I promise."

"You may not want to, but sometimes life turns out different than you expect. It already has."

"My life crumbled in a way I never realized could happen when my parents were killed. I went from being a carefree teenager to one who carried a tremendous burden as their only son." Rayhan closed his eyes for a moment. She thought he might not continue, but then he cleared his throat and let his gaze settle on her. "I had been raised to honor them and make my life a tribute to our home and family, but I was so busy being a sixteen-year-old boy whose only thought was a field trip. I wanted to fit in with the rest of my American friends, and I failed to remember what was important."

Liz studied his face. His soft brown eyes glistened, laden with unshed tears. "You don't need to do this if it is too painful for you."

"I have not told you the whole story of the day my parents died. I learned a lesson I'll never forget."

Liz stood in front of him, close enough to touch him, but hesitated, wondering if he would say more. "Rayhan, you didn't do anything wrong. Everyone makes decisions they regret, but you were only a kid." She touched his arm. "You're being too hard on yourself, just as you are now, about us."

"They died in a traffic accident on the way home after dropping me at school. I bolted from the car and I never told them much more than goodbye, let alone that I loved them."

"I can't possibly comprehend what you've been through, but I do understand. I've learned lessons, too, about missing that last opportunity to tell someone how you feel." She dropped her head and brushed her hand against her cheek. "Sometimes there are no second chances."

He covered her small, soft hand in his large one, which had become callused from his archaeological digs. "Let's just wait and see if we can work this out, okay?" He reached up and touched her cheek and moved closer.

Liz stepped away. "No. Your uncle is unhappy, and you feel that by loving me you've brought misfortune to Jahi."

"I admit it, I was wrong. Let me try to make it right."

"Then we need to ask for God's direction."

He closed the gap between them and pulled her into him. He brushed her forehead with his lips. Liz closed her eyes as his lashes fluttered against her cheeks. He placed his mouth on hers and she tasted the sweetness of his lips. Her entire body tingled as she responded to his kiss.

THE PILLS DONNIE had given Liz forced her into a fitful sleep, but her eyes fluttered open and squinted to adjust to the pale, yellow glow of the lamp. She wondered if Rayhan's apology and his kiss had been real or a dream, and sat up with a jolt as she became reacquainted with her surroundings. She had insisted Rayhan and Jahi not follow tradition, and they ate dried fruit and thick slabs of crusty, baked bread; the aroma filled the room. Liz thought Donnie had come back from below, but he had positioned himself out of her line of vision. The door to the stairwell stood open.

Dizziness overtook her as she rose from the cot and, with trembling knees, she sat down and moaned. She couldn't remember when she'd last eaten. "Jahi, please?" she said and pointed to her mouth. He jumped up and brought her a slice of the fresh bread the priests had brought. The light taste of olive oil and sweet spices filled her mouth. Jahi sat down beside her and leaned against her. Her hand encircled his shoulder while he nuzzled close.

"He's homesick," Rayhan offered.

"Me, too. This trip didn't turn out like I'd expected, but then I would have never met you two if it had."

"Inshallah," he said.

"What?"

"Fate. We met by fate. The rough translation is: if God is willing."

Liz smiled at Rayhan and rested her cheek against the top of Jahi's head. God's will. Liz prayed for God's will. Had Rayhan sensed it too? Liz shook her head, confused. Her plan to embrace his lifestyle and his customs seemed so easy at first. If he had been sure of their love, why, then, did he think he had been wrong? It had been Rayhan's idea in the first place. *Then last night when he kissed me—wait, did he kiss me? Did he think it could all be mended so easily?* There were just too many unanswered questions.

Her thoughts of Rayhan were interrupted as Donnie approached. "We're ready," he said. "There is a long corridor, then another door with an impression of an ankh. It could be the way out, but if it isn't, at least we can hide there until Ahmad has given up and left."

"What were you doing back there?" Liz said over her shoulder toward the open door.

"I rigged up a stiff piece of paper and a string to drag sand across the door once it is closed. That way it will appear we've vanished." Donnie raised his hands in front of his face and flashed them at her, open palmed. "Poof." He smiled. "Now, it's your turn. What's this Eye of Horus thing and how am I supposed to trick Ahmad with it?"

"Horus is thought to be the prince of the sun. I had one of the priests deliver a message to Ahmad that I want to see him at noon tomorrow."

"When did you have time to talk to a priest?"

"While you were in the back. They woke me when they brought in some food."

Donnie shook his head. "Do you know how dangerous that was?"

"I know..." She drew her hand across her lips. Her mouth went dry, and for a moment she couldn't speak. *What had she done?* She cleared her throat. "I took a chance and put us at risk, but I had to have Ahmad here at twelve. It's when the moon will begin to eclipse." Liz shifted Jahi into her lap as Donnie listened to her plan. "At that point, I'll quote the translation of a piece of papyrus I read at the museum. In fact, it was from a project I had been working on with Addie." She paused and thought of her friend and how they had worked on the recent display. "I'll take enough of it out of context to scare Ahmad, then you'll pitch some of your flash powder at him and we'll escape down the hole. We'll have less than ten minutes."

"Nice. I couldn't have planned that better myself, but I want you to go with me right now and see if you can open that second door." Donnie came to her side and lifted Jahi off her lap. "We also need to take what we want and place it in the shaft." Donnie tickled Jahi and the child's blissful laughter lightened her heart. "Can you stay here and guard the door, little man?"

"I want to help." Rayhan joined them, took Jahi into his arms, and sat him down. The child scurried to his cot. "What do you want me to do?"

"Liz and I will go down to open the door and you and Jahi start packing the basket. I'm going to string what's left of the striped blanket over this opening here." Donnie pulled a small cord from his black pouch and began to fashion a curtain. "If someone starts to come in, call her name and I'll have enough time to climb back up the steps."

Donnie reached into his pouch and pulled out a shiny cellophane package. "Come here, Liz. I need to wrap you up."

"What are you going to do?"

"It's dirty down there. Go behind the curtain and let me re-bandage your shoulder before we go down." He held up the small plastic package. "This will protect your wound. I want to check it, too. Make sure it's okay."

"Let me do it," Rayhan demanded. "I should be the one…"

Donnie cut him off. "I think I've seen a few more bullet wounds than you have, and I have something in my bag that will prevent infection." Donnie sighed. "We need to get this done. We're wasting time."

For one brief moment, Donnie, Rayhan, and Liz grew silent, sharing a common thought. They looked at each other and the room weighed heavy with apprehension.

Rayhan broke the silence. "Inshallah, Liz."

Liz answered him as she slipped behind the curtain. "Inshallah."

"Let me see that shoulder," Donnie urged at her reluctance to peel her t-shirt away from the injury.

"I'm sure the priests put something on it." Liz winced as she uncoiled the bandages below her sleeve. "I feel uncomfortable having you see me like this."

"Here," he said. He handed her a strip of the material he'd cut from the main blanket. "Cover yourself with this and expose your upper arm. I need to see if it is infected."

Donnie turned his back and Liz pulled her shirt from her arm grimacing where the dried blood had bonded the shirt to her skin. "See, it isn't too bad." A clean hole pierced through the skin of her upper arm, and a narrow slit on the other side where a small caliber bullet had come through, the skin around the wound red and swollen. A light smear of some greasy substance covered her entire upper arm. Whatever the priests had dressed it with had worked well.

Donnie retrieved a small vial of clear liquid from his pouch and removed the cap with his teeth. "This might hurt." He kept a firm grip on her arm, pouring the liquid over the wound.

"Ouch. What is that? It looks like salad oil and smells like pizza."

"Close. It's oregano oil, a natural antibiotic. Let me bandage it again, then I'll put the plastic wrap over it. It will stay clean until we can have someone examine it."

Liz stood still, waiting for Donnie to finish, but they were interrupted by Rayhan's urgent voice. "They're coming," he said from the other side of the curtain.

"They arrived quicker than I thought. Stay here. Act like a girl for once." His expression let Liz know he meant business. She stayed put when Donnie dropped the curtain between her and the outer portion of the room. A loud exchange between Ahmad and Rayhan caused her optimism to fade that Ahmad would leave them alone until tomorrow.

"Where is she? I want to talk to her and ask her who she thinks she is, demanding my presence." Ahmad grumbled.

"Leave her alone, she's resting behind the curtain. We gave her some privacy, and you should do the same," Rayhan answered him. When the skin-to-skin pop reached her ears, Liz knew Rayhan had just received a blow. "You—"

"You wanted to see me." Liz drew back the curtain and glared at Ahmad, hoping to break up their fight. "I didn't expect you until tomorrow."

"You are *my* captive." His glassy eyes appeared an unnerving yellow in the lamp light. "Why are you ordering me to see you?"

"I wanted you to be aware that Horus will capture the sun tomorrow." Liz stared down at her less than spotless, once white, tennis shoes and mustered up her courage. "You are a smart man, maybe you already know."

"You, an American and a woman, know of Horus' powers?" Ahmad turned to her in amazement.

Liz knew her plan would work. She had him hooked, and Donnie could distract Ahmad. "Horus hath become the divine Prince of the Boat of the Sun, and unto him hath been given the throne of his divine father Osiris." Liz quoted from the papyrus. "He shall come forth by day, he shall not be turned back at any gate in the underworld, and he shall make his transformation."

"What do you mean? How can you open the gates to the underworld?"

"Not I, Ahmad. Horus is coming tomorrow at twelve. I only wanted to warn you. Be here tomorrow. He plans to snatch away the sun."

"I don't believe you. This is some kind of trick."

"If you don't believe me, then wait until tomorrow."

"Stupid woman. You know nothing." He stormed across the room toward the door and turned with a large swish of his tunic, his sword banging against the door jamb. "How do you know this?"

Now he doubted himself. Perfect. Liz assumed Ahmad had no formal education, his people a nomadic group of rebels who had been hired by the scar-faced man Liz had seen at the restaurant and again at Bani Suwayf. Where Ahmad had learned to speak English was anyone's guess, but there were plenty of Americans in Egypt who could have easily taught him.

"I have read the signs." Liz glowered straight into his hardened face. He glanced away from her, but not before the fear in his eyes cut her to the core.

"At twelve, then. Prove yourself tomorrow at twelve." He slammed the door so hard dirt shook loose from the plaster ceiling. The bolt slid into place and the locks hinged shut. Donnie and Liz hurried toward the curtain.

"Wait. Liz. Let me go." Rayhan rushed to her side.

"No. I'll be fine. Donnie has wrapped my shoulder, and you need to stay with Jahi in case they come back." Liz reached over to him and took his hand. She squeezed it in hers and searched his ardent, brown eyes. "It will all turn out fine." She wanted to say that she promised, but she knew that might be impossible. She promised it in her heart. With God's help, they'd all find a way out of there.

"Hurry, Liz. We don't have much time." Donnie gestured toward the hatch in the back of the room.

She reached the door first, and waited for him to open it. Liz didn't want to disturb the intricate contraption he had rigged up at the hinged side of the door. "You must elaborate on what this is for." She pointed to the thin string woven tight through a thick piece of paper.

"Not now, Liz. You'll see how it works tomorrow. We need to hurry."

She scrambled down the steps and reached the bottom of the stairwell. The dirt floor beneath her felt powdery and soft. Liz saw the imprint of Donnie's shoes and other, recent footprints. She trekked against the sidewall far into the tunnel, but the unnerving feeling of utter solitude overtook her, and she turned to see that

Donnie hadn't followed her, but stood about three steps down from the opening.

"You aren't coming?" Liz called back in a hushed voice.

"Can't. I have to make sure your friend doesn't reappear." Donnie stood steadfast and waived his hand for Liz to go on down the corridor. "Go on. There isn't anything but a door down there at the end."

Liz shined the beam of Donnie's flashlight in front of her. She had the same sweaty-palm feeling she'd had during her dream where she searched for Addie and Gary and they were just beyond her reach. Now her dream had turned into reality, and with equal fright, a nightmare. Liz continued along the narrow path.

She approached the carved, wooden door and fumbled for the ankh. It slipped out of her hand, and landed with a plop on the soft, dirt floor. As she shined the beam toward her feet to find the key, she spotted something lying in the corner. Liz bent to pick up a small piece of torn yellow and white cloth. She froze. Every scrap of strength drained through her into the floor. Liz steadied herself against the wall and slid down to sit on the dirt. A square of Gary's shirt, his favorite Hawaiian shirt—the one he had on the last time Liz saw him and Addie at the San Francisco Airport. What had it been, less than two weeks?

Had Liz read the signs wrong? Were Addie and Gary still here, hidden somewhere, maybe in the room she prepared to open? She had been so certain they were in Alexandria. She had figured out all the clues, all the riddles.

The men from the church had brought them here to be safe. This had to be the meeting point. According to the riddle they were to be moved *before the waning doth begin*. Liz put her head against her knees. *Think.* She pressed her back against the cold, stone wall.

The phase of the moon was wrong, so they couldn't be here. Or could they?

Liz scrambled to her feet and placed the key in the door. It fit with perfect connectivity, as it had the other times she'd used it. The door pin grumbled and moved, and Liz forced her power into her good shoulder and pushed against the heavy, wooden plank. She half-expected Addie and Gary to be standing there waiting.

The room resembled the other secret chambers. The ceilings were painted in soft muted murals which dated back thousands of years. Old, jagged pots and dishes sat on a side table, and unusual pieces of furniture lined the walls. Any other time, she would have been excited to be in that very place, examining the artifacts, dating and cataloguing them, but on that day, her eyes could only focus on one thing—Gary's shirt, torn and blood-stained, lying on the floor.

Liz bent to pick it up and stood immobile, glued to the spot where the crumpled garment had been discarded. She forgot why, only minutes before, she'd come down the steps. Liz folded the shirt and carried it with her, evidence, if need be, but she shook off the thought. There had not been any sign of Addie. *Had she made it here? Were they together now? What had happened?*

Liz's hands shook. She needed a place to sit down and stumbled to a nearby stone bench. Her entire body began to shake with uncontrollable sobs while the coldness of the rock crept past her clothing and into her soul. What if Addie and Gary weren't in Alexandria? What if Liz never found them? Had she risked all these people's lives for nothing? "God?" Liz said. Her voice shook on the verge of losing control. "Are you listening to me? What am I supposed to do?"

Nothing but the empty, hollow echoes of the subterranean room met her ears. Liz drifted barren and without purpose as her thoughts mimicked the swirling sand drifts outside the monastery's fortress. Addie and Gary were gone. If they weren't in Alexandria, could she ever forgive herself? Her thoughts turned to Rayhan and she remembered what he had told her: *Inshallah.* He had been so sure, so positive they were right for each other, and then he let her go without, she assumed, thinking it through, but he wanted God's will.

A peace Liz couldn't describe washed over her. She sat in this room some twenty feet below ground due to God's will. The urgency to find if this room could be a way out or a hiding place surged through Liz's consciousness, giving her strength to move ahead. Reciting the Twenty-Third Psalm seemed appropriate. Liz began, "The Lord is my …" With a sudden swoosh, what little light coming from the upper floor disappeared from the hallway. Donnie had closed the door. Trapped. *How am I going to get out of here?*

Had Ahmad came back? How were they going to explain why she wasn't there? Could anything else go wrong?

Liz shined the high-powered beam around the darkened chamber and hunted for some sort of escape route. She found an oil lamp and a box of matches on a table. Liz struck a match and, with a careful hand, held the flame to the wick as the soft, dim glow reflected against the walls. Against the far partition stood a large bookcase, a desk, and a table. The opposite wall had been filled with shelves populated by pottery and bottles and an occasional book. The entrance she had used offered the only exit.

She carried the lamp across the room and out of the corner of her eye, caught a glimpse of a small, thin strip of red material running the full length of the bookcase. Footsteps echoed in the corridor and she darted across the expanse. Ahmad had found out—his men were coming. Cornered, she had nowhere to go. She grabbed a thin-necked jug from the shelf and held it above her. Liz blew out the light and held her breath.

Someone stood in the doorway, but the lack of light made it far too dark to see. The shadowy figure backed into the room until he stood about three feet in front of her.

Liz stepped toward her assailant and gripped the pot when Rayhan whispered, "Liz? Where are you?"

She grabbed the flashlight from her pocket and shined it in his eyes, letting the jug fall to the floor and shatter. "About ready to hit you over the head, that's where. Why did you shut the hatch?"

"The priests came in and brought more provisions, and Donnie came from behind the curtain. Jahi peeked around the blanket and beckoned to me. I shut the door, just in case Ahmad was with them." His face relaxed, and then he grinned at her. "Thanks for dropping the weapon."

"You're not funny. You scared me to death, but since you're here, I need some help. I may have found something." Liz motioned to the bookcase. "Could you move that?"

"Redecorating, are we?" He relit the lamp and had brought it over to the side of the room where she stood.

Liz held up Gary's shirt, which she clutched in her left hand. "All the blood; he must have been hurt pretty badly."

"That's not good." Rayhan's face grew somber. "Any sign of your friend, Addie?"

Liz shook her head. "No, I'm afraid not. I'm trusting she made it this far."

"Where did you find the shirt?"

"A small scrap was in the hall, the rest of it on the floor in front of the door. He has been here. The riddles are leading the way. It's more proof they're in Alexandria." Liz patted Rayhan's wide chest. "Come on, move the bookcase."

He strained, pushing against the stone, but the case moved no more than six inches.

"I guess it's heavier than it looks. Could you wedge it out somehow?" she said.

"I think it's made out of stone. I don't want it to go over. It will make too much noise and Ahmad will find us for sure." With another shove, Rayhan increased the gap between the bookcase and the wall to twice the size it had been before. "Can you get behind it and see what you were looking for?"

Rayhan held the lamp above his head and she pulled back the velvet curtain to reveal another door. The wood had the recessed mark of the ankh and Liz slid the cross into place and pushed. The door opened into another stairwell and at the top, a tiny patch of dark, star-filled night sky.

CHAPTER ELEVEN

"CAN YOU SEE anything?" Liz whispered to Rayhan. He stood above her, halfway up the steps.

He stopped and turned back in her direction. "Not much. I think the opening is blocked off with something. I'll try to move it." He reached back to her and asked, "Could you hand me the flashlight?"

She set the lamp down on the stone ledge and discovered each step had carved letters from a language she didn't recognize. Her urge to investigate further put on hold, Liz reached into her back pocket, charged up the gap which separated them, and gave him the long, black-handled beam. "Here."

"I'm going to the top," he said and turned to ascend the stairs. "You stay here and listen."

"Okay. There's something I want to check out anyway." She narrowed her eyes to peer at the steps and placed her fingers into the groves of the chiseled marks. Liz fumbled through her pockets where she hoped to find paper and pencil for a rubbing. "You all right up there? I need to find something." She pivoted to take the steps back down into the secret room.

"There isn't time. We need to get back to Donnie and Jahi in case something happens." He came back down the steps. "What did you find?"

"These stone slabs have some sort of inscriptions, but I can't read them. It goes all the way to the top. You didn't count the steps, did you?"

"Liz. Drop the Egyptology session and let's worry about getting out of here. I'll look at your rubbings later. Maybe either Talmar or I can figure it out."

"It could be something important. Something I need to find Addie and Gary." Liz reeled with her own delirium. "You're right, but I'd really like to know what they mean."

"I'll read it later. Let's go." He grew silent as they walked toward the door to the tunnel, then stopped and grabbed her arm. "There's a bit of a problem."

She ignored him. *I don't need another setback. What if the inscriptions on the steps are another clue?* They'd reached the first door before she'd convinced herself they weren't. "What's our problem?"

He took the lamp from her and sat it on one of the tables, blew it out, and shined the flashlight toward the door. "The exit from the stairwell is blocked by rocks. There is an opening at the top, but too small to crawl through. Does Donnie have anything to blow it open?"

"Blow it open!" Liz turned to him as they entered the corridor, panting in short gasps. "He's not carrying dynamite, is he?"

He opened the hatch and Liz saw his face as he grinned. "He has black powder."

"I'm not asking." Liz reached the top of the steps, shook her head, and walked off. When she pulled back the curtain, Jahi tackled her knees and almost knocked her over.

"Lizzz," he whimpered.

She bent down and peered into his dark, brown eyes. A tear splashed down his cheek. "What's wrong?"

"Scared," he moaned in hesitant English.

"Yeah." Her gaze found Rayhan. "Me, too."

"He's worried. You two were gone a long time. It is almost midnight," Donnie said.

Liz took Jahi's hand, walked him to her cot, and patted the blanket where he sat down next to her. She pulled him close. "We're fine."

Jahi snuggled into her, yawned, and closed his eyes with a big sigh.

"He's tired," Donnie said. "We all should get some sleep."

"Sorry, but we have some rocks to move," Rayhan called from the back of the room.

"Rocks?" Donnie glanced between Rayhan and Liz. Puzzled, his forehead creased.

"We found a way out, but it is blocked. The barricade was either put there by nature or intentionally to keep us in here. We have to make a large enough opening so we can climb out and with precious little time once the eclipse starts."

Rayhan made his way to the table and surveyed their evening meal. There were hearty bowls of stew, bread, and a plate of dried fruits. A large dent had already been made in the meal. "This any good?"

"Yes. Jahi and I have eaten," Donnie said. "We didn't know when you'd be coming back."

"Most people would have waited." She frowned at Donnie. *Hasn't he learned anything from their customs?* "But I realize you aren't just anyone."

"What did I do?" Donnie grumbled. "Sorry, I'll follow the etiquette book when we're back in civilization."

Liz turned to Rayhan. "When you have eaten, take Donnie, and see what you two need to do. I'll stay with Jahi."

Rayhan finished his stew, rolled a portion of dried fruit into a cloth, and stuffed it into his pocket. He broke a thick chunk of bread from the fresh loaf, which he laid on the table next to the flashlight. He rummaged around in the basket, made sure everything they needed had been secured, and hoisted it up on his shoulder. "Let's go." He grabbed the bread and the flashlight and nodded to Donnie.

"It's my turn to tell you to be careful." Liz smiled at Rayhan. He nodded and fell into step with Donnie. They reached the curtain and she remembered the carvings. "Wait, Rayhan. See if you can read the writing on the steps."

Donnie glared. "Have you lost your mind?"

"It could mean something. Humor me."

The two men disappeared behind the curtain and Liz went to Jahi. She tucked him into his bed and sang to him. Liz wondered if he understood the words or if the soft strains of the lullaby and her presence soothed him. Before long, he closed his eyes and drifted into the sweet sleep of innocence. Liz took her bowl of stew and sat near the window. The food had turned cold, but temperature didn't matter. Famished, she ate her meal, and wiped the bowl clean with a piece of torn bread. She listened, but couldn't hear any sounds from the back or below her. A thankful prayer graced her lips. The process to enlarge their escape route must be accomplished in silence.

After a while, Liz became drowsy, and even the light, cool desert breeze that drifted through the window did not keep her heavy eyelids open. She left the bowl in the window sill and found her way to her cot.

The next morning, Rayhan nudged the edge of her bed with his knee and startled her out of a sound sleep. "Wake up," he whispered. Covered from head to toe with dust and dirt, a large brownish stain blazed across his shoulder. Liz reached to touch it, and he winced. "Ouch."

"What happened?" As she looked at him, tears filled her eyes with sympathy for their shared injuries.

"It's not blood, maybe just a bruise. I think it came off some of the painting on the walls."

"Hematite," Liz said.

"Oh yeah. Just paint," he said as he dusted off the powder.

"It's used to make the paint." Liz corrected him and rubbed her eyes. "Did you move the rocks?"

"We made the opening big enough for Donnie to crawl through. The rest of us won't have any trouble. We found the jeep. There doesn't seem to be anyone guarding it." Satisfaction radiated from his face.

"Where's Donnie?"

"He's cleaning up behind the curtain. Knowing Ahmad would notice how dirty we are, I convinced the priests we needed some soap and warm water. You must have been beat. You slept through everything." Rayhan handed her a bowl of porridge and Liz inhaled the sweet smell of cinnamon.

Donnie came from behind the curtain, joined them, and ladled out a bowl of the breakfast gruel. He motioned to Rayhan. "It's all yours," he said and pointed to the back of the room. "I see you've followed the American tradition of eating without me."

"See how easily I fit in to your society," Rayhan said as he handed Donnie the lid from the porridge container.

Donnie nodded a thank you, then said, "Liz, Rayhan read the inscription on the steps. You'll find it interesting."

"*I am the light of the world: he that followeth me shall not walk in darkness, but shall have the light of life.* John 8:12," Rayhan quoted and smiled.

Liz couldn't speak. She cleared her throat and tried to dislodge the emotional upheaval that ran through her and settled there. The priests must have used the same passageway to help Addie and Gary escape from the monastery. If so, then they were the ones who covered the opening.

"Do you think Addie made it here?" Donnie pulled the curtain open.

"I do. I have to. What time is it, Donnie?" came from her mouth in a soft whisper.

"Eleven. We have an hour." He walked over and sat down on her cot. "Tell me again how we're going to pull this off?"

"When Ahmad comes to the room, I'm going to take him to the window and show him the beginning of the eclipse." Liz rose and stood by the small window ledge and tilted her head to make sure the angle of the sun was correct. "We'll have about three minutes of total coverage. Things will cool off and I'll tell him that Horus has come."

"If he doesn't believe you, then what?" Donnie said. The corner of his mouth twitched.

"Then it's up to you to distract them enough with some sort of explosion, and we'll make a run down the steps." Liz pointed to the black pouch around his waist. "Use some of that flash powder, something to avert his attention. I've been told you have plenty.

We'll only go as far as the first room, then leave tonight after dark. I just want him to think we disappeared."

Rayhan broke into her explanation. "It isn't safe to travel at night, Liz. I've explained to you before there are robbers on the road, especially out this far."

"We have no choice. We'll just have to be careful." She turned to Donnie, who had part of the contents of his bag strewn across her cot. He measured out portions of two powdery substances. "Do you know how to hot wire the jeep?"

"Well, unless someone slips you a key, I don't have any other answer for you."

"Do you?" she demanded.

"Sure." He didn't look up. "I won't have time to access the rear of the vehicle's key-start mechanism, so I'll just smash it to get to the rotation switch."

"Sounds like you've done that before. Like only you could." Liz said. "We'll have to apologize to Richard and fix it for him when we get back." Liz pointed to the curtain. "Hurry, Donnie, you don't have much time."

She walked around the room and checked if they had everything. Liz didn't want it to seem as if they'd packed to leave, but there were certain things they had to have, the most important, the Book of Hours. "Where's the prayer book, Rayhan?"

"Safe in the basket; we took it down last night."

She walked over to the Egyptian blanket, the makeshift curtain which partitioned the room, and fingered the fine woven material where the corner had been ripped into bandages for her arm. "I hate to leave this. It was a beautiful gift."

Jahi pulled on Rayhan's shirt and had him bend down close. Jahi whispered something into Rayhan's ear that caused him to grin.

"Jahi says his mother will make you a thousand blankets when he gets home."

She went over to Jahi and smoothed down his dark brown hair. He turned his face toward her as Liz spoke. "You're worth thousands of blankets, Jahi. I'm sure she misses you and is worried. You'll be home very soon."

"Lizzz?" Jahi questioned.

"After we go…" Liz began, but stopped. She didn't want Jahi to accidentally give away their plans. "After we go back to Cairo, I'll take you to your mama."

"Then what will you do?" Rayhan asked.

"Go home with Addie and Gary. I may still have a job. If not, I have enough connections to find something in antiquities."

"I'm sure you could find something here." He walked to stand beside her. "I wouldn't mind if you had a job once—" Rayhan stopped.

"Once what, Rayhan? Once we were married? That was what was supposed to happen, but you think you did something wrong by loving me, then you cast what we had aside. How am I supposed to feel?"

Rayhan reached for her. "I'm sorry. I felt putting Jahi in danger was my fault."

"If it was anyone's fault, it was mine. We aren't being punished because something happened to Jahi, but I can't be with someone who gives up on what's important."

"Liz, I didn't. It may have appeared that way to you, but I do know what's important." Rayhan's words flowed to her in a whispered plea. "I tried to tell you earlier. My family is the most important thing in my life, and I want you to be part—"

Donnie came back into the room and interrupted their conversation. He picked up the packet he'd made, straightened the cot, and said, "It's time."

Liz took the boy's hand and delivered him to his cousin. She looked at Rayhan and spoke quietly, "We'll talk later." Then she knelt down. "Jahi, stay with Rayhan. In the next few minutes, the moon will come between us and the sun." Liz didn't want to scare the boy, but she wanted Jahi to comprehend what might happen and not be alarmed if they became separated. "It's going to be dark and you and Rayhan need to stay together. I'll stay with Donnie. Don't say or do anything. Do you understand?"

Jahi's eyes widened. He nodded his head and took his place beside Rayhan. She crossed the room and placed her forearm on the window ledge. Liz bent to see the angle of the sun and observed the moon had begun its path. A small crescent bite blackened the celestial fireball.

Her stomach boiled as she tried not to think of what might happen when she faced Ahmad. Would he kill them if they didn't escape? Or did Ahmad still need her? The taste of salty fear rose in her mouth. It had to work. She had to have faith not only that would God protect them, but in herself, and she desperately wanted to believe in Rayhan.

The door slammed against the wall and Ahmad roared, "Who are you to predict such things?"

With a quick movement of her hand, Liz motioned for Rayhan and Jahi to move back toward the curtain. She shuddered at Ahmad's explosive entrance and shifted to confront him. "I did not predict this, Ahmad, it is written in your own ancient tongue. I only told you it would happen. In the next few minutes, the sun will disappear and the sky will be black. Can't you feel the coolness? Horus is coming."

Ahmad crossed the room and stood inches in front of her. She felt his hot breath and stared into his demonic eyes.

"I don't believe you," he growled.

Liz inhaled and summoned a calm reply. "It doesn't matter if you believe me or not, Ahmad, it's happening. Go to the window and see for yourself."

At that point, Rayhan's six-year-old charge couldn't control himself any longer. "Lizzz."

They all turned to where he pointed. On the wall, in paint flecked with pyrite, a hieroglyphic of a falcon with a large, flaming ball in its talons glimmered before them. Liz didn't know why she hadn't seen it before. The process mixture of the Egyptian Blue must have been wrong, which caused the original painting to disappear over time. When the cuprorivaite element of the paint dissolved, it left the glittering quartz sand, which could only be seen in the half-light left from the sun. The drawing gave them an unexpected edge. Ahmad turned from her to view the wall. He then rushed to the window as the coronium appeared around the edges of the solar body. The loops of magnetic flux swelled from the surface and filled with hot plasma.

Ahmad let out an aberrant, guttural sound. He turned and stepped toward her. Liz nodded to Donnie, who threw the packet he'd prepared, and the four of them rushed behind the partition.

The substance Donnie had mixed caused a larger explosion than Liz expected, and they entered the hatch and closed it without pursuit. Liz handed Rayhan the ankh. "Open the door and wait for us in the room. I'll knock three times. If we don't come soon, go on with the plans. Find your way back to Cairo and tell Richard what happened. Tell him where Addie and Gary are."

Rayhan opened his mouth in protest.

"Go! I'm staying with Donnie."

"No. Both of you come with me." Rayhan pointed the beam of his flashlight down the corridor.

Liz picked up the boy and moved to stand on the flat, sandy soil at the bottom of the tunnel. Rayhan and Donnie stood on the steps in total darkness. Donnie stuck his thumb on the flint of a disposable lighter and he handed Rayhan the cord that dangled on one side of the hinged door. "Here," he said, "pull with a slow, steady hand and this will draw sand across the door and cover the opening."

Liz now understood the cardboard contraption he had made. The men maneuvered the string toward the end opposite the hinges and pulled sand across the hatch. They were almost finished when one side of the cord snapped and went slack. "Donnie?" she whispered, perspiration dampened her lip.

"It will have to be good enough." He pulled his side through, along with the cardboard panel, and discarded it on the floor then motioned toward the corridor. "Run."

Her heart pounded an echo through her body as they ran down the tunnel. Her movements played out in slow motion while they sprinted toward the door, which took less than a minute. Only once did she glance back into the darkness. *Let the hatch stay closed.*

Liz pointed to the ankh and Rayhan unfastened the lock, which allowed them entrance. She shook off the nerve-grating escape from Ahmad and drank in their first moments of freedom. "We've made it."

"We're not out of here yet," Donnie's face, illuminated by the sputter of lamp he'd just lit, showed the slightest hint of worry. "It's a long way between the opening at the top of the stairwell and the jeep."

God wouldn't have delivered them from Ahmad and brought her so close to finding Addie and Gary to abandon them now. Her strength and courage renewed, Liz knew they'd manage.

Jahi and Rayhan sat against the wall as Rayhan told another one of his stories. He moved his hands in expressive gestures, and Jahi giggled, unaffected by the afternoon's events. Liz shook her head. Even now, she found it difficult to accept that these quiet, unpretentious people had opened up their hearts and put themselves in harm's way for two lost Americans. They lived by their faith, and that belief could cost them their very lives. With their unfettered gift of courage and servitude all of them had chosen to put her crisis before anything else. They had asked for nothing and given so much, especially Rayhan.

Her thoughts drifted back to Talmar and Ini—were they in danger because of her? And Richard? He could lose his job at the Embassy. Liz felt he had been duty-bound to assist her, perhaps out of his grief and guilt; but the others delivered a gift from God, a gift of great value. Their lives were in peril. Only a week ago they had all been strangers. A quick prayer escaped her lips. *God, grant us all one more day.*

Liz brought herself back to the present and Donnie's concerns. "We'll make it. If anyone is watching, I'm sure we can figure out a way to find the jeep. Besides, we're walking up the very steps that promise to show us the light," she said and pointed to the message engraved into the stone in the stairwell.

"When we leave, Liz, then what?" Donnie sat at the table with the lamp, the contents of his bag dumped out. He dug through the objects as he searched for something.

She moved from where she stood and joined Donnie. "Rayhan? How long will it take us to get to Alexandria?"

"About five hours, perhaps faster traveling at night."

"Are you familiar with the Church of Alexandria?"

"Yes. We make a pilgrimage there every year. Jahi has been, too."

"We'll drive to Cairo." Liz said to Donnie, who continued to search for something. "I don't suppose you have another disposable cell phone?"

"Yeah, I brought two. I figured we'd have to ditch one of them along the way," he said, but remained constant at his task.

Liz grew impatient. "What are you looking for now?"

"I had this little bag of paper clips. I can't seem to find them."

"Paper clips?"

"Well, since we're stuck in here until dark, I was going to make some airplanes for Jahi. Paper clips weigh the nose down and they'll fly well in here with the tall ceilings and all."

"Paper airplanes?" She shook her head in disbelief.

"It will pass the time and take his mind off..." He stopped. "What were you saying about a cell phone?"

"We'll have to stop for gas in Cairo, and I want to contact Richard so he can meet us there. We may need to change cars. He might be able to pull some strings to help us locate Addie and Gary."

"Ah. Here they are. Now, I need some paper. Can I use some from Gary's notepad? It's in the basket."

"Sure. Use the blank pages."

"I need to speak with Richard, too." Donnie stood and walked over to the basket. He shuffled through the wicker container until he found the tablet, sat down beside her, and handed her the notebook. "You tear out the pages, then I won't mess up anything you want to keep."

Liz thumbed past the note Gary had written and the detailed entries on Horus and the walk in the light. Then she tore out several blank pages and handed them to Donnie.

"Here. Is that enough?"

"That will be fine. Want to join in?"

"No. We have several hours to wait. Go ahead, occupy Jahi."

Donnie leaned close to Liz and whispered in her ear. "I'll keep Jahi busy for a while. You and Rayhan need to talk. He loves you, you know."

"When did he tell you this?"

"We had a long talk while we moved the rocks last night." Donnie paused and then continued to whisper to her. "It's obvious. He knows he messed up, Liz. It's hard for him. He's walking a tightrope between his customs and ours."

Liz glanced up at Donnie, surprised he'd come to understand Rayhan. "Okay. I'll talk to him."

Lost in thought, she listened, but heard nothing from overhead or the hallway. She assumed they were about twenty feet underground and insulated from any noise. Ahmad and his men had either been so frightened by the eclipse that they did not search their room further or the sand over the hatch had worked and they hadn't seen the opening. It didn't matter what had happened, gratitude flowed through her, and she felt safe for the first time in days.

Donnie had assembled his gauzy-winged aircraft on a long, wooden bench. He and Jahi busied themselves in the fine art of defying gravity. Rayhan sat on the floor with his back against the wall. Liz searched and found a quiet place for herself at the small table near the entrance. When she placed the notepad on the table top, written on the back cover in Gary's tight, neat penmanship, "The journey of faith begins with one small step."

Liz rose and walked to Rayhan. He tilted his face up to her when she reached him. She put out her hand and he took it in his. Rayhan scrambled to his feet and they walked to an alcove away from Donnie and Jahi.

CHAPTER TWELVE

LIZ AND RAYHAN moved to an area where they could be alone. Her wound forgotten, she stretched her injured arm to feel for the wall in the dimly lit room and crumpled forward in pain.

"Are you all right?" Rayhan put his hand on her good shoulder.

"Yes." Liz rubbed the area near the bandage. "My range of motion is compromised more than I thought, but I'm okay." She glanced around the small entrance. The room where they'd left Jahi and Donnie had high ceilings and seemed cavernous compared to the ante room where Rayhan had moved the bookcase and they'd found the stairs to freedom. Somehow, the smaller room of the two seemed perfect for their intimate conversation, and her heart raced, anxious to speak with Rayhan, but terrified to hear his words.

Rayhan whispered, "I do know what is important."

Liz tampered down the storm raging within her in the hope she wouldn't sound hysterical. "Our customs set us apart, Rayhan. I thought I knew enough and could understand. Because of Jahi's incident with the snake, you decided it was better to dump me." Liz swallowed hard before she continued. She had to tell him what weighed on her heart. She loved him. *Just when did it happen? When she first heard his voice on the phone? When she saw him at the airport?* "It isn't your fault Jahi snuck into the back of the jeep and came with us. None of us could control what happened."

Rayhan pulled her into his arms. "I feared I was being punished. I know now that I wasn't. It was my own guilt." He kissed her forehead. "Last night when Donnie and I came down here to move the rocks, we talked for a long time. We prayed together, and I realized God did not punish me for following my heart."

"Your uncle does not approve of our relationship, and neither will most of your friends or the people here. Are you ready to give up your life here and come to the States with me if it comes to that?" Liz stepped out of his embrace. Her heart pounded in her chest and tears began to prick her eyes.

He took her hands and brought them to his lips and kissed her fingertips. "Are you ready to come here and live with me and give up all you know?"

They both whispered, "I am" and, as they melted into each other's arms, her heart beat against his chest, the rhythm in fusion with his. They had sealed themselves to each other and they would find a way, somehow, to be together. She felt his fingers caress her cheek and she pulled herself from the safety of his arms. "We need to think about getting out of here."

"I know. I want to show you something."

"What?"

"I need the prayer book from the basket," Rayhan said. He took her hand and walked back to the larger room. Frantic, he dug through their belongings twice, then put his head in his hands.

"What is it?" she asked.

"It's gone. I've been studying the layout of the monastery from the drawings in the back of the Book of Hours." He stopped. "I placed it in here myself, last night."

Rayhan rushed past her toward Donnie and Jahi. She reached them as Rayhan said, "Donnie, did you take the Book of Hours last night?"

"Didn't you pack it up before we came down here?" Donnie asked.

Rayhan didn't answer and crossed the room to the boy. Rayhan squatted down in front of him. "Jahi, did you take the book?"

Jahi's eyes filled with tears as he nodded to his cousin.

Rayhan hugged him. "Where is it?"

"On my cot," Jahi whimpered.

"I have to go after it." Rayhan rose and left the room

Liz found him sitting in a small niche near the door. She moved closer to him and chose her words with care. "No." Fear gripped her as she leaned against a table for support. "We're almost out of here. We're going to be there in a few hours. Why do you need to see it now?"

"I've been studying the diagrams of the secret rooms. I need the layout of the church at Alexandria."

The entire time they'd been captured, he had studied the Book of Hours. Liz thought he had been reading the prayers.

"What if you're caught?"

"I found a priest's robe and head covering over there in a chest." He pointed to the back of the large cavity where they'd taken refuge. "If Ahmad is still here, he won't recognize me, and I can find the book and meet you at the jeep. If I'm caught, I'll somehow make my way to Alexandria."

"Why is it so important? Can't you just wait until tomorrow?"

"It belonged to Talmar, an ancient copy and an important artifact. He trusted us with it, with a great secret. We cannot let it fall into the wrong hands. And I had found the layout of the secret room at the Church in Alexandria, where the priests would hide your friends. There is no sanctuary here in Egypt, no amnesty or protection." Rayhan stopped and brushed over her with his gaze. "Addie and Gary might be in danger, not only from Ahmad, but from our authorities, depending on who Ahmad is working for or with. I marked the page. If he or anyone else finds the book, they'll know exactly where to look."

Liz brought her hands to her face and choked down the panic growling in her throat. She moved away from Rayhan. How could she let him do this? Her stomach churned. They were almost free; Jahi just hours away from being delivered home. Liz turned back. "I can't let you risk your life again. You were caught once trying to help me." She tilted her head up and saw the persuasive expression in his eyes.

"I must. From the layouts of the other monasteries, the secret rooms are not shown, but I've noted a tiny mark on each one of the diagrams. It is in the exact location in the three churches we've been in this far." He drew his hand across his mouth before he continued. "Without the book, I won't know where to go when we're there."

Liz found the tablet and handed Rayhan a sheet of paper. "Show me."

He made a quick sketch. "Here, like this one." Rayhan's slender finger pointed to a sign on the page.

"It's marked on each of the floor plans and identifies the three secret rooms we've been in?" He nodded, as Liz analyzed a tiny letter "a" he had written on the diagram. "This is similar to the Greek letter, but the slant is different."

"It is the old fifth century Christian Egyptian alphabet. The letter means alpha in both languages."

"The beginning," Liz said just above a whisper. "I appreciate all you've done for us, but we'll find the location where Addie and Gary are being kept while we're there. I can't let you go back for the book—it could cost you too much." *It would cost me, also.*

A troubled pall crossed Rayhan's face, and he walked from the table to the bookcase that hid the stairwell. From the shelf he pulled an old, worn Bible. When he returned to her, he read, *"So let your light shine before men that they may see your good works, and glorify your Father who is in heaven."* He glanced up at her and continued, *"Blessed are they that suffer persecution for righteousness' sake: for theirs is the kingdom of Heaven."*

Rayhan stood frozen, quiet, and thoughtful, before he closed the Bible and brought it to his chest. He paused and studied her with a deep, leaden sadness. "Regardless of what happens with your friends, the sacred book must be returned. We cannot leave it behind. It will be my good work, my way to glorify God, my way to show you who I am."

"But you don't need to prove anything to me." Liz fought back tears.

"This is important to me. The book cannot fall into the wrong hands. It will be okay, Liz. I promise." Rayhan reached out and took her hand. He cupped her face and gazed deep into her eyes. "I'll be fine."

Liz gave in. "All right, but first we must discuss this with Donnie. The precision in the timing of your mission, and our escape must be exact. It is essential you be extremely careful."

Rayhan glanced through the door at Donnie and Jahi where they played on the floor, then back to her, his face darkened. "Jahi..."

"If anything happens, I'll take care of him. We'll take him back to Cairo and his family." Liz touched Rayhan's arm, her resolve faltered. *I hope he isn't doing this to please me. I must trust him that he wants to glorify God with his actions, but he doesn't have to go.* "Wait. Isn't there another way, without you endangering your life?"

"I have stumbled in my faith and my convictions. I endangered Jahi's life and most likely lost face with my family." Rayhan turned pleading eyes to her. "I want to prove I am a good man, worthy of you."

He took her into his arms and kissed her. She clung to him as trepidation rippled through her. *What if I lose him?* Terror rose within her at the thought that she might never see him again. Their tested love could reach an untimely end. Her eyes filled with tears and she rushed to say the words before her throat clogged with her sobs. "I love you."

She chose to support his decision and would defend him in the confrontation it would bring when they told Donnie.

"I love you too. I have since you walked off the plane and I'll love you forever, no matter what happens." He kissed her again then pulled away. "I'm going to do this."

DONNIE'S VOICE ECHOED his disapproval once Rayhan revealed his plans. "No. I'm serious about this, Rayhan. You cannot go back up there looking for a book. If Ahmad finds you, he'll kill you and could come after the rest of us." Donnie shot a heated glance in her direction, then turned back to Rayhan. "I won't let you."

"I've made up my mind, and I'll suffer the consequences. The secrets of the book must be protected." Rayhan stared Donnie down. The two men stood not more than a foot from each other, and Liz thought Donnie might take a swing at Rayhan. His resolute face turned in her direction and waited for her response.

She closed her eyes and shuddered. "Let him go," Liz insisted. "It's important to him."

"I don't like it and I don't mind saying so." Donnie's eyes clouded over with concern.

"The Book of Hours cannot fall into Ahmad's hands, and besides, I need it to find the secret room in Alexandria. It is essential to rescuing your cousin," Rayhan said.

Donnie softened. "Go ahead, but I won't give my approval if that's what you're looking for."

"Point taken. Now, how much longer do we have to wait until nightfall?" Liz changed the subject and hoped to quell their argument.

"It's about seven-thirty. We have an hour." He pivoted around to Jahi, who played on the floor. "We should feed the boy. I don't think there's enough food for the rest of us. We don't have a lot of water either, but it shouldn't take us long to return to Cairo, not the way I plan on driving."

Liz pointed Donnie to the table, then turned and spoke to Rayhan. "Come over here. We need to talk."

Once they were seated, Liz scrutinized both men. "I will be following your lead, Donnie. Jahi is my main concern during our escape, and I will take care of him. After we clear the opening to the stairwell, what should we do?"

"We will only be able to take what we can carry. The basket and its contents will have to be left. Rayhan, how long will it take you to find the book and then reach the jeep?"

"No longer than twenty minutes." Rayhan searched Donnie's eyes. Liz wondered if he wanted confirmation that his motives were understood. "I'm sorry, Donnie, I have to do this. Please understand."

"Just be safe. We need to leave here together and not have them follow us any too soon." Donnie shifted his gaze to Liz. "We should begin gathering what we want to take, prepare Jahi for what is about to happen, and move the shelves before Rayhan goes topside."

Jahi and Liz made a game of assembling their things while the men moved the bookcase away from the stairwell. Liz decided which of their meager possessions would be the most important to take and after she gave them to Jahi, he laid them in a straight row next to the basket. She took out the dried fruit and the bread left from that morning and told the boy he needed to eat. "Tomorrow, you'll be home. You'll see your Umm, your mother."

A lighthearted impish expression danced across Jahi's face, he smiled. "Tomorrow."

She could only hope she spoke the truth.

Rayhan had disappeared for a short time and returned in the priest's robe and hood. When he joined them, he reached down to Jahi, spoke to him briefly in Arabic, and walked toward the door. Rayhan turned and whispered to Liz, "I'll be back soon."

"God go with you," Liz said to the sound of wood scraping the threshold.

The door between her and Rayhan closed with a soft click as Liz felt Donnie's presence behind her. She turned around; a knot grew in her chest. Donnie's displeasure with Rayhan's decision had grown into a credible force. "Before you start in, you need to understand that Rayhan felt he had to do this to serve God. He sees it as his duty. I tried to talk him out of it, and I couldn't." Liz paused. "Before you get upset with me, try to consider his beliefs."

"I do, but this endangers us all. Did you think about that?"

"I did. You can't talk someone out of something if it's what they believe. It's better that he goes with our permission than for him to take off on his own and we find out later we left him behind. God will take care of him and us, Donnie. You have to understand that." Her belief in God had become the glue which held her together. Liz couldn't struggle anymore. She had to give it over.

Donnie took off his hat and drew his hand over his hair. He hesitated for a moment and rubbed his eyes with his thumb and forefinger, stopping to squeeze the bridge of his nose. "Okay. Let's get on with this. The clock is ticking."

CHAPTER THIRTEEN

Donnie went to the table and removed his waist pack. He assembled a few things and then put a multi-tool—a combination screw driver, pliers, and perhaps a knife and fork—into his front pants pocket. Liz tore Gary's notes from the pad of paper and with great care, folded them. She found a long, black sash in the bottom of the basket and fashioned herself a sling and inserted the notes inside, close to her body. Liz picked up the two foot square package and tied it in an old remnant of cloth that she and Jahi had prepared to hold their belongings.

Donnie and Liz climbed the steps and crouched at the entrance. The evening sky began to color with crimson tones that would soon give way to darkness. The moonless night lay out before them, the jeep straight ahead in their path.

"I'm going out first to hot-wire the jeep. You and Jahi stay here and I'll signal you when I'm ready. I'll start it up once you're there. Remember, make as little noise as possible." Donnie burst out of the opening, ran low to the ground, and jumped in the side of the vehicle.

No more than five minutes had elapsed since he disappeared behind the side panel, but it seemed an eternity passed before he sat, took off his Stetson, and waved in her direction. Jahi and Liz scrambled out of the stairwell and ran across the sixty-foot expanse from the safety of their hiding place and into the vast openness of the desert evening. Liz kept the boy in front of her as she crouched over him and provided him with what protection she could.

Once they were seated, Donnie and Liz in the front and Jahi on the floorboard between her feet, Donnie fired up the engine. No sign of Rayhan. Liz turned around toward the monastery and back to Donnie.

"I'm sorry, Liz. We have no choice. We have to leave him." Donnie lowered his head, then placed it on the steering wheel for an instant. "He knew the risks."

One lone tear slipped down her cheek. She reached down and pulled Jahi close to the seat between her feet. "I know," Liz gasped. Her heart ripped from her chest, a corporeal pain burned from within. *Within a week I have lost my best friend, fallen in love with Rayhan, and found myself on this incredible adventure. Now I must face the possibility of losing him, too.* Liz turned to Donnie and then once more back at the monastery. "Can we wait just a few more minutes?"

Jahi reached to her from the floor. "Rayhan?"

She didn't know what to say to the boy, and gratitude flooded her when she didn't have to explain the whereabouts of his cousin for long. As Donnie began to drive off, a loud whistle came from the side of the building, and Rayhan ran, robes flapping, toward them. "Donnie, wait!" echoed from Rayhan's lips and into the hollowness of the night.

Liz grabbed Donnie's arm. "He's coming," she whispered.

The muffled sound of harsh-toned voices floated over the dunes and met their ears. Rayhan's whistle had not gone unnoticed and her apprehension churned into a frenzy. Liz feared Ahmad hadn't left after the eclipse. She'd hoped he would have given up his desire to find her friends, but Ahmad's determination proved to be as strong as hers.

The loud crack of a rifle hastened Rayhan's pace as bullets hit the sand behind him. Donnie doubled back, and Rayhan dove for the jeep. Donnie gunned the engine and sand flew into the night sky.

"Yah, yah, yahhhh," came from Ahmad's lips as his legs gripped the sides of a powerful, Arabian stallion. The movement of Ahmad's hand commanded the whip with authoritative force, urging the horse toward them. Behind him, a covey of his rebel followers rounded the corner of the monastery at full speed.

"Get down!" Donnie yelled.

She bent over Jahi just as a shot shattered the windshield. The jeep fishtailed though the sand, found the road, and they sped toward Cairo.

Liz glanced over at the speedometer and the pointer on the gauge disappeared, buried in the right side of the dial. On edge, she wanted to convey her concern to Donnie, but decided to keep it to herself. The road splayed out before them, straight and even with no other traffic. They needed to put a substantial distance between them and Ahmad, and Donnie could accomplish the task.

Liz jerked back from the black hole of panic she'd tumbled into. Rayhan sat behind her, safe, and she moved her attention to Jahi, who had a death grip on her leg. Liz reached down and unwound his arms from her knee and pulled him to her lap. He nuzzled into her injured shoulder. She winced and moved him over to the other side, and he rested his head in the crook of her arm.

Rayhan had shed his priest's robes and sat in the back seat in silence. The darkened shadowy moon made it difficult to see his face, and she wondered if his heart had stopped racing. Liz turned toward him and yelled over the roar of the engine, "You okay?" She reached back and grasped his hand.

He leaned forward before he answered, "I think so." She felt the pressure as he squeezed her hand. *His hand didn't even shake. Amazing.*

"What happened?" she bent close to his ear to ask.

"I found the book without incident, but on my way out I saw Ahmad and his men far to the back of the monastery tending their horses in a shaded enclosure. That is probably why they did not hear or see you leave. I was able to walk along the side of the building, unnoticed, but when I whistled and started across the sand, they saw me."

"You ran pretty fast. I don't think I could have done that."

"Oh, you would if you had to. I felt the sting of the sand on my legs from the bullets that nearly hit near me. That hastened my departure." He leaned forward in his seat a little more. "I'm all right. How's Jahi?"

"He seems okay, just frightened like the rest of us."

Donnie, who had kept his eyes on the road and his foot on the accelerator, reached over and tousled Jahi's hair. They exchanged smiles, but neither one of them spoke.

The coolness of the desert evening caused an icy shiver to run the length of Liz's spine. Her shoulder pulsed, and when she touched the sleeve of her shirt, she felt a sticky dampness inside the sling. She had likely torn open the wound at some stage in their escape, but her main concern centered on Addie and Gary. *Would they be in Alexandria?* Liz was so certain that's where the clues led them. *What if they weren't there?* Liz prayed they hadn't given up on being rescued. "How much longer?" she questioned Donnie.

"If I can keep up this speed, no more than three hours." He glanced at the gauges—green, gleaming dials in the half-lit dashboard. "We have enough gas to make it to Cairo." Donnie reached into his bag and handed her a familiar black and silver rectangular object. "In about an hour, call Richard."

"What should I tell him?"

"I want a number of things. When you make the call, you'll repeat what I need. I'm still running things through my head. I'll let you know then." With that, Donnie fell silent and returned to concentrate on the road ahead.

Jahi crawled over the center console dividing the two front seats and curled up near Rayhan's side.

She rested her head on the back of the jeep's seat cushion and pulled her cap over her eyes. She pretended to sleep, but teetered on the edge of that black hole and prayed Addie and Gary were well in body, mind, and soul. She believed they'd all be together again. She thanked God for Rayhan's safe return. She wanted to take him in her arms, kiss him, and, as he had done to her, and tell him she would be by his side forever, no matter where that might be. But their situation prohibited her.

"Great," Donnie yelled into the night. "Just great." He veered the vehicle off the pavement and slowed on to the dirt shoulder.

Liz sat up in her seat and turned in his direction. "What are you doing? We can't stop now."

"I think I saw a flash of light back there. I'm not sure, maybe another set of headlights." He narrowed his eyes as he trained them on the rearview mirror. "We might have to take out across the open desert."

Liz jerked around and tried to spot what he'd seen. "Do you see anything?"

"No. Maybe I'm just getting tired, but there was something—a reflection, a glint. I don't know. I only saw it an instant." Donnie shifted in his seat and pushed back his hat. "I'm exhausted."

"Do you want Rayhan to drive?" Liz queried. "We could stop for a second."

"No. We'll…. Wait, there it is again." Donnie gripped the steering wheel with both hands. "Ahmad's back there. We're going to have to lose them." Donnie shot a quick glance out onto the side of the road, trying, Liz assumed, to find somewhere they could hide or make their way out into the desert and safety.

Rayhan reached over and put his hand on Donnie's shoulder. "Keep going. They won't catch us."

"How do you know that?" Donnie shouted. "They can't be more than a couple miles behind us."

"Because I had one of the priest's loosen the oil drain plug. They'll never make it to Cairo."

Liz turned in her seat and gave Rayhan a look of astonishment. "How did you manage that?"

"I had something to trade that the priest wanted. We made a deal," Rayhan shouted back in their direction. "He had to check out Ahmad's vehicle for him, so I asked a small favor."

"What did you trade him?" Her curiosity had gotten the best of her. "When did you have time to find this out?"

"I saw him in the hallway when I first entered the monastery. He recognized me and took me to the room where we stayed. While we were there, some of Ahmad's men were in the hallway. The priest and I assumed the position of prayer, and I asked him then." Rayhan sat back.

"What did you have to pay him for his favor?" Donnie yelled back over his shoulder.

Rayhan moved his leg in between the seats to show them his bare feet. Until that moment, Liz hadn't been aware of his lack of footwear.

"I gave him my shoes." Rayhan chuckled. "I had them sent from the States."

"I thought priests wore sandals." Donnie shook his head.

"They were. Designers to be exact."

"Ouch! I'll send you a new pair when we're home," Donnie called back to Rayhan. "Those must have set you back $200."

"Not quite. It's okay."

"No. I'll send you a pair, maybe two. There's a store that carries them not far from my house." Donnie glanced again at the side mirror. "I don't see them anymore. It must have worked." He turned to Liz. "Call Richard."

Liz punched in Richard's number and waited for him to answer. His home phone rang ten times, and she'd almost given up when a muffled noise on the other end returned Richard's sleepy voice.

"Richard, it's Liz McCran. We're in trouble."

"Liz. Thank God, you're safe. I've been frantic."

"Donnie wants a few things. Could you help us?" Then she added, "We don't want to cause you any problems."

"Never mind that now. You must understand, I couldn't become involved before, but if you're in danger, it changes things. I'll do as much as I can. What is it?"

Liz searched Donnie's face and repeated his words. "A vehicle, ready to go to Alexandria, with tinted windows if possible, Jahi's parents, a change of clothing for Donnie, Rayhan, and myself, food and water, and an Embassy escort. If you can't come, maybe someone else." She paused. "Oh, and shoes for Rayhan."

"What?"

"Never mind. I'll explain later, just tell Al Abdul to bring Rayhan a pair of sandals."

"I can do that," Richard eagerly said into the phone. "How much time do I have?"

"About an hour. Where should we meet?" Liz paused. "I'm sure Ahmad has connections."

"Ahmad Lasammi? He's dangerous, Liz." Richard's voice became agitated. "How do you know of him?"

"He held us captive for a couple of days. He's somewhere on the road to Cairo with a blown engine, thanks to Rayhan."

"Well, that won't stop him for long. Meet me at the church in Cairo. It is safe there."

"Richard, one more thing. Could you bring a doctor? I think I might need someone to check my shoulder." Liz closed the cell phone before he could ask any more questions.

CHAPTER FOURTEEN

DONNIE TOOK HIS eyes off the deserted highway and pulled to the side of the road.

Liz rubbed the sleep from her eyes and asked, "What are you doing?"

He didn't answer and reached over to the back seat and jostled Rayhan. "Hey, wake up and take the wheel for a while."

Rayhan shook himself awake and moved the sleeping Jahi from his lap. "Are you okay?"

"I just need some sleep. Wake me just outside of Cairo and then I'll be fine."

Liz and Donnie exited the vehicle and Rayhan jumped from the back of the jeep and slid into the driver's seat. Liz shook her head and wondered why the sudden change of plans. "Wait a minute," she said to Donnie and pointed to the back of the vehicle. She pulled him out of earshot of Rayhan. "I don't get it, you're fine."

"Did you and Rayhan make up?"

"When did that become your business?" She bristled. She had a sudden desire to guard her relationship with Rayhan. *Why do I want to hide my love now? We'd been out in the open about the engagement. We've even posed as man and wife.* She turned back to catch a quick glimpse of Rayhan and smiled as tears filled her eyes. Their love had become real and tangible, even though they'd spent little time alone, never really courted, and hardly ever kissed. Electricity generated through them both when he held her close. Yet she seized in her heart guardianship of their love. *It had become a special secret.*

Her mother had told Liz when she had her first high school crush that sometimes a love becomes so great between two people no one else can break the aurora surrounding them, the invisible barrier shielding them from the world. Her parents had such a love, and now Liz and Rayhan had built their fortress.

"I was hoping my little talk with him did some good, that's all."

"He told me you two spoke last night." Liz changed the subject. "Stopping like this is stupid," she said as they walked the short distance to the jeep. She gestured to the back seat. "Climb in, go to sleep, whatever." Reaching to touch his arm, she whispered, "Oh, and Donnie, thanks."

Once they were underway, Rayhan glanced at her, then leaned over and spoke, his voice just above a whisper. "Liz?"

"I think I may have opened up the wound. My shirt's damp and plastered against my skin." Liz saw his jaw set. "No. Don't even think it. I'm going, even if it is on a stretcher."

"I wasn't going to say anything. I know better. I'm just worried."

"I'm fine. Richard can have someone look at it and we'll be on our way." He ran his hand through his hair and Liz picked up on his frustration. "Really."

"It wouldn't matter if you weren't. You're too stubborn." He reached over and pulled her baseball cap down over her eyes. "Just let me know before you pass out or something."

"You'll be the first." Liz smiled at him in the dark. She confirmed Donnie had closed his eyes. "I think they're both asleep," she whispered.

"Are you sure?"

"Jahi hasn't moved, and I think Donnie's nodded off, too."

Rayhan took her hand and brought it to his lips. "This has been an incredible journey. We still must find your friends."

"How much longer?" Liz asked

"Forty-five minutes, tops. I can't take the jeep down the narrow road to the church. Can you walk that far?"

"I'm okay. Once we give Jahi back to his parents, I can breathe a little easier. We'll just have to worry about ourselves and whatever trouble we get into."

Rayhan glanced back over his shoulder at the pair sound asleep in the back seat. "Have you thought this over at all? What are you going to do?"

"I'm not sure. I don't expect it to be easy. I'm assuming you can find the secret room, if that's where they're keeping Addie and Gary. I'm sure Ahmad or one of his group will be there to meet us. I don't know…we'll just see how it goes."

"You want me to do something? I still have a case of light bulbs and a small amount of the exploding powder." Donnie mumbled from the back seat.

"A case of light bulbs?"

"Yeah." He grinned. "They sound like guns going off if you drop them just right."

Liz thought for a moment. "I have an idea. It may not work, but we have to have some sort of a plan."

"What? Is it feasible?"

"I don't know. I hope so." She paused. "When we arrive, we'll split up. I want Richard to go in with me, you take that case of light bulbs and stay outside, and Rayhan can find Addie and Gary." Liz moved back in the seat and pulled the damp cloth away from her skin. The sight of the bandage soaked in blood made her weak. "If we run into trouble, you can start throwing the light bulbs."

"That's a pathetic plan, Liz." He glanced in her direction. "Then what?"

"I don't know, Donnie. I'm not sure who'll be there, friend or foe. I just don't know."

"We're walking into this blind. They have weapons, we don't. I don't think that me throwing light bulbs around is going to do much. Do you?"

Rayhan tapped her shoulder. "Is tomorrow Wednesday?"

"Watch the road. I think tomorrow is Wednesday." She turned to Donnie. "Isn't it? Why?"

"It is close to the Feast of Ascension, forty days after Easter. If we go immediately to Alexandria tonight, the streets will already be packed with worshipers."

"Perfect," Donnie chuckled. "Then I have all I need."

"What are you going to do?"

"Don't worry. I have a plan now. You two find Addie and Gary, and we'll be on our way out of Alexandria before anyone realizes we were there."

THE WINKING LIGHTS of Cairo created a welcoming glow in the distance and Liz hesitated to ask Donnie any further questions. She had no idea how to foil Ahmad a second time. Donnie's ideas were a little offbeat, but he'd already proven they could work.

The jeep found its way into the city and moved with mechanical dexterity down the narrowing street to the church. Finally, Rayhan parked the vehicle and they walked the remaining quarter of a mile on an old, cobblestone road. Donnie carried Jahi, who had slept the last hour, and Liz leaned into Rayhan as he supported her. They neared the church where a candle flickered in the window.

When they reached the large, wooden door, Donnie placed his free hand against the thick, smooth plank. He nudged it open and Talmar stood in the narthex.

"Keefic," he whispered. "Yel-la."

Rayhan's staccato translation met their ears. "He welcomes our return, but we need to hurry."

Richard stood at the front of the chapel, along with Jahi's parents and another American man. Richard moved in her direction. He held out both arms and pulled Liz into an unexpected embrace. "After you told me of Ahmad, I didn't think we'd see you again."

Her knees wobbled and she sought out Rayhan. "I was afraid I might not see you again, either." Her voice quivered and she walked in the direction of Jahi's parents. "I'm so sorry."

Donnie motioned for Amisi to join them, and she moved to his side, nearer her son. Al Abdul lifted Jahi into his arms.

"I trust he wasn't too much of a burden," Al Abdul said, his voice stiff and noncommittal. "I hope you find your friends and you all return to America."

Tears stung Liz's eyes as Jahi's parents turned to leave. She had failed to win Al Abdul's approval, and she feared she might never see Jahi again. He'd awake tomorrow in his own bed, and she'd be gone. He'd carved a place in her heart that she would never forget, and she only hoped he'd remember her, too, and that maybe someday they'd meet under different circumstances.

Rayhan placed his arm around her. "Wait. She isn't returning to America, Uncle Abdul. She's staying here with me as part of our family. If you do not approve, then I shall go with her."

Al Abdul glared at them and spoke through clinched teeth. "I do not think that is wise. You," he said, his eyes burning straight into Liz, "risked the life of my son."

"No. She didn't. Jahi was a stowaway and we had no idea he was with us," Rayhan told his uncle. "If any one of us is responsible for Jahi being brought home safely, it is Liz. She rescued him more than once."

Amisi put her hand on Al Abdul's arm and searched his face with beseeching eyes. Al Abdul glanced between Liz and Rayhan and, at last, back down at his son, asleep in his arms. "All right. I approve, but—" Al Abdul was cut off by a flashing glare from his wife. He turned to Liz and spoke. "Be safe in Alexandria and bring Rayhan back to us, too." Amisi and Al Abdul left the church and above her veil, Liz saw Amisi's eyes twinkle with a smile.

"Liz." Richard placed his hand on her shoulder and directed her toward the other American gentleman. "This is Doctor Bain. He works in a children's clinic here, but he supplies most of the medical needs for the Embassy staff." Richard pointed to her bloodstained shirt. "I assume that's why you needed him. Let the doctor see your arm."

Liz followed the men into a hallway and out of the chapel before Richard spoke again. "Can we talk while he dresses your shoulder? There is a private area in the back. I'll sit outside the door and explain what I can do for you. I had Al Abdul relay your wishes to Talmar and he'll update Rayhan and Donnie as to what will happen when you reach Alexandria."

Liz entered the small room and positioned herself on a stiff, folding metal chair, where she stripped off her shirt. The grimace on the doctor's face told her the news wouldn't be good.

"You seem to have torn open the wound, but I guess you knew that, or you wouldn't have asked for me."

"How bad is it? It isn't going to stop me. I want you to know that."

"Okay, little lady. I'm just going to patch it up and examine you. I wasn't going to stop you from doing anything. The wound is deep, but clean. You've had good care so far. The plastic wrap probably saved your life."

"My friend, Donnie, thought of that. In fact, he's thought of a lot of things."

"Liz?" Richard shuffled outside the door. "Are you sure Addie and Gary are in Alexandria?"

"If they aren't, then I don't have a clue." *Or any hope*, Liz thought for an instant. But she couldn't think that way. *God give me hope and strength and courage. Give it to all of us.* "I was given several indications they would be there."

Richard cleared his throat and Liz saw his shadow outside the door. "He could hold the priests captive if Ahmad reaches there first. I can't call ahead on a supposition. My jurisdiction only reaches so far. I want to help you, but it has to be done with the utmost care."

"Ouch," Liz groaned as the doctor bound the wound tighter than she'd expected. "We won't do anything to cause you any problems, Richard, I promise."

"What are you going to do?"

"Donnie has figured something out, but I want you to go with us. Rayhan seems to think he knows where Addie and Gary are. You and I can deal with whomever we need to while the two of them are working out their plans." Her gaze went to the doctor, who studied her shoulder. She reached out and put her hand on his arm. "Will you come, too? I think Gary may be hurt."

Richard broke in before the doctor could answer. "No, Liz. He can't. If Addie and Gary need medical help, it can be arranged in Alexandria. We can't have the fine doctor in any deeper than he already is."

The doctor turned to leave the room after he finished wrapping her shoulder. "Thank you," tumbled from her lips. He gave her a hesitant, fatherly smile when he reached the door. "I won't forget your kindness."

Liz strained to understand the muffled voices of the two men, then Richard spoke up. "There are clean clothes for you on the table. Donnie and Rayhan should be ready. You need to go."

"Richard, you never told me what we were going to do."

"The car Donnie wanted is parked in the back of the church. You'll drive to Alexandria and be there sometime around midnight. I don't know if you can do anything before morning or not. The streets are packed for the feast, and you'll have to approach on foot."

"Rayhan warned us of that, but I think that Donnie wants to use the crowds of people to his advantage."

"Quick. Change your clothes." Richard walked away from the door and his footsteps echoed in the hallway.

To her surprise, Liz had a tunic and traditional head covering lying on the table. She drew her arm with a slow deliberate move through the sleeve and pulled the garment into place. She slid into sandals and joined the men. Donnie and Rayhan were dressed in traditional garments as well—loose-fitting shirts, ballooning, white pants, and sandals. Rayhan showed Donnie how to wrap his head.

Richard stood by the side door, the keys to the car in his hand. "Your rooms have been emptied and your things sent home. In the back seat of the car there is a briefcase with four tickets to San Francisco."

Startled by what he had said, Liz turned and stared at him. "You aren't coming, are you?"

"I can't, Liz. No one must know that I had any part in this. The ramifications of all of this reach far more than you know. If your friends are where you think they are, then find the airport as quickly as possible. As far as I or anyone else involved knows, you were never here."

"But...what if we need your help?"

"You've done fine so far. It's in God's hands now."

"I can never thank you enough—you know that." Liz moved to Richard and hugged him with her good arm. "What about Rayhan?"

"He can drive you to the airport. I've arranged for him to leave the car in the parking lot. He will be picked up and brought back to me at the Embassy. I've made plans for him until this all blows over. No one knows that, either."

"Why did you decide to help us?"

"Your plight touched my heart. I wrestled with my involvement, but once you were in danger I had to step in. Rayhan has been such an asset to me during my assignment here. I had to help him, help all of you."

"Bless you." The words stuck in her throat as they said their goodbyes. "If I need to find Rayhan, will I be able to do that?"

"Maybe. I'm not sure." Richard eyed her. "He'll be safe." Then Richard smiled and Liz knew he understood. "I'm certain we can make the necessary adjustments to his security. He's a good man, Liz."

"I know."

RAYHAN DROVE WHILE Donnie and Liz occupied the back seat. Richard's wife, Inez, had packed enough fruit and sandwiches to feed them twice over, along with several small bottles of water. They were stopped once at a check point and through what Liz could understand of the conversation, Rayhan told the officer they were on their way to the Ascension Feast.

The guard grumbled in Arabic and let them pass.

"What did he say?" Donnie asked.

"Christians." Rayhan answered. "They don't like our holy days, but they let us celebrate them. It's a trade off. Both groups honor the others' days of worship."

They arrived in Alexandria just after midnight. Rayhan drove through the throng of worshipers which, at the late hour, had not dissipated. The building sat illuminated by spotlights and shone white and brilliant, silhouetted against the night sky. Because of the festival goers, Rayhan parked in an open lot and they pushed through the crowds toward the church.

"Can you walk the two blocks, Liz?" Rayhan queried as they moved along with the masses. "Can I help you?"

"I'm fine. We shouldn't talk to each other, just walk."

Rayhan grabbed her arm. "Stay with Donnie. Don't be the brave one. Let me or him. You must be safe. I could not go on without you." He gazed into her eyes, but did not give her time to answer before he stepped into the crowd.

Donnie and Liz followed as Rayhan wove in and out of the pilgrimage. Dressed as they were, the trio blended in. They walked past a policeman and Donnie stumbled into him, righted himself, and bowed in apology.

"Watch it. You're going to get us caught," Liz whispered.

"No. I'm not." He grinned at her from under his keffiyeh. "That was part of the plan."

Once inside the sanctuary, Liz looked around. The ancient pristine architecture heightened her keen admiration and marvel. The tall arched walls reached majestically toward the ceiling. The interior of their refuge was bathed in golden light and fine linen covered the altar. Serenity filled the chapel and the pungent smell of incense sweetened the air. The far wall had been draped in an intricate, woven golden cloth and behind the pulpit, a raised, ornately carved platform displayed a modern cross with an ancient inscription in each of the four corners.

Liz leaned over to Rayhan and asked, "Could you translate the words on the cross?"

"Jesus Christ, the Son of God." His voice hushed in awe.

A sudden wash of reassurance poured over her. They had come to the right place. Talmar's ankh, the original Egyptian Christian cross, his name imprinted on the back and spelling it backwards: Ramlat, the home of Sheba, the house of David, the lineage to Christ. The final clue: *use the ankh to find the sign.*

Rayhan moved up the center aisle of the church through the parishioners, crossed himself and walked to a priest who stood near the side of the altar. The priest's eyes widened and he nodded. Rayhan motioned for Donnie and Liz to join him and they followed down a small, constricted hallway. Rayhan raised his hand to his lips and whispered, "Stay here." Then he disappeared down a darkened passageway with the priest.

Liz trembled. Her head spun and lightheadedness swallowed her. I can't faint now. I have to hold on. In just a few hours, we will be on a plane going home. The passports are in the briefcase; another change of clothes in the car. No one will think we are any more than American tourists on a vacation. *Please God, let this work. I've come this far.* Addie and Gary are somewhere in this building, somewhere very close. *Let us see this to the end. Let it be Your will that we all return home safely and don't spend the rest of our lives here in prison, implicating all of those who have helped us.*

The curtains rustled behind them and Liz saw the glint of the blade in Ahmad's hand. She froze beside Donnie as Ahmad approached. Donnie slipped his hand inside his tunic and retracted a clinched fist. With another long step, Ahmad stood in front of them. He raised his knife and Donnie blew a fine mist of powder into Ahmad's face.

"Run, Liz. We have to find Rayhan. Hurry."

Her feet slapped the tile floor as they ran in the direction Rayhan had gone seconds before. The hallway, lined with tall marble pillars large enough to hide a man behind, allowed Donnie to duck between two columns and pull her to his side.

"Do you know where Rayhan went?"

"No. He knew where to find the secret room. That's all he told me."

Another commotion erupted at the end of the pathway and loud voices rolled toward them, shouting in Arabic. Donnie yanked a device he had apparently taken from the policeman out of his tunic and bound it to a transistor radio with a piece of duct tape. He flipped the police transmitter into the on position and turned the volume up on the transistor, then he tossed them out a nearby window. They continued on until the tiled floor joined another walkway.

"What did you do?" Liz asked between ragged gasps.

"Jammed the police communication," he said with such nonchalance, the action took on an odd normality.

"Great."

They ran through an archway and out into a garden at the back of the church. They cut through a sturdy hedge and were halfway across the grass when Liz saw Addie. She supported Gary's weight against her as they stumbled into the open.

Liz controlled her urge to raise her voice in victory. Addie stood not ten feet from her. They'd found them. Thoughts raced through her brain, but the only words she could utter were, "Where did you come from?"

"Back there." Addie motioned over her shoulder. "Someone let us out of the small room the priest had taken us to." Addie reached out to Liz. "How did you wind up involved in this?"

"We had to find you. Donnie is here, too." An immersion of thankfulness flooded the void threatening to devour her spirit. "Are you two all right? Are you hurt badly?" Liz asked, but froze. What happened to Rayhan? Had he been captured? She had to find him. She ran back into the church, but tumbled forward, caught by a tunic-clad arm. She turned her face to Donnie, who she thought had broken her fall, and Rayhan's face came into focus.

He embraced her. "I told you I'd be okay."

Addie shot Liz a questioning glance, and she winked. "We'll talk later."

"He is the one who rescued us," Gary said. "How did you know how to find us?"

"I have studied the layout of this church, but I wasn't expecting to find one of Ahmad's men standing sentry at your door."

When she noticed the cut on his face had been reopened and his cheek took on the purplish hue of a fresh bruise, she asked, "What happened to the guard?"

"Rayhan knocked him out somehow and locked him in the room where we were being kept," Gary offered.

Donnie grinned at Rayhan. "Sleeper hold?"

Rayhan nodded. "I don't know how long he'll be unconscious—that's all the more reason for us to hurry."

Liz swelled with unmistakable joy. She had never loved and admired a man as she did Rayhan, who had placed himself in danger, once again. He had rescued and protected Jahi, foiled Ahmad at the monastery and won her heart. Liz took Addie's hand in hers. They had survived.

Donnie and Rayhan supported the injured Gary between them and moved away from the church and into the swarm of revelers on the street. "Can you stand alone?" Donnie asked.

"Yes. Is it much further?"

"Not far. I need Rayhan for a minute." He yanked Rayhan in front of him as he pried a small metal plate from the light post.

"Cover me," he said. He had trimmed up his plastic library ID card with a Swiss army knife while he hurried down the street and shoved the pieces in the sprockets timing the traffic light.

Someone yelled at them in the distance, but Liz didn't turn around. Gary blacked out and crumpled to the pavement.

"Gary!" Addie screamed and leaned into Liz. They staggered to his side.

"I have him," Rayhan said, lifting Gary into his arms, and cradling him against his chest. The group hurried across the street, dodging cars on their way into the parking lot. Rayhan settled Gary into the front seat of the vehicle next to Addie and handed the keys to Donnie before he walked to the rear of the vehicle to join Liz.

Ahmad and a group of men approached the traffic light in a military vehicle. The light had turned red minutes before and jammed traffic coming from the direction he traveled. Donnie maneuvered away from the parking lot and out onto the street.

"Donnie!" Addie exclaimed. "It's good to see you. You two are going to have to explain all of this when we're home."

"There isn't much to explain. The Embassy called Liz, she called me, and here we are."

Addie patted her cousin's arm. "We were afraid no one would find us."

"Gary helped by leaving the notebook and combined with Liz's knowledge of Egypt, everything lead us to you. We had a lot of help, didn't we?" Donnie glanced into the mirror at Rayhan and Liz.

Rayhan took Liz's hand and kissed her palm, then cupped her face and brought it to his. Their lips touched and Liz forgot the world around her.

"Masha'allah." Rayhan nodded as he spoke to Donnie.

"What did he say?" Gary returned from the darkness that enveloped him and rubbed his forehead.

"God has willed it," echoed Rayhan and Liz.

Liz had learned so many times in her life—God's timing isn't our timing. But they weren't out of danger yet. Donnie entered the gate to the airport where several large, yellow barricades blocked their approach. Once the uniformed personnel spotted the vehicle, four armed Egyptian policemen moved from the guardhouse toward them. Her heart turned over and Liz gripped Rayhan's hand.

"We've been caught." Liz's voice wedged in her throat.

"It appears to be that way, doesn't it?" Donnie said. "We'll be deported, but Rayhan is probably going to prison."

Rayhan groaned. "Or worse." He looked at Liz and squeezed her hand.

"All over a piece of paper and an envelope I never delivered," Gary added.

Stunned, Liz leaned forward in her seat to speak, but Donnie voiced her exact thoughts. "You still have it?" He shook his head. "How did that happen?"

"Once it became a priority to move us out of danger, Moustafa's driver and the others never mentioned it. When I awoke at Moustafa's, my jacket was gone."

Liz laid her hand on Gary's arm. "Was it in your jacket pocket? How did you find it?"

"We were separated at Apa Bane, but right before we were taken there, Addie saw my jacket on the floor of the driver's car. The same car they used to rescue us. I folded the envelope and put it under the inner sole of my shoe."

Their quick conversation stopped with the light tap of a police baton on Donnie's window. He pushed the button and the panel glided downward. The officer spoke to Donnie in English and pointed to a side street flanked by police cars. Donnie nodded and slid the window shut.

"Now what?" Liz said.

Donnie's face grew apprehensive in the rearview mirror. "I have to fall in line with the police cars and follow them. Where, he didn't say."

Donnie turned to face Addie and Gary. "We may still need that letter. It might be essential. If we have to, we can bargain with it to make sure we all go home."

Donnie entered the side street behind the police procession; three in front of them and three in back. Liz's stomach roiled and her mouth went dry. She sat in silence. *How were they going to get out of this?* The parade of police cars stayed on the airport grounds, but drove to a distant building, away from the terminal. Another group of men, dressed in black suits, white shirts, and black ties came to the car when it reached the parking lot. One of them indicated for the group to stay in the vehicle.

When all the policemen exited the cruisers, they came to either side of the sedan and escorted the entourage into the building. Liz reached over and grabbed the briefcase with their tickets, astounded no one tried to take it. The two wheelchairs on the sidewalk surprised her even more.

Gary eased into one of the chairs, but Liz and Addie refused assistance. They entered the building in single file, flanked by the officers, and were led into a large, comfortable room. Liz saw a small jet on a thin stretch of tarmac as well as a gleaming black limousine with Egyptian flags secured to the front fenders. A quick breeze rippled across the landing strip. The flags fluttered.

A high-ranking police official, judging from the decorations on his uniform, stood at the end of the room. He walked toward them and cleared his throat. He examined each one of them, and Liz steadied herself. "Mr. and Mrs. Wright, I understand you were asked to deliver something on your visit to Egypt, and in so doing, caused a rather, shall I say, uncomfortable incident."

"Yes," Gary spoke. "It was my fault, sir. I had no idea what the letter contained and, unfortunately, both the person who gave it to me and I thought the information was harmless."

"The letter?" the officer questioned. His right eyebrow rose, which made his face take on a quizzical appearance. "Where is it now?"

Gary reached down and removed his shoe.

"But—" Liz began, stopped by a quick glance from Donnie. She feared Gary would give away their bargaining chip.

Gary made eye contact with Donnie, who nodded his head in agreement. The letter moved from Gary's hand to the official.

Liz cringed, worried for all of them, especially Rayhan. The man fixed his perplexed stare on Gary and Addie. "Do either of you read Arabic?"

They shook their heads. The officer turned the letter over in his hand, walked to the door, and whispered something to a waiting assistant. With finality, he said, "Then you did not know of the letter's contents." He handed the envelope to the man on the other side of the door.

"Well, now that the evidence is safe, we can move on to the pleasantries," the officer paused. "My name is Captain Badru. I have served many years with the Alexandria Police Department, the last ten of those years in pursuit of Ahmad.

"It seems you've done me a favor. In fact, you've done all of Egypt a favor. Ahmad and his men are a dangerous lot." Badru moved across the room to a large desk and picked up a stack of papers. "We captured Ahmad and his group in that traffic jam you created. He has a long history of, shall we say, less than admirable situations."

Liz found her voice and spoke up. "We may go, then?"

"Yes." Badru came to the front of the desk and sat down on the corner. "The original plan has been altered. An officer will take Rayhan to a safe location for a few weeks. Perhaps even out of the country. Once Ahmad's trial is finished and the rest of his men rounded up, then Rayhan may return to Cairo."

Liz glanced at Rayhan and a smile filled his face for the first time since they'd left the chapel. "The rest of us?"

"The jet will take you to Paris. There, arrangements have been made for Mr. Wright at the hospital, and Mr. Barnes and Miss McCran may fly to the States." Badru walked among them and handed out the necessary documents and papers they'd need. He turned once again to Gary. "There will be a doctor to attend you and Mrs. Wright when you reach France, if necessary, before transport by ambulance to the nearest medical facility." He pointed at Liz's arm. "You, too, Miss McCran."

"Thank you, Captain Badru," she said, her voice wrought with multiple emotions—relief, gratitude, love. Her friends were safe, their ordeal over. Liz's eyes settled on Rayhan. What would become of him? Their relationship? They'd fought hard to stay together. Now, circumstances they could no longer control would separate them.

"Once this is settled, you'll all return as the guests of the people of Egypt. As I said, you have done the nation a great favor by allowing us means to catch Ahmad."

"Captain Badru," Liz ventured. "Mr. Moustafa...was he..." She stopped, not wanting to hear.

The captain nodded, and with a solemn note to his voice, said, "I'm sorry, Miss McCran, I cannot tell you about Mr. Moustafa. It's classified." A hint of a smile caught his lips, which assured her Moustafa, too, had been taken somewhere out of danger.

The group made their way onto the tarmac where a car waited, and beyond it, the private jet. Donnie stopped and talked with the captain, then rushed to Addie's side. "Give me a quick smooch, cuz-o-mine. I'm staying here."

Liz glared at him in disbelief. "What?"

"I'm going with Rayhan and make sure he returns to Cairo in one piece," he said with a smile. "I owe you that much, Liz."

"Take care of yourself, then." She choked back a sob and whispered, "Thank you, Donnie, for everything." She brushed a tear from her face. "You did an amazing job, and I'm so thankful you're staying with Rayhan. I hope we'll continue to be friends." She gave Donnie a quick hug and left him to say his goodbyes to Addie and Gary.

Liz ran to Rayhan, who waited at the foot of the jet's boarding steps. "I guess this is it," she said.

Rayhan pulled Liz away from the others. The couple stood in the shadows, tucked under the wing of the plane. "I want to stay with you," she said and gripped his arm as her heart tore in her chest.

"It isn't safe. You know that." Rayhan brought her into his embrace and kissed her. "Donnie and I will watch out for each other. The time will pass quickly."

Liz rested her head against Rayhan's shoulder. "What about your uncle?"

"I think my aunt has set him straight, but I don't care. You're all that matters to me."

Their time grew short and Liz glanced back at the others. "I have so many unanswered questions, but I believe my quest brought me to you." She kissed him on the cheek. "From the very beginning, you touched my heart."

Rayhan took her hand. "Here, I have something for you," he said as he caressed her fingers. "Do you know about the betrothal ceremony?"

"Yes. Where rings are exchanged?"

Rayhan pulled the gold ring from his finger and slid it onto the middle finger of Liz's right hand. "This will have to do for now. Go back to the States with Addie and Gary. We will make plans for our wedding when it is safe."

"But where?"

"Inshallah, Liz. Wherever it is God's will."

Addie, Gary, and Liz boarded the plane, where she claimed a window seat and hoped to catch one last glimpse of Rayhan. The black limousine raced along beside them as she pressed her hand to the window. She caught sight of the gold ring mirrored against the glass and could no longer contain the tears she'd withheld. Liz remembered the final words of her pastor's sermon she'd heard long ago. *Let God work in your life according to His plan.*

The plane left the tarmac and Egypt grew smaller beneath them. Liz settled back in her seat, weaving her plans to return to the country and the man she loved.

EPILOGUE

THE DAYS TURNED into weeks and the weeks into months, and Liz had no contact from Rayhan. In fact, there had been no communication from Donnie or Richard. Liz began to think it had all been a dream.

Liz sublet her apartment before she left for Cairo and since she had no time frame on her impending marriage, she lived with Gary and Addie. Liz collaborated with Addie on a small project at the museum while Gary worked from home, and the Wright's annual July 4th party not only celebrated the holiday, but Gary's return to work. Liz sat in the shade under a large oak tree in the backyard. She thought about Rayhan every day, every moment, and when Addie approached her, Liz couldn't hide her mounting pain.

Addie handed her a glass of lemonade. "You'll hear something soon. Please come over and join us," she coaxed.

"I wouldn't be good company." Liz gazed down into her tumbler, then brought it to her forehead and pressed the cool glass to her skin. "It's been three months. You haven't heard from Donnie, either, have you?"

"No, but Donnie's wise to the world. They'll be fine."

Liz could hear the quiver in her voice as she spoke. "I just wish we'd have a message from someone—something." She stood up and set her drink on a small table. "I'm going in and lie down."

"Do you want anything to eat?"

"No. I'm fine." She raised her hand and waved to Gary. "Go help him grill the steaks."

Addie stood and faced Liz, gave her a quick hug and walked away.

No word came through August, September, and most of October. She stood in the window as the last of the rust-colored leaves fell onto the brown, dried grass. The earth had begun its annual winter preparations, and her heart grew weary. Clouds drifted across the sun and she shuddered from the cold. She spun the gold betrothal ring with her thumb. *Where is he? Why hasn't anyone heard?* She understood the Egyptian government had put him into the equivalent of a witness protection program, but she never imagined it would be so hard to wait.

The rumble of the engine of a delivery van met her ears as it rounded the corner and slowed to a stop at the curb. A uniformed man retrieved a shoebox-sized carton from the back of the truck and walked to the door. She opened it before he stepped onto the porch.

"Delivery for Liz McCran." He held out the box and the electronic tablet for her to sign.

Her eyes traveled to the sender in the upper left hand corner where Richard's name appeared. "Thank you," she called to the retreating driver and took the box to her room.

Her hands shook as she sliced into the tape which bound the package. She tore off the lid and laughed out loud. Letters from Rayhan spilled out onto her desk. No other explanation from Richard, but at that point, she didn't care. Liz arranged the letters into chronologic date order and tore open the first one:

My Dearest Liz:

I have no idea when you'll receive this, but I plan to write as often as possible. I can't tell you where we are, but Donnie and I are doing well. I'm seeing parts of the country I didn't know existed, and he's turned into quite the nomad.

I love you. Remember that. I don't know when this will be over, but we have to believe we'll be together again.

You're in my dreams, my heart, my soul.

Love, Rayhan

She traced his signature with her finger and brought the note to her cheek to summon a sense of him. Liz read fifteen additional letters. They were short notes, really, vague as to where they were and what they were doing, but filled with his love. She reached for the next stack when the doorbell rang. Addie and Gary were at work, and she rose to answer the door a second time. A telegraph agent stood in front of her with a telegram.

"Ms. McCran?" the young man asked.

"Yes," Liz said and she signed for the document. The driver returned to his car and drove away. She held the envelope against her chest, afraid to open it. She went inside and closed the door and leaned against it to keep out the rest of the world. *What if it was bad news?* She ran her fingernail under the seal.

Liz:

The trial is over STOP Someone will contact you soon STOP

Richard

Her stomach lurched when she glanced at the date. Three days ago? *Who will contact me? Rayhan?*

"Protocol and international relations," she said into the open space of the empty house. Troubled, she returned to her room and the stack of letters, her one connection to Rayhan.

She had begun to read the remainder of the second stack when the doorbell rang a third time. "I'd really like to read these without all these interruptions," she huffed and went again to the entrance.

She yanked the door open and a man, dressed in a dark blue suit, had his back turned, so she couldn't see his face. "May I help you?"

"I think so," he said and spun around.

"Rayhan!" she shrieked and collapsed into his arms. He kissed her eyes, her cheeks, and finally, her lips, as she clung to him and grasped for control. She feared he might be an illusion. Liz pulled away and drew him into the house. He kissed her again in the foyer.

"I just received your letters a couple of hours ago, and then a telegram. When did you get here?"

"I came straight from the airport. I left as soon as possible after the trial. I couldn't wait any longer. Six months is a long time." He picked up her hand and kissed her fingertips, placing his thumb on the golden ring on her finger. "I want to replace this." He paused. "I mean…"

"Six months is a long time, Rayhan, but I believed in you. I believed in us."

"Then, I want to do this properly." He reached into the pocket of his jacket. He held a black, velvet box in his hand, and when he opened it, her eyes widened at the size of the diamond. "Will you marry me, Liz?"

Tears welled as he slipped the ring on her finger. "Yes," she sobbed. "Yes." She melted into him and he held her close. She could feel his heart beating against hers and he smelled of musk and ginger.

She tingled from head to toe and wanted to stand there forever, but he let go and held her at arm's length. "You look so good," he said.

She blushed and led him into the living room, where they sat side by side on the couch. She didn't bother with the lights. The faint, fall sunshine created a soft glow in the room. She stared into his eyes, removed the betrothal ring, and placed it onto his finger. "The cycle is complete," she whispered. Then she remembered. "Where's Donnie? Addie will be disappointed you didn't bring him with you."

"I have a lot to tell you." Rayhan moved close and pulled her into his arms again. "Donnie is in Cairo. He has a job with the government and a fine house in the city. He wasn't kidding when he said he wanted to stay."

"Who gave him the money for the house?"

"The people of Egypt were very grateful for the capture of Ahmad and his men. The house and the job were their gift to Donnie. I must say, he impressed many of the authorities. The job he was given isn't one normally taken by an outsider."

"You helped, too." She searched his face and remembered the large part he had played in the capture of Ahmad. She didn't want it brushed aside and forgotten. "Weren't you rewarded?"

"Yes." Rayhan hesitated. "I only asked for a three things. Donnie really was the hero."

She reached up and touched the scar on Rayhan's face. His humility only endeared him to her further. "What did you ask for?"

"The funds to finish my education, my own apartment in Cairo and most important, plane tickets to bring you home."

"Your own apartment? You aren't living with your uncle?"

"The apartment is ours, Liz. You'll live there until the wedding." He tilted her chin toward him before he kissed her again. "The reward money for Ahmad was to be split between Donnie and me, but Donnie wouldn't hear of it. He gave me his portion as well, for us. I bought the ring and took the next flight out."

"Your uncle? Is he willing to accept us? Our marriage?"

"He and Aunt Amisi are planning a large engagement party when we return." Rayhan pulled her to him and kissed her long and hard. "God works in mysterious ways, Liz."

She nestled into his chest and placed her hand against Rayhan's heart. "Yes, He certainly does."

AUTHOR BIO

Victoria Pitts-Caine is a native Californian and lives in the bountiful San Joaquin Valley. Her varied interests include genealogy and exotic gemstone collecting both of which she's incorporated into her novels. While her genre is inspirational, she likes to refer to herself as a Christian Romance Adventure Novelist.

The author has received recognition in both fiction and nonfiction from: Enduring Romance top 10 picks for 2008, William Saroyan Writing Conference, Byline Magazine, Writer's Journal Magazine, and The Southern California Genealogical Society. Her first novel, Alvarado Gold, was published in 2007.

Victoria is a former staff technician for the environmental sector working in air pollution control. She is the mother of two daughters. Victoria and her husband enjoy travel, church service, and emergency radio communications.

Thank you for your Prism Book Group purchase!
Visit our website to enjoy free reads, great deals, and
entertaining, wholesome fiction!

http://www.prismbookgroup.com

4723997R00138

Made in the USA
San Bernardino, CA
04 October 2013